The Best Trick

The Best Trick

THE BANK ROBBERS
BOOK SIX

ANNIKA MARTIN

Reading order

Chapter One

THE FOUR OF US WERE SITTING OUT ON THE GRAND patio of our Northern California woodland Airbnb hideaway when the call came in.

Or maybe I should say that Thor and Odin were sitting; I was lying between the two of them with my head on Odin's lap and my feet on Thor's lap, a favorite configuration of mine.

Thor was massaging my feet.

Odin was feeding me the occasional champagne grape, my favorite kind of grape, what with that bright burst of flavor.

And Zeus was sprawled in the big patio chair, which we'd taken to calling his daddy throne, watching with lazy satisfaction, because he loved when things were right with us almost as much as he loved making things right.

Everything stopped when Zeus's phone did its chirpy little tone.

We all came to attention; I even partly sat up. It really was weird when a call came in, being that we cycled through new burner phones every month.

Who would call us?

Zeus grabbed the phone off the rough-hewn outdoor coffee

table and answered it. He listened to whatever the caller was saying with a thoughtful expression, then, "That is a really tempting offer, yes...yes...no, we have a shindig in L.A. we're committed to." The person on the other end talked some more and Zeus nodded and mumbled more thanks.

Of course we weren't committed to any shindig in L.A., and we never would be. A major part of the job description for "internationally wanted fugitives" was to *not* let people know where you'd be ahead of time. We would never commit to anything or RSVP to anything, and we hardly even ever attended parties, unless you considered traveling the world, robbing banks, having group sex, and staying in posh hotels while solving the occasional mystery to be a party.

Which, if I'm going to be honest, could very much be a party at times.

"What was that all about?" Odin asked when Zeus ended the call.

"The owners had the next week suddenly come available and were asking if we wanted to stay on."

"And you said no?" Odin asked, sounding a bit outraged.

"Of course, I said no," Zeus said.

"We love this place," Odin said.

Zeus gave him a hard look. "Yet we've been here ten days already."

The four of us had solemnly agreed never to stay more than ten days at a place.

To be fair, at the time we agreed on that rule, we'd just narrowly escaped grisly deaths at the hands of Denko, our mortal enemy. There's nothing like narrowly escaping a grisly death to make you get serious about safety measures.

"Maybe so, but this is one of the safest places we've ever been," Odin said. "And one of the best. A few more days. We could at least discuss it."

I waited to see what Zeus would say, because I, too, loved this place.

A lot.

It was rare that we felt truly safe for long stretches of time, but this place was out in the middle of nowhere surrounded by trees as tall as skyscrapers, making for a "highly defensive layout," as Zeus called it.

Even the birds helped in our defense, being that they tweeted when there was any kind of weirdness out there—an amazing alarm system, even better than Odin, who was always so wildly hyperaware of our surroundings.

The nature was spectacular—we saw moose and deer and even a few bears. There were definitely lots of woodland animals around, not the least of which were Thor, Zeus, and Odin, when we got to re-enacting my very favorite cartoon porn fantasies.

I'm happy to report that playing out a torrid capture fantasy never got old, even though it always ended in the same way.

Moreover, it was one of the poshest places ever—surprising, I know, considering we stayed at the finest hotels in the world, and also surprising considering the fact that there was not even a hot tub on the premises. But it was like a beautifully furnished Cabela's, and that suited us at the moment.

The guys and I had gotten into mountain biking around the mountainside. After a number of races and challenges, Thor was the champ in the category of long-distance mountain biking, meaning that he had the best endurance; however, Zeus held the award of fastest mountain biker—he had the most explosive athletic power, what with his tree-trunk legs and incredible muscles.

And if there had been an award for the most creative mountain biker, Odin and I would've shared that, considering how often we snuck out of the races to hang out and enjoy the scenery or take a naked dip in one of the pristine mountain streams.

The four of us would spend our nights grilling elaborate feasts, which we'd devour on the porch that overlooked rugged mountains. Then we'd go on to devour each other, and I don't mean that in a praying mantis way.

"Why not cancel the next place and pay the penalty?" Odin asked.

"We'd be breaking our ten-day rule," Zeus said.

"What's the *fucking-g* problem with staying a few more days?" Odin said—unsurprising, being that he'd never met a rule he didn't want to break.

"Procedures and rules keep us safe, and breaking them makes us less safe," Zeus said, also not surprisingly, being that he'd never met a rule he didn't want to enforce, marry, and possibly even tie up and fuck in a long and delicious way.

"I'm tired of us being so rigid and brittle," Odin said. "Let's stay for a while longer just this once. Why not?"

"Because we can't." Zeus's harsher-than-usual tone surprised me.

"That's a bullshit answer," Odin bit out.

"Yeah, well, that's the answer you're getting," Zeus growled. "We leave tomorrow. End of story."

I cringed—this was exactly the kind of response that Odin hated.

Thor and I had a nonintervention policy when Odin and Zeus went at it, but honestly? Odin had a point.

And...woodland adventures!

"Screw that," Odin said.

"Hey, I'm tired of being on the run, too," Zeus said. "I want it to be different, too, but do you know what I don't want? For us to die.

That's what the rules are there for."

"Rules are not smarter than us," Odin said. "They don't know that this is a good safe place where we can stay a bit longer."

"God!" Zeus thrust himself up out of his chair. "You know what I'm tired of? Having to fucking enforce the rules when you act like a goddamned teenager. I can't go back and change the past, so you're gonna have to deal with reality, and that includes following the rules."

Odin swore and stormed into the house.

Zeus stormed in after him.

A lot of fights came down to this same basic struggle—Odin wanted flexibility, and Zeus wanted law and order. But the two of them were being more intense this time.

Maybe because this hideaway had been so amazing.

When you've been on the run for so long, safety is a beautiful feeling.

Never having to look over your shoulder, never having to paste a really stupid nose onto your face and then glue the nose ruffle all over your cheeks, and then it itches, and then when you pull it off, it leaves red marks on your face.

I sighed dramatically and looked over at Thor, because Thor and I sometimes bonded when Odin and Zeus fought, but Thor was staring grimly into the middle distance, face ashen.

"What's wrong?"

He shook his head like it was too awful to verbalize and stared into the gloom some more.

Had I missed something? I hung back, giving him his space.

With his bright blond hair grown to his shoulders, he looked like a slightly feral Nordic reindeer herder, a look I definitely approved of, but something was off with him lately.

Thor was the peacemaker of the group, but in certain moods he could be the wild card, going from stable to recklessly unhinged in two seconds flat.

This mood felt different. New, somehow.

I'd had this sense lately that being on the run was grating on him. I sometimes forgot that he hadn't always been part of an armed-to-the-teeth, bank-robbing squad whose members all took their names from comic book gods. In fact, he'd been a nerdy doctor. A science geek. A man who dedicated his life to helping others. Healing was in his nature, and I knew he missed doing that.

Odin burst out the door, bottle of scotch in hand. He grunted unintelligibly and headed into the woods, disappearing into the gloom.

Moments later, Zeus burst out and stomped after him.

They did that sometimes when things between them were rough—they went out, talked about everything and got really drunk.

I heaved myself off the couch and went up behind Thor, wrapping my arms around him and setting my chin on his shoulder. "There goes OZ to do manly score settling," I said, trying to cheer him up. I'd even used his snarky nickname for Odin and Zeus—OZ.

He didn't crack a smile.

"No, wait, excuse me—*stalking* off. They definitely stalked, wouldn't you say?"

Thor had recently observed that Odin and Zeus always stalked around.

He remained silent, sullen and stiff under my embrace.

"Come on, the heavy, deliberate steps? The trunk-like legs of manly men, the sense of great purpose. If that's not stalking..."

"This is bad," Thor said, shaking me off and doing a little stalking of his own—into the house.

I followed, pulse racing.

He went to the refrigerator and grabbed a beer.

"What's up, Thor?".

"This can't go on, that's what." He twisted off the top and chucked it angrily across the room.

"What are you talking about? This is good. We're good." I plopped myself down into a comfy pine-and-plaid chair. "They're going to work it out—they always do. Come on, baby, we're a happy badass criminal family."

Thor just scowled. He sometimes got unbalanced when he couldn't practice medicine for long stretches of time. Was that it? Being kept from his heart's calling for too long?

And fabulous as our travels were, we all missed having a real home—there was that, too. We all missed our hideout in the Hollywood Hills where we'd spent a few blissful months playing house. We got to decorate the place in our own way and have friends over and not worry about breaking stuff. It was the closest we ever felt to being a normal family.

I missed my girlfriends, too—the Gigis, an awesome jewel-thief girl gang. But now that our enemies knew about our hideout, I wasn't sure when we'd ever be able to return there.

Probably never.

Thor continued to scowl at the forest.

"They'll be back with Odin grudgingly acknowledging the wisdom of a chain of command, and Zeus acknowledging the wisdom of flexibility. You know that's how it ends."

Thor sank heavily onto the couch and plopped his feet onto the coffee table, inconsolable.

"Right?" I pressed.

He shook his head.

"Is this about Odin and his sleep issues?" I asked. "Are you worried about that?"

Again, he shook his head.

I put on the new Marvel movie. Comic book movies always cheered up my guys...over and over and over. How many times could my guys watch a comic book movie? We were well into double-digits territory on that one. Though to be fair, I had made them watch *Miss Congeniality* easily a dozen times.

Was it about Odin's sleep issues? Thor desperately wanted to help him; I knew it was really bothering him that he couldn't help him.

Odin had these sleep issues where he'd thrash around at night. One time, in Rome, I'd gone into the bedroom and stretched out next to him while he was snoozing, and he'd bopped me in the face. It was a total accident, obviously—the man was sleeping, after all, and I should've known better—but Odin was mortified.

He'd refused to sleep with me ever again—the slumbering type of sleep, anyway.

I hated that, because Odin had endured a lot of trauma in his life, and one of the few things that enabled him to have any kind of peaceful night's sleep was when he and I slept next to each other.

It had meant so much that I could help him in that way.

Sleeping side by side was off the table now, no matter how much I begged him to give it another shot. It had only happened once, and I would have gladly risked it to see that he had a peaceful night's sleep.

Thor was desperate to help Odin have a non-thrashing sleep, constantly seeking out cures and remedies. He was a doctor with one patient to focus on, much to Odin's dismay.

Recently, he'd created this special harness out of seat belts made to fit around the bed, with the idea that it would help Odin keep still so that he could then sleep next to me without worry.

Odin had found being strapped like that intolerable.

Odin and Zeus returned three hours later, slapping each other's backs.

Zeus drunkenly informed us that Odin was the best guy ever, and Odin drunkenly informed us that Zeus was the best guy ever, and then they drunkenly wrestled.

Afterwards, Zeus announced that the gang would have a meeting soon about being more flexible, but not a drunken meeting, and Odin announced that sticking to the rules had saved us a lot.

And then they raided the refrigerator.

I gave Thor such a triumphant look, like, *I told you.*

But he still looked upset. What was up with him? Was it something more than Odin's increasingly dire sleep situation? Something more than Zeus's philosophical struggles about too much structure versus the tyranny of structurelessness?

࿇

Odin and Thor and I scrambled to be packed and ready to go ahead of time the next morning so that we could relax for a few last blissful moments on the woodland porch of awesomeness.

I was stretched out on the comfy outdoor couch with my feet on Thor's lap, reading a book that was incredibly exciting. Thor was also reading a book. He had it balanced on my ankles—some kind of medical book, or else it was a sports biography. In other words, not at all as fun or exciting as my book.

Odin was in Zeus's man throne with his sketchpad, doing one of his amazing sketches.

Zeus came out and just stood there for a minute being ignored by us, because we had exactly twenty minutes left in our favorite place.

"Twenty minutes. I want to be on the road by eight," he finally said, all grumbly.

We three grumbled back. We didn't need to be reminded. Also, hungover much?

"Well, are you packed?" Zeus asked. "Is everything set? Isis, linens handled?"

"Yuppers," I said, not looking up. Putting the used linens and bath towels in the proper place was my job after staying at an Airbnb.

Zeus turned to Odin. "Recycling handled?" Recycling was Odin's duty.

Odin just kept on sketching.

I frowned. Why was Zeus so eager to get on the road? If he thought somebody was onto us, he would have said.

Also, we were totally responsible when it came to leaving an Airbnb in amazing condition.

We had to be responsible Airbnb customers. We had painstakingly created different identities under which we would rent them, and it took a lot of work to create those identities—you had to set up Facebook profiles and disguises and get a bit of an internet footprint. If one of the identities got a reputation for leaving Airbnbs in bad condition, nobody would rent to them.

Sometimes we were two separate couples vacationing together. Sometimes we were a family of four with Thor as an old woman, which he totally hated. We had another identity where Odin and I were half-siblings. Sometimes just two of us rented a place and asked permission to have friends drop by.

"Odin?" Zeus asked.

Without so much as looking up, Odin said, "I'm a highly trained lethal operative capable of running simultaneous operations across five continents. Why don't you take a guess if I've managed to get the *fucking-g* recycling out on time?"

"I'm sorry if I'm a highly trained lethal operative who always checks on everything," Zeus said.

"I'm sorry if you're a highly trained lethal asshole who's ruining our last few minutes on the porch," Odin bit out.

I tensed up.

Zeus frowned. And then he said, "I guess I am being a bit of a lethal asshole."

"Highly trained lethal *fucking-g* asshole," Odin mumbled.

Zeus snorted.

I relaxed, because that was what we did—we had fights and resolved them with humor. It showed the health of our relationship that we could always do this.

I looked over at Thor, thinking this would hearten him, but he looked like he'd seen a ghost almost.

What the hell?

Odin brushed the pencil shavings off of his artwork. "This was a good place," he said. "I like a place with a porch, like we had in L.A. Will Malibu have a porch?"

"A porch *and* a private hot tub," Zeus said.

All eyes turned to me at the mention of a hot tub. I smiled and shrugged. "Whatevs," I said playfully.

Odin narrowed his eyes. "Did you just say 'whatevs' about a

hot tub?"

"That's what I said—whatevs," I sniffed. "It means whatever, but more like I don't care."

"That's what I thought you said," Odin muttered darkly, closing his pad.

I sighed like it was all so incredibly tedious, but inside I was glittering with excitement, because Odin was in a dangerously sexy mood now.

"Yeah, whatevs," I said haughtily. "Hot tubs aren't all that they're cracked up to be." Of course, I was teasing. Hot tubbing was one of my favorite group activities.

Odin came over and loomed over me. Thor closed his book —loudly.

I suppressed a huge grin. Spicytimes ahoy!

"No way. We're not starting anything," Zeus warned. "Not starting anything. We don't have time."

"Right, and I really don't see what the big thrill is with hot tubs," I continued breezily. "Everybody is always so excited about them, but what are they, more than a giant vat of warm water? My book is so much more exciting than that. It's a historical taking place in the Regency times when people knew how to act properly. Unlike now. Men simply don't know how to treat women nowadays, don't you agree?"

Zeus looked nearly apoplectic.

Few things were more enjoyable than taunting my guys when there was no time to have sex.

Three pairs of eyes raked my skin. Taunting unlocked.

I planned to continue my evil taunting in the car, and they would have to wait, slowly going crazy. There was no better recipe for an explosively delicious manwich.

Zeus planted his fists on his hips. "We'll be there by dinnertime, and then we *will* go in the hot tub." He narrowed his eyes at me.

My belly tightened.

Chapter Two

TWENTY MINUTES LATER, WE WERE SPEEDING DOWN THE road, all testosterone and sexual tension in a silver Jaguar that we'd paid cash for, courtesy of a recent withdrawal we'd made from a First National Bank in western Nebraska. And yes, we're talking about a withdrawal using automatic rifles and Donald Duck masks.

Thor and I rode in the back, as usual, with Zeus driving and Odin riding shotgun.

As ex-super-secret covert-intelligence-agency spies, Zeus and Odin tended to monitor other cars whenever we drove places, sometimes obsessively. You could blindfold them at any time, and they'd be able to name the make and model of all the cars that had been behind and in front of us for miles, complete with a detailed critique of their turn-signal-usage style.

But was Zeus glancing at the rearview mirror more than usual? Was Odin scrutinizing the side mirror a little too often?

"Is something feeling off out there?" I finally asked. "Seeing anything?"

"Just your sexy face," Zeus said to me in the rearview mirror.

"Seriously, are you looking in the mirror a lot? Because I think you are."

"No one's out there," Zeus said. "We got this."

"Re-entry stress," Odin said. "We were safe back there, and now we're back out in the world."

"Hey, fuck you," Zeus said. "We're safest when we move around."

They glared at each other for a second and then went back to vigilant man mode. Thor sat there with a dark look on his face, working on weird-Thor-mood number three.

"Who are we for this one?" I asked.

"We'll be the Newsomes," Zeus said. "We'll change at that rest stop you like. Tejon Pass."

I groaned. The Newsomes, who we sometimes called the Snootersons, loved art and cheese; their disguises were effective but very elaborate. As Sarah Newsome, I wore cheek fillers, which clamped over my teeth, dramatically changing the shape of my face. Basically, Sarah Newsome had chipmunk cheeks and bushy dark eyebrows and awesome dark corkscrew curls. As Sarah Newsome, I was in a relationship with Zeus, a slightly pudgy personal trainer with shaggy blond hair named Theo Talbott.

Thor played my father, Jeff Newsome, an elderly art gallery owner. He had to wear powdery gray stuff in his hair, makeup that made his skin look weather-beaten, and a beret. Odin was my half brother, artist Jerrod Newsome. As Jerrod, Odin got a bushy beard, bushy eyebrows, a man bun, and fashionable, blue-rimmed glasses.

The best identities have some true things about you. Thor knew a lot about fancy culture. Odin did, too, and he was an amazing artist. I knew a lot about artisanal cheese from the sheep farm where I grew up. I had even started teaching online classes, using the Sarah Newsome persona, because why not? Sarah Newsome was a large, artisanal cheese-making chipmunk.

"What if I skipped the makeup?" Thor tried.

"The owners might be there," Zeus warned. "They seem interested in art, as it turns out."

"They can ask me about cheese, but they'd better not want me to discuss art," I said. "My favorite kind of pictures are dogs playing pool, painted on velvet."

Odin groaned.

"Hey, that curly fries restaurant is coming up!" I said. "Curly fries! We haven't had them in ages!"

"I'd like to get there on time and get situated," Zeus said.

"Situated for what? We have nothing going on. And, dude, curly fries!" Zeus was usually as excited about curly fries as I was, and we knew and liked this restaurant, in part because of the lack of cameras in and around it, as well as the plentiful escape routes— an important restaurant feature when you're on the run.

"I want to be settled," Zeus said mysteriously. "Be settled and get the lay of the land and all that."

"What are you not telling us?" Odin demanded, turning to Zeus. "You're in this big hurry. What the hell? Is there something concrete that you're responding to?"

"Wait, like a threat?" I asked. "Excuse me, but a girl likes to know whether her mortal enemies who want to kill and torture her and her three husbands are closing in."

Zeus sighed. "It's nothing."

Thor and I narrowed our eyes at each other. Something was definitely up with Zeus.

"A guy likes to know that, too," Thor said.

"Out with it," Odin said.

"You'll see," Zeus said. "It's a surprise."

"Wait, what?" I asked. "What about our no-surprises rule?"

"Yeah, what the hell?" Odin complained. "You get to break the rules, but we don't? Hell no."

"I'm alerting you to the fact that it's a surprise," Zeus said. "So therefore, it's not really a surprise."

"That's still a surprise," Odin said.

"Okay, let's call it a can't-miss-weekend thing we need to do that will be fun," Zeus said.

"If you don't tell us what it is, then it's a surprise," Thor put in.

"No," Zeus said, "because now you know something is coming. A surprise is unexpected. If you're expecting it, it's not a surprise, is it?"

"What the thing *is* will be a surprise, therefore it's a surprise," Odin said.

"Not if you know it's coming," Zeus insisted.

"Will we be surprised?" Odin asked. "Answer me that."

"What is the exact definition of surprise?" Thor asked. "Surprise means 'to be surprised.'"

"No, I disagree!" Zeus said. "It means unexpected."

Thor and Odin pulled out their phones.

I groaned and grabbed my book.

My guys were major control freaks—bullheaded and bossy—which worked out great for sexytimes, but it led to a lot of arguments that devolved into issues of terminology, which were about as thrilling as the square dance channel. Zeus lost the surprise argument but still wouldn't tell what the surprise was. He did, however, agree to stop for curly fries. We ordered a metric ton of food and got back on the road.

The sun was getting high in the sky, and the flat, brown landscape stretched out as far as the eye could see. I was definitely looking forward to some sunset cocktail hours. "Do you think the hot tub at this place has a view of the sunset?" I hoped so—sunset-view hot tubs were the best, and considering Malibu, it wasn't an unreasonable expectation.

"If I don't tell, will that qualify as an illegal surprise?" Zeus asked.

"Oh my god!" I threw a wadded-up curly fries bag at his head. No way was I letting them start up the definition-of-surprise debate again. I had to distract them. "Surprise or no, I'm looking forward to this new place. I can't think of anything better than reading my exciting historical book with a nice glass of wine. Just nothing better. It just doesn't get better than that. Me alone with my book...mmm. Nothing better."

Odin twisted around to give me a dark look.

Thor snickered and set a strong hand on my thigh. "Nothing better than that? You can't think of anything better than that?"

"What could possibly be better?" I teased. "Oh, wait, curly fries. I guess there's that."

Zeus growled, pinning me with his gaze through the rearview. I could feel it like a physical thing, pressing in on me.

"What?" I protested. "What could be as awesome as a book, wine, and curly fries?"

More man-growls.

"Oh, wait! Chocolate?" I teased. "Is that what you're trying to tell me? Chocolate?"

Thor shook his head sadly. "Oh, goddess. You are heading down a very bad road."

I bit my lip excitedly. A sad headshake from Thor always foretold of scathingly sexy things.

"You can't think of anything better than that?" Odin asked me.

"What could possibly be better than that?" I teased. "Oh, are you talking about that hot tub again? Been there, done that."

"Goddess," Thor rasped, inching his hand near to my sex.

Odin had turned all the way around in his seat, facing backwards now. So much for seat belts.

"Give me that ereader," he said.

"This?" I asked, holding it up.

He tried to take it from me, but I wouldn't let it go. I was just laughing, and then he twisted it out of my hand. Out of nowhere he had a necktie, and he was tying my hands together, all deft movements like the ex-secret agent that he was.

"Hey! How am I supposed to eat my beloved chocolate and curly fries with my hands like this? Those things are my main pleasures in this life!"

Thor squeezed my thigh. "You sure about that?"

Odin tied my hands to his headrest. "Goddess, you are going to exhibit the proper attitude soon, I promise you."

"Wuuuuuut..." I whispered impishly.

Once my hands were tied, Odin leaned way back into our space. He grasped my nipples. Excitement shot through me like fire.

"Erp!" I said.

"Thor, push up her skirt," he commanded.

"Hey!" Zeus said. "Keep that seat belt on. You're gonna get us cops on our ass."

"Cops on our ass," Odin said. "That's why God gave us gas pedals."

"Yah," I gasped, enjoying the feel of Thor's wicked fingers pushing up my skirt, feeling excited about what would come after.

"Do her," Odin said, "but don't let her come."

"What?" I whined.

"Oh, Ice, you have done it now," Thor said, ripping my thong to useless scraps, fully baring my mound to the cool wind whooshing in the window. He cupped it with rough hands.

I gasped.

Odin clambered all the way into the back seat, installing himself on the other side of me from Thor. He pushed down my shirt and bared my breasts. "We are going to make you beg so hard, you'll forget all about chocolate and curly fries," he said, pressing something cold and hard to one of my nipples, and then the other.

I gasped. An ice cube!

He tossed it aside and touched them with warm fingers.

"You will forget all about them," Thor said.

"I can't imagine how that could ever happen," I somehow managed. "Can't...imagine..." I said, arching my pelvis into Thor's hand. He pressed a finger into my wetness, and I nearly exploded with pleasure.

"Tell us what you really want," Odin said.

"Maybe it's a surprise," I bit out as Thor zeroed in on my hard little nub. "What…" I said, pulsing under my guys' delicious ministrations. "Please," I whispered.

"Please what?" Odin said.

"Please let me come," I whispered.

"You break so easy," Odin said, doing a just-right twisty thing to my nipples that tweaked the pleasure center of my soul.

"Tell us what you love the most," Thor commanded, doing a reverse circle thing on my sex that made my mind go blank.

"Your hands on me," I panted. "I love your hands on me, and your cocks!"

"Be more convincing," Odin growled, tweaking harder.

I was about to come. Seeming to sense this, Thor halted all festivities between my legs, and not only that, but used his hand to prevent me from squeezing my legs together and finishing myself off. "You are a very bad girl," he rasped into my ear.

"I know—a terrible girl! What are curly fries again?"

"You think we can't tell when you're just saying something because you want to get off?" Odin said. "We can tell, goddess. We won't let you use us for your sexual pleasure. That's not the kind of men we are."

I snorted. That's exactly the kind of men they were.

Thor started up his little circles, Odin did more things to my nipples, and I begged some more.

So that's how we passed that next part of our car ride, with me on the verge of coming.

We stopped at the rest stop to change into our disguises, but that did little to dampen my excitement.

By the time we arrived at the Airbnb, I had chipmunk cheeks, awesome corkscrew hair, and an off-the-charts horniness level, plus a bit of dizziness thanks to the route we took, which involved a hillside of hairpin turns laid out like remnants of Silly String from a toddler's birthday party.

Chapter Three

The owner, Sue, came out of the house as we pulled up.

My guys always preferred that nobody see us, even in our disguises, but I always liked when the owner met us—otherwise it meant that we'd gotten into our disguises for no reason. Like getting dressed up and having no place to go. Who wants that?

"Showtime," Thor grumbled, putting on his beret. He and I got out of the car and introduced ourselves to Sue, a fiftysomething woman with moon boots, lots of bracelets, and a strangely intense gaze.

"Glad you made it up that crazy road in one piece!" she said, shaking our hands. She showed us the code and ushered us into the place while Zeus and Odin stayed behind, making a big deal out of unpacking the car, but probably really scanning for trouble. We were always most vulnerable when we first arrived at a place.

Sue led Thor and me into the living room. "We were really excited to hear that you were art collectors," she said, waving her hand toward three small prints that hung over the sofa. "Rembrandts. Not the originals, of course. We have one tiny original of his in our home, though."

"Amazing," I said.

"How did you acquire it?" Thor asked.

"Christie's during the recession," she said. "I mean, 2009, what a year to buy art, right? We've been eyeing his sketches forever, but getting our hands on that one..."

I winced because one of the things you definitely don't want when you're masquerading as something like an art connoisseur is to meet somebody who's an actual freaking art connoisseur. Odin needed to be here. Odin was an amazing artist, and he knew as much about Rembrandt as he did about introducing chaos into dangerous bank takeover robberies. He was the ultimate Renaissance man.

But Thor handled it with his usual charm. He smiled, confident and breezy. "That's what I call a damn fine investment."

Sue smiled happily. "Are you looking for anything in particular? Are there any area artists that you're looking at?"

"No, not really," I said. "It's just more of a tour, and, if something catches our fancy, we may want to talk to the artist a bit more."

"You can cut the act," she said.

"What's that?" Thor asked, still sounding all breezy, but his guard was up.

"Oh, I know exactly what you're doing," Sue said. "I know who you are and what you're up to."

My heart pounded. "Excuse me?"

"I think you're here to buy," she said. "You've identified an area artist who's going to be hot, and you want to buy up their work before anybody else figures it out and snaps it all up."

"No, that's not it at all!" I said, maybe with too much energy.

Playfully, Sue narrowed her eyes. "So you're not going to give me any hints on who you're looking at?"

"Sometimes we like to explore an area without a preset agenda," Thor said. "It keeps us open to discovery. When you go into a place with fixed ideas, you don't always see everything."

I grinned up at Thor. This was the kind of thing my guys said about casing a bank for a possible robbery—they preferred to look around without a preset idea of how best to rob it. "Indeed," I said.

"Yes, indeed," Thor echoed. We said the word *indeed* when we were masquerading as the Newsomes. I wanted to take his hand, but he was my father when we were being the Newsomes, so I settled for an appreciative look.

"Mmm," Sue said, not entirely convinced. She led us onward.

"Preconceived ideas and a preset agenda calcify the mind to hidden opportunities," Thor said. "Sometimes when you set out to zig, the best thing is to zag. That's our motto."

More bank robber talk. I bit back a smile. "Yes indeed, though sometimes both zigging and zagging can be ever so tedious," I said, with the extra impudence that I knew would get him going.

"Hardly," Thor said pointedly, another Newsome word. "I can't say that I've ever seen people find both zigging and zagging tedious."

"Don't worry, your secret's safe with me," Sue said.

We headed across the three-season sun porch and out onto the back veranda with plush seating and trellises that overlooked the hillside leading down to the ocean. There was a fence all along the edge of the property, there, no doubt, to protect drunken renters from tumbling down the hillside.

But the main attraction was clearly the hot tub—it wasn't any ordinary hot tub, but a magnificent in-ground tub lined with colorful tiles that looked as if they'd been collected from all over the world. The thing was surrounded by lush flowering trellises and lots of plush seating.

I was definitely seeing some hot tubbing in my future—hopefully soon, being that I was still buzzing from the car ride.

Was this Zeus's big surprise? The best hot tub ever?

"Most of our guests spend their time out here. It's a favorite place, a magical place," Sue said.

"It's absolutely spectacular," I agreed.

Sue showed us the control panel, hidden inside a fake rock. By then Zeus and Odin had arrived, oohing and aahing over everything. It was always better for the attention to be off of us and on the scenery or another person, though in this case, there really was a lot to ooh and aah over.

"I guarantee we'll be spending a lot of time in the hot tub," Odin said, giving me a look. I put on a confused expression.

Sue pointed to a pair of huge, ancient trees with a hammock strung between them and, beyond it, an amazing view of the ocean. Shivers went over me. An amazing hammock with an amazing view where I could sit and read.

Was *that* the surprise?

I took Zeus's hand. "I love hammocks," I said.

Sue beamed. "There's nothing like a hammock with a view," she agreed, and we had a moment of silent bonding over that.

"Just give me my book and a nice view and that is better than any experience ever," I said, restarting my taunting program.

Zeus grumbled, squeezing my hand.

I slid a sideways glance at Odin. A grin had spread over his handsome face. He was in the mood for trouble.

Yay!

"Nothing that I can think of," I added.

Sue showed us how to use the porch grill, completely not necessary considering my guys could build a grill out of things from a dollar store and make it fly to space if they wanted. But we acted really eager and interested, and I said a few more things about how much I couldn't wait to sit on the hammock overlooking the cliffs.

The energy was building like crazy.

If Sue noticed anything, she didn't comment, and finally she took off.

"I thought she'd never leave." I took out my cheek implants and pulled off my wig. "I'm going to go unpack," I said, though I had no intention of doing any such thing. And I definitely knew my men wouldn't be doing any unpacking unless they were unpacking sexy new moves that they'd dreamed up during a certain frustrating car ride.

Odin came to me, eyes dark and serious there in the afternoon sunshine. "Oh, goddess," he said.

"What?" I asked innocently.

"If you have to pee, you'd better do it now," Zeus chimed in.

Odin shot him a dark look and came to me. He took off his glasses, slow and sexy, and set them aside.

Gasp!

He grabbed my hair then, and slowly he wound it around his fist, winding it up hard.

Shivers skittered up my spine.

He yanked my head to the right, all the better to plant a tender kiss upon the delicate skin of my neck. "Thor," he said in the deep rumble that always spelled trouble. "Make sure Sue is truly gone and then find something to bind this one's hands."

Gulp and gasp!

"Zeus," Odin continued, "please strip our goddess, one button at a time. Please undress her, and make sure she feels you undressing her. Make sure that she knows that we are now baring her body, getting ready to use her for our pleasure."

Pulse racing with excitement, I pulled Odin to me and kissed him while I still had use of my hands. "Oh yeah?" I mumbled into the kiss.

"Yeah."

Zeus came up behind me. "Oh, goddess," he rumbled into my ear, reaching around to my shirtfront. Clumsy fingers began to undo my buttons. He pulled my shirt off, and then yanked my bra down under my breasts.

Odin took a nipple between two rough fingers, rolling and squeezing it.

Breeze tickled my skin. The earth seemed to tilt on its axis.

Manwich time!

"We will not be able to let you off easy, not for this," Odin said. "We are in charge here, and it is not for you to work us into a lather, not for you to twist our minds up with sexy thoughts while we're trying to travel between hideouts. To consume our minds with the desperately dirty things we will do to you. Do you think it is for you to do that?"

With trembling hands, I reached down to undo Odin's buttons. "Kind of?" I teased.

Zeus rumbled behind me, expert fingers undoing my fly. He reached his hands down to grab my entire crotch. "What will I find under there?" he whispered roughly into my ear. "When I pull these pants off?"

"If you don't know the answer to that, we might have to look into a cognitive test," I said.

"Oh, you are pushing it now," Odin said in a scolding tone. "Pants, all the way off," he commanded. "Strip her all the way, Zeus."

By now, I was quivering with anticipation, and excited to taunt them further. If worse came to worst, I could always use my safe word, Mississippi.

Zeus made me step out of my jeans in the grumbly and surly way that always turned me on. Eventually I was totally naked, being carried, fireman-style, by Zeus into the three-season porch. Thor appeared with some silken lengths of rope. He tied my hands behind me.

Odin bent me over a tallish buffet-type thing so that my ass was exposed to Zeus and Odin and the warm Pacific breeze blowing in through the open windows.

Would we not even make it to the hot tub?

Rough hands pushed my legs apart. Large fingers invaded my sex, pressing between my legs, sliding the juices around, arousing me.

I gasped, on the verge already.

"This is what I knew that I would find," Zeus grumbled, stroking me. "A wet pussy craving to be punished for impudence. One wet pussy that knows it belongs to us and only us, craving to be punished."

Thor came around the front of me, sliding a hand over my hair. "You know that we have to do this," he said. "You taunted us so much in the car, it has to be balanced out."

I whimpered, playing the sorry ingenue, trying not to smile. It would've been really bad if I'd laughed, and it was so hard not to because I loved the we-must-punish-Isis game. And especially the we-must-punish-Isis-in-a-harsh-and-sexual-way game, and the we-must-do-shockingly-dirty-things-to-Isis game—which, needless to say, is not available in your local toy stores.

Slowly, Thor began to undo his pants.

I was only half paying attention, what with Zeus making me mindless with pleasure with what he was doing to my clitoris back there.

"You must not come, yet. Things will not go well," Odin said.

"Well...Zeus can't keep doing that, then," I said in a strangled voice. "Omigod," I added, panting, pure pleasure thrumming through my veins, electricity building behind my eyes.

"Zeus gets to do whatever he wants," Odin said, slapping my ass, which sent me reeling with extra pleasure.

I focused on sheep breeds. There was the Merino, the docile Texel sheep, the Suffolk, the cute Valais blacknose.

"Your body is ours to use for our pleasure," Odin muttered threateningly. "If we want to press our fingers to your pussy, to explore all of your pussy that we own and enjoy, that is what we will do. Understand?"

"Okay," I gasped.

"And if we want to bring you to the verge of orgasm, to feel every vulnerable nerve ending in your clit stand at attention for us, primed to explode with one more stroke, we will."

"Uhhhh..." I said.

Zeus stroked on.

Romanov...a regal breed of sheep.

"If we want to bring you there and stop moving, and forbid you to come, that is what we will do."

"Okay," I whispered, mind melting. Would I have to move to presidential birthdays?

"And if we want to bring you to the verge of orgasm and then *not* stop moving, but to continue to stroke and own you with rough, careless hands, then that is what we will do."

Oh, Odin could be wicked! I was on the verge of orgasm. I was very nearly weeping with the effort not to burst into orgasm.

Taking his cue from Odin, Zeus began to stroke me carelessly.

We would definitely not be making it to the hot tub.

In front of me, Thor continued to fumble with his fly, and then he stomped out of his pants, revealing his sexy, muscular legs and his beautiful golden cock, sprung up at attention. He knelt, facing me. "Ice," he whispered.

"What?"

Warm, smooth fingers slid up my neck and under my chin. "I'm going to need your mouth on me," he said gravely. "I'm going to hold your head and shove my cock deep down into your throat, and it is going to be rough and fierce," he said.

Gulp, I thought happily.

"Zeus, do you think it is time for the new toy?" Odin asked behind me.

Double gulp.

Zeus's fingers disappeared. Now something cool and oily pressed in circles around my asshole. I squinched my eyes shut tight as it pushed in slowly. It was some sort of toy, large and cool and smooth.

"Do you understand why we have to fill your asshole?" Thor asked, a rhetorical question if I'd ever heard one.

"Uhhhh," I said, not able to expend resources on speech while a cool, bulbous thing was being pushed with maddening leisure into my asshole. "More," I gasped.

"Answer."

"I don't know," I breathed. "I'm still thinking about those curly fries."

With a decisive movement, the toy was shoved all the way in, past Go, past Boardwalk, past the guardian ring of muscles into the best Park Place ever. My ass was filled, stretched. I gasped at the delicious intensity of it.

A large hand roamed over my butt cheeks.

Odin.

I braced for the sting that I knew was to come, the exquisite sting of an Odin slap. "What did you just say?"

"C-curly fries."

Slap.

"Thor, stand up and grab her hair," Odin commanded. "Show her how you want her to suck you. Push all the way into her. You know how she likes to be used hard." Odin turned to me here. "Isis, you will take him down your throat while I spank you, and you will let him feel no teeth, or things will really go bad."

Thor pressed his cock into my mouth and all the way in.

"And things won't go bad in a good way, so don't get any ideas," Thor added, gripping my hair, fucking my mouth.

"And you must not come," Odin commanded, slapping my ass again. The slap seemed to vibrate my clit from the inside out. I don't know if it was the toy inside my ass or Odin's wicked hand slapping the outside of my ass or what, but the darkest pleasure pulsed through my veins. Sweat dripped down my spine, tears streamed down my face. It was too good and I was running out of sheep breeds!

"She wants to come," Thor said.

"Do not," Odin said, slapping my ass harder now.

I moaned, senseless.

Not coming was a ridiculously tall order, but hey, I could chew gum and walk at the same time. Though *chew gum* probably wasn't the image I needed to be having while my mouth was all over Thor's sexy cock.

I squeezed Thor at the root, and suddenly he was coming, crying out. He petted my hair, over and over, senselessly petting it like a man dying of some mysterious cause and petting my hair was the only way to stay alive, the only way to breathe.

Right then Zeus turned me over and climbed on top of me. In one fluid movement, he pushed apart my legs and thrust his huge cock into me.

"Yesssssss," I hissed.

"You're so hot like this," he said, thrusting. He took hold of my nipple, giving it a twist.

"Uhhh!" I cried. "I won't last! I can't!"

He did it again and I exploded in an orgasm, crying out in a seagullish way, which I didn't intend, but what can you do?

"Uh-uh-uh," Zeus grunted, and I knew he was coming along with me.

"Fuck, goddess," Odin gasped. "I cannot last with you like this. Your pleasure slays me." He came somewhere, lord knows where. And then Thor untied my hands. I felt warm and pliant and happy.

"I guess the hot tub was good," I said.

Odin hoisted me up over his back and carrying me—not to the hot tub, but to the pool.

"Nooo!" I cried.

He threw me in, naked. I grabbed a floaty bed and floated in the glorious sunshine. It was incredibly peaceful until my guys stripped off all of their clothes and did cannonballs into the pool, splashing ridiculously, nearly toppling me.

Because that is what you get with guys.

Chapter Four

WE SWAM FOR A WHILE, AND THEN WE ORDERED A HUGE haul of food from the grocery store and unpacked. Zeus was excited to grill some of the local fish.

The guys grumbled about needing to brush up on their art history and art scene intel. Just in case Sue came sniffing around.

"Well, luckily, I'm just the cheese expert in this identity, so I don't need to know about art. Yay! I'm really going to check out the hammock for sure," I said, turning to Zeus. "The amenities of this backyard, just all of this, it's a wonderful surprise. It really is."

"What do you mean?" Zeus asked.

"You said there would be a surprise at this Airbnb, right?" I said. "Wait, it's not the hammock and hot tub? That's not the surprise?"

"I didn't say the surprise would be *at* the Airbnb," Zeus said.

I could sense Odin and Thor perking up. They would not be at all thrilled with the idea that the surprise was yet to come. But nobody wanted to be in a fight after the last fight.

I grabbed my book and went out and sat on the hammock. It was everything. I read and napped, and soon delicious aromas were wafting my way. So I went and joined my guys, and we had a sumptuous meal. Later, Zeus and Thor took a walk down to the beach, and Odin and I hung out on the couch.

I got back to my book. Odin was looking at the magazines and brochures that Sue had out on the side table. Suddenly he let out a huge, loud man-groan.

I looked up. "What's wrong?"

"I think I found the surprise," he said ominously, holding up a small brochure.

"What is it?"

He handed it to me. It was a brochure advertising romantic hot air balloon rides for two up and down the coast. The operation was owned and managed by a ballooner named Harley. With the romantic balloon ride for two, apparently, Harley packed a couple a picnic basket with a bottle of champagne and snacks and flew up with them over the coast. The pictures showed the couple toasting with champagne glasses.

"Make a champagne toast to your beloved against the backdrop of the Pacific Ocean as you soar above the treetops," the brochure read.

A romantic balloon ride for couples. Zeus catnip if I ever saw it.

"Damn," I said.

Balloon rides generally seemed like fun, but I could see the un-fun way in which this one would all unfold, and I was sure Odin did, too: Zeus would decide that the four of us, as a romantic unit, should be able to go up in the balloon together, and if it wasn't allowed, there would be trouble.

Big trouble.

Zeus's willingness to fight for our love wasn't always the best thing ever, let's just say.

Zeus went on a long run the next morning, and Odin and I showed Thor the balloon brochure.

"Damn," Thor said, draining his coffee.

"My sentiments exactly," I sighed. If only the balloon rides were geared toward groups!

"*Fucking-g* tailor made for Zeus to freak out on," Odin said.

Thor nodded. "Zeus did mention he wanted to do an excursion tomorrow. Something about us getting on our disguises and going into town. This must be it."

Odin started scrolling around on his phone. "The website for this Airbnb mentions romantic balloon rides as something people visiting the area like to do. He knew about it before we got here. This is definitely the surprise."

"Why this?" I asked. "It could be almost anything."

"Goddess, don't you remember? You said it was your dream last year," Thor said. "You said, 'it would be so amazing, floating through the clouds. Perfect silence. And with all of us together, it would be even better.'"

"I said that?" Sure, I could see myself saying something like that, but I definitely didn't remember it.

Odin nodded his head. "Yes, you said it last year in New Mexico." He turned to Thor. "But I believe she used the phrase, 'perfectly quiet.'"

"No, it was 'perfect silence,'" Thor insisted.

"I just can't believe you two remember that much detail," I said.

"We remember everything about you," Thor said. "How could we not?"

I just sat there grinning stupidly, heart overflowing with love. Being in a relationship with three hot guys who remembered my every word and acted as if my every whim was a command engraved in stone was better than all the hammocks and curly fries in the world.

Most of the time.

I studied the brochure some more. All the pictures were of couples. "Maybe this balloon guy'll bend the rules for us."

"This man's entire business model is based on couples. Rides for couples. Two seats in the balloon. I don't see him bending the rules, do you? Who has ever bent the rules for us?"

"But look," I began hopefully. "There's not even enough room in this balloon for five people! Zeus will see that!"

"There's room if one of those people is holding a gun," Odin said.

"Harley could refuse to drive it," I said hopefully.

"Zeus and I have a dozen different types of flight licenses between us," Odin reminded me. "Zeus could take that thing up drunk and blindfolded with both hands tied. I know I could."

I frowned, trying to picture exactly how either of them could possibly fly a hot air balloon in that condition. "Would it be wrong to ask for a demo of you guys doing that for my birthday?"

"Be serious. Zeus is going to want this for you, goddess," Odin continued. "This has to be the surprise. 'Surprise not at the Airbnb'—that's how he phrased it."

"Forewarned is forearmed," Thor said. "We'll talk to Harley. We'll ask him to cancel Zeus's reservation. Maybe we'll buy up Zeus's time slot, make it worth Harley's while. Maybe we can get Harley to call Zeus and tell him that the balloon's broken. Zeus'll never know it was us who put the kibosh on it."

"Right, good," I said. "Zeus would've made the reservation under Theo Talbott, *that* we know."

"This is why I hate surprises—this," Odin grumbled. "Fucking-g balloon ride."

"He just wants to fight for our relationship," I reminded Odin. "Fighting for our relationship is Zeus's love language."

"My love language is whatever doesn't result in a hassle with a stranger followed by a state-wide manhunt," he grumbled, with a dark look at Thor. He was talking, of course, about the infamous "couples' massage" incident which, to be fair, Thor *had* started when he pointed out how terrible it was that all four of us couldn't have a romantic couples' massage together.

"I didn't know he'd go crazy about it," Thor protested.

"Yes, you did," Odin said.

I looped an arm around each of them, there on the couch. "We protect each other's dreams," I said, reminding them of our wedding vows. "As well as each other's right to be totally messed up if we wanna be," I added, which was not in our wedding vows, but was something we sometimes reminded each other of.

Thor smoothed a lock of my hair—my natural red hair, shoulder-length these days. "I love us, too. I love you," he said, smoothing my hair some more, but not in the scurvy-cure way this time.

"Backatcha," I said, resting my head on his shoulder.

We were all four a little bit messed up. It's why we worked as a gang—we loved each other's messed-up-edness. We protected each other's messed-up-edness from the world.

Odin got up to make snacks. Thor and I followed him to the kitchen.

"We need to jump on this now," Odin said. "Zeus'll be out on his run for another hour. I say we go now."

"We could say I wanted to shop at the boutiques," I suggested. "If Zeus gets back before we do, he'll feel like he dodged a bullet." My guys hated boutique shopping.

"Perfect," Odin said.

"But we'll have to actually stop at a boutique to make it be true," I informed them. "And do some actual shopping. Maybe even bring home some proof, like a cute new sundress."

They groaned.

I wrote the note, and then the three of us shambled on our Newsome disguises. Ten minutes later we were on the road, heading away from the coast toward Harley's hot air balloon service, which would be opening in an hour. We were hoping to catch him before his first ride.

After what seemed like forever of us driving inland, we pulled into Harley's place, a dusty expanse of fenced-in land that was mostly barren except for a large metal warehouse-type outbuilding.

"Balloon rides by appointment only except Sundays noon to six" was hand-painted in block letters on the side of it.

A bearded man in overalls worked at a pump-type contraption at the far corner near an old red pickup truck. He stood and squinted as we drove across to where he was, regarding us with open suspicion.

Odin pulled up and parked next to the truck, and we got out.

"Rides by appointment only," he said, wiping a large wrench with a rag, roving his eyes over elderly Thor with his beret, arty Odin with his man bun, and me with my breasts.

"Are you Harley? Are you in charge here?" Thor asked.

The man poked his tongue into the inside of his cheek, making a bump that appeared and then disappeared, and then appeared again. He didn't like our questions or the way we looked—that's what I was getting from the cheek-poking thing.

"Who wants to know?"

"Has anybody by the name of Theo Talbott made a balloon ride reservation?" Thor asked. "It would have been for a couples' romantic ride, probably for tomorrow, though we're not really sure."

"My customers' reservations are none of your business," he said.

"Of course," Thor said, taking a diplomatic tone. "We just wanted to tell you that, if you're renting a balloon ride to this guy, you might want to rethink it. He has a history—"

"What did I just say?" Harley barked.

"We wanted to save you some possible hassles," Thor suggested.

"We just don't want anybody to have trouble," I put in.

"And who the hell are you to define what trouble is?" Harley asked my breasts. "What do you know about trouble?"

My breasts had seen a fair amount of trouble, that's for sure, but that was the sexy kind of trouble. The kind of trouble Zeus would cause if Harley didn't want four people up in his balloon would not be the sexy kind of trouble, that's for sure. Meeting Harley now, it wasn't much of a stretch to imagine that he wouldn't enjoy having the four of us up in his balloon for a romantic ride—not even a PG one.

"Who are we to define what trouble is?" Odin asked. "We're people who know Theo Talbott, that's who. He shouldn't be allowed up in a balloon—he's going to be a problem up there. If you have a reservation, I would strongly suggest canceling it. We'd be more than willing to pay you to make up for the loss of the ride. Maybe even throw in a bit extra for your willingness to be flexible."

Thor said, "We're truly trying to protect you—"

"Do I look like I need protection? Is that what you *folks* think?" Harley spat out the word *folks* like he didn't want it in his mouth too long. "The only problem here is I got some ponces thinking they can tell me how to run my own business, telling me who I can and can't take up in my own balloon, but last I checked it was a free country and I can damn well take up whoever I want. This Theo and his lady want a romantic hot air balloon experience? I'll give them the hot air balloon experience of a lifetime."

More like Zeus would give Harley the hot air experience of a lifetime, but of course I didn't say that, and neither did my breasts.

"Look," Odin said, "how about we pay you double the fee to rent Theo's spot?"

This was plan B. Money. It was also plan C, D, E, F, and G–Z.

I handed a stack of bills to Odin, more of the stash from the First National Bank in western Nebraska. We didn't have a lot of money from that heist left, but the three of us were willing to pay a lot of money to avoid the type of romantic hot air balloon experience of a lifetime that Zeus might end up creating.

Harley eyed the money, poking his tongue into the side of his cheek—poke, poke, poke. It looked like a little animal was trapped in there, trying to push its way out. A vole, perhaps.

"That's double and then some," Odin said.

"You think you can come in here flashing your money around,

telling me what to do? No. You come back here with the sheriff and a court order, and then we'll talk. Now get out."

I exchanged glances with Odin, who shook his head darkly. He turned on his heel and walked back to our car. Thor and I followed. Odin swung into the driver's seat and Thor got into the passenger side and I slipped into the back.

"I thought we were going to offer him more money," I said.

Odin backed up the car and headed out to the main road. "He wouldn't accept more money," Odin said. Odin tended to know these things. "We have to prevent Zeus another way."

"How?" I asked.

"I don't know," Odin said.

"Maybe I'll pretend like I'm coming down with something," I said, turning to Thor. "But not enough for him to ask you to make me a health shake."

"What's wrong with my health shakes?" Thor said. "They're good for you. And delicious."

"Um..." I said.

"Fine. Go with vertigo," Thor said. "Vertigo would ruin a balloon ride, and health shakes don't do anything for it."

I wrapped my arms around him. "You are brilliant!" I said, giving him a big kiss.

"What about me?" Odin complained.

"You'll get a kiss when you say something brilliant. Which I'm sure will be soon." I was feeling good. Vertigo was the perfect excuse to get out of the balloon ride.

Chapter Five

ODIN BUGGED ZEUS ABOUT THE SURPRISE THAT NIGHT, just because it would be weird not to bug him about it, and I started planting the vertigo seeds, complaining of dizziness when I stood up from the table.

Zeus looked concerned. "You're not coming down with something, are you?"

"Oh, no," I assured him. "It's just a touch of vertigo. It's nothing, really."

"Maybe you need one of Thor's health shakes," Zeus said.

"Yeah, maybe that would be beneficial," Thor said impishly.

"No, vertigo isn't the kind of thing that a health shake can help," I said, glaring at Thor. "It's a low blood pressure thing. As long as I don't do anything weird like bungee jumping or a gymnastics routine on a trapeze, I'll be fine."

"Do you think the hammock could be aggravating it?" Zeus asked Thor.

"Probably not. Unless she was trying to stand up in the hammock," Thor said, redeeming himself somewhat. "Being off the ground standing like that would be very bad."

Zeus looked at him like he was crazy. "Why the fuck would Isis stand up in the hammock?"

Thor shrugged.

"No standing up in the hammock. It's decided!" I exclaimed, hopefully ending our weird conversation.

&

Thor and I were at the breakfast bar when Odin dragged himself out of the bedroom he'd claimed as his.

"Did you even sleep?" Thor asked.

Odin grumbled, grabbing a coffee cup. A *no* if I ever heard one.

"Did you try the meditations I gave you?" Thor asked.

"Yeah," Odin said.

"Both of them?" Thor pressed. "Twenty minutes twice a day, and the progressive relaxation one before sleep?"

"This doesn't just go away with a snap of the fingers," Odin barked.

"But if you'd give them a try," Thor said.

"We'll see, okay?" Odin snapped.

Thor stared into his coffee. Was Odin even trying the meditations? Thor was a dedicated doctor with exactly one patient—Odin—and he was desperate to help him. Maybe too desperate.

"I bet they would help if you tried," I said. "We have to find a way for you to sleep with us."

"After what happened in Rome?" Odin scoffed. "Impossible."

"Nothing's impossible," I said as Zeus strolled in from the veranda.

"About time you losers woke up." Zeus refilled his coffee and glanced at weary-looking Odin. He, too, was worried about Odin's sleep issues, but he didn't want to say anything. Instead, he asked about my vertigo.

"Not much change to report," I said.

"Mmm," he said.

I think we were all feeling pretty confident that the vertigo would get us out of any balloon rides, but then, after lunch, Zeus said, casually, "I think we should go into town. I think we should get our disguises and go to town and walk around. I might have found something fun for us to do."

"What would that be?" Odin asked.

"You'll see," Zeus said.

"What do you mean by 'into town?'" I asked. There were several little towns around, one of them near Harley's.

"Just into town," Zeus said.

"Is this our surprise?" Thor asked.

Zeus shrugged.

"Come on," I begged. "A hint?"

"You guys suck the most. Yes, it is the surprise, okay?" he said, annoyed.

"Is it going to aggravate my dizziness?" I asked.

Zeus frowned. "I hope not. It's just some walking around."

"Perfect!" I said happily.

We got into our Newsome disguises and piled into the car. Odin and Thor and I exchanged relieved glances as we headed in the opposite direction from the Harley balloon emporium, eventually heading up along the sea.

Disaster averted!

"Is your vertigo okay with all of this driving?" Zeus asked at one point.

"Way better," I said. "I think the fresh air and scenery is doing wonders for it."

Next to me, Thor rolled his eyes. I brushed some of the powder from his sleeve. His old man hair and mustache required a lot of powder. He smiled and his face cracked a little.

Sometimes we argued about which of our Newsome disguises was the most uncomfortable. Odin had the bushy artist beard and man bun hairpiece and shaded glasses, and he often complained that he was hot. I had that stuff that fit around my teeth and made my cheeks different, plus a wig and fake brows—it was a lot! Thor mostly had face makeup and hair powder. Zeus had to wear padding to give him a belly, plus the wig. But please. Cheek puffers!

After forty minutes of driving and a few twists and turns, we ended up on the outskirts of a little town called Oak Corners.

"We're here!" Zeus announced.

"Is this the surprise?" I asked.

Zeus looked at me, disgusted. "What, some random town? What the fuck kind of surprise would that be?"

"I don't know," I said.

We drew closer. There seemed to be some kind of outdoor festival going on, judging from the number of people on the sidewalks and how hard it was to find a parking space. We finally found one and got out.

Zeus seemed extremely excited.

"Is *this* the surprise?" I asked.

"When you see it, you'll know it," he said.

I was just excited that there were no hot air balloons anywhere. But what was the surprise?

Zeus had his phone out and was following directions, heading north. I walked by his side as though we were a pair, and Odin and Thor walked together some ways behind us, acting as if they didn't know us. This way of walking had become second nature to us, being that one of the first things ZOX agents and the police who worked with them would be looking for would be three men and a woman.

Not that people would be on the lookout for us in random places. But you never knew. And Odin and Zeus still seemed to be looking over their shoulders more than usual.

We turned a corner onto Main Street, nearing the center of the small town. It was there that I spied the huge banner strung between old-fashioned streetlights, emblazoned with the words

"Oak Corners Artisanal Cheese and Wine Festival" and, below that, "AAGSCI."

I spun and grabbed Zeus's arm, grinning so widely I'm sure my chipmunk cheeks were the size of two baseballs. "The American Artisanal Goat and Sheep Cheese Invitational!" Which we in the business pronounced ag-see.

"That's right," he said.

We'd been spending so much time running from place to place I hadn't kept up with the world of artisanal cheeses. I'd forgotten it was even this weekend, or that this year's festival was on the West Coast.

"This is one of the most prestigious small-farm cheese events in the world!" I exclaimed. "How did you think of this?"

Zeus smiled mysteriously.

At the center of town, Zeus showed his phone to a guy at a table. The guy handed over four bracelets. Zeus discreetly passed two of them to Odin and Thor. I hooked my arm in his and practically dragged him toward where cheesemakers and other vendors had set up their tables and booths to display their wares.

"Hope you're hungry," Zeus said.

"For cheese?" I exclaimed. "Always! Thank you," I added.

Zeus's mysterious smile wore on. Was there a further surprise? Were they giving romantic hot air balloon rides at the festival?

"My sisters and I always dreamed of Sunny Sisters Sheep Farm being invited to compete," I told him. "It was on our dream board."

He just smiled some more.

We tasted an amazing gouda at the first table, and then some really interesting blue cheeses. Zeus bought me a soft, hot pretzel covered in melted Swiss cheese, and I nearly died of yumminess. I turned and caught Odin's eye and pointed to the booth, meaning, *you two need to get yourselves these things.*

We headed up the street. In addition to the many cheese tables, there were cheese-themed Christmas ornaments, cheese knives and serving sets, plaques with cheesy cheese sayings, and lots of other cheese-themed crafts that made me wish we had a permanent home to decorate.

We stopped and bought some fresh cider—luckily not cheese flavored—and proceeded on to the local high school football field where the main judging event was apparently being held.

Tables were set up all over the playing field, arrayed in four long rows up and down. The place was crowded already, and it wasn't even noon. There were even clusters of people sitting up in the bleachers.

"This is such an amazing surprise, Zeus," I said.

"Oh, it gets better," he said mysteriously.

My heart began to pound. "What? Tell me!" I didn't dare hope...

Zeus handed over a program he'd snagged. "Why don't you look on here and see who's up for a class C small-farm sheep gouda medal?"

Hands shaking, I scanned the list, and there, listed in the field of ten finalists, was Sunny Sisters Sheep Farm.

"They're here!" I whispered. My first impulse was to take off sprinting, to run all around looking for my sisters—who I hadn't seen for what felt like a lifetime—but of course that was impossible.

Zeus looked at me sadly, following my train of thought. "You know you can't..."

"I know," I said.

It would be far too dangerous to make contact with my sisters in such a public place. It was always possible that ZOX was on our tail, and the last thing we'd ever want to do was lead them to my sisters. ZOX had no idea who I was or where I was from, and it was important to keep it that way. If they knew who my sisters were, or the fact that I would do anything for them, they'd use that information ruthlessly.

"But they're here. You'll get to see them competing—from afar, anyway," Zeus said.

"I'll get to see them achieve a dream," I said.

Odin and Thor had caught up to us. We lingered discreetly in a cluster of people watching a cheese-making demonstration.

Odin lowered his voice. "Your sisters will kick the living shit out of everybody in this place," he stated.

"Maybe you could at least say hi to Vanessa," Thor suggested to me.

Vanessa was the oldest of my three sisters, and the most chill of the group. Unlike my younger sisters, she knew I was alive.

"There's no way they're, you know," Thor added, meaning there was no way ZOX was on our tail right now.

"We don't know that," Odin said. "We have to follow the protocols we've developed. It's how we keep ourselves—keep everybody—safe."

Such a Zeus thing to say. I smiled approvingly, loving that he wanted to show his commitment, to keep things smooth after their fight.

We watched out for each other. We supported each other. That's what kept us strong.

"Yeah…" Thor mumbled with a significant glance at Odin and Zeus. "Right."

"'Yeah, right' what? Is there some reason to be worried?" I asked, because Thor clearly had something on his mind.

"There's always reason to be worried, is there not?" Odin said.

"Look, here they are." Zeus showed me the festival map, finger tapping a spot with his big, meaty finger.

I examined the map. The Sunny Sisters' table was near the far corner of the field, third from the end of a row of small sheep-cheese producers near the concession stand. I wanted to go over there, but my sisters would definitely recognize me no matter how good my disguise was. What's more, my sister Vanessa had met Odin, Zeus, and Thor last year—she might see through their disguises, too—especially if they showed up together. We decided that Odin looked the least like himself, so we elected him to go over to their table, get some of the cheese samples, and maybe even talk to them.

"Ask them how they feel about their chances," I said. "Ask them what their favorite cheese is right now and if there are any new offerings on the horizon."

Odin nodded.

"Wait, no, ask them..." I pressed my fingers to my forehead, wanting the perfect question. "Hold on, let me think."

Strong hands settled onto my shoulders. "You want to know how they are, and if they are happy," Odin said.

"Yeah, but..." It's not like he could ask them that.

"Am I not a professional *fucking-g* interrogator?" he said to me. "You think I can't conduct a casual conversation where I figure out how three girls are doing and get some fun details of their lives?"

"Okay, yeah. Try to get a lot of fun details. Everything you can," I implored him.

"I will, goddess." Odin set off.

Chapter Six

The three of us stayed back in the group watching the demo. I studied the map some more, staring at my sisters' table—number 803—just wanting to go there with Odin. After way too much time doing that, I forced myself to look at the rest of the map. I recognized the names of some of the big players in the cheese world. The larger producers were assigned to long tables on the ends of the rows to accommodate the crowds. There were also tables with industry experts here and there, most of whom would be judging. Some of them, like me, taught online cheese-making classes, but way more popular ones than my measly little classes that I didn't advertise. A few had YouTube channels about cheese.

Zeus and Thor and I checked out the tables on our side of the field. A few of the judges were milling around—you could recognize them by their white coats. The cheese industry is big on white coats. We were on the goat cheese end of things, and we tasted a lot of amazing cheeses. That artisanal cheese world was becoming more and more sophisticated—and more and more competitive.

The three of us were just moving from one goat farm table to another when the voice rang out: "Hey! I know you!" My antenna went on alert because the voice seemed familiar, and definitely seemed aimed at me.

Gulp! Had somebody recognized me?

But I knew enough not to look up.

I could feel Zeus's gaze on me. I could feel Thor straighten.

This was a cheese festival, after all—it was no doubt crawling with Wisconsin people—but who could possibly see through my disguise? What's more, I was presumed dead. I hated that we'd had to fake my death, but it was the only way to protect my sisters.

It was just last year that we'd let Vanessa in on the secret that I was still alive. My sisters had needed our help solving a mystery, and it was unavoidable. But Vanessa never would have told another living soul our secret.

Zeus grabbed my arm and began to walk casually away.

The voice followed us. "Hey, wait!" the voice said. "Sarah! Sarah Newsome!"

I could feel the relief in Zeus's large frame. Somebody had recognized me from a cheese-making class. Not great, but way better than being recognized as my former self. I spun around, plastering a smile on my chipmunk face.

An attractive, big-boned, middle-aged woman came up to me. She had long black hair with a wild gray streak right down the front.

"Yes?" I said.

"I thought it was you! I'm Babs 123. I took your class online last year? My neighbor recommended it. She's here somewhere. She'll be so excited that you're here."

"Oh, Babs 123. I remember you!" I said. "How is the quest to make the perfect smoked mozzarella going?"

Babs caught me up on her cheese-making journey. She'd moved on to cheddar and recently tried her hand at gouda. I introduced her to my boyfriend, Theo Talbott, aka Zeus. Thor had disappeared into the crowd, probably monitoring from a distance.

Zeus seemed relaxed, so I relaxed, too. It wasn't the worst thing in the world to have been recognized as my online cheese-making-teacher persona; in fact, it showed that the alternate identity was working out. My guys were always saying that we wanted our alternate identities to be viable. That's the word they always used. A viable alternate identity would be crucial if we ever really had to disappear.

Still, it was a little disconcerting.

Babs dragged me over and introduced me to her sister, who was talking to a pair of goat cheese judges. Her sister was just as excited as she was.

One of the judges, a man with white hair and a dark mustache, turned to me. "You teach cheese making?" he asked.

"Not in any big way. It's just a hobby," I said.

"It's not a hobby for Sarah, it's a passion!" Babs said. "She knows everything about cheeses."

The other judge had perked up now. She was in her thirties with short blond hair and a serious gaze behind her thick glasses. "Sarah, I don't want to impose," she said to me, "but one of our judges couldn't make it, and we need a third for the aged goat cheddar competition. We'd love it if you could step in…if at all possible. I'm technical, and Cal is aesthetic; as an educator, you'd do overall."

"Oh, I don't know," I said, turning to Zeus. "It's such an honor, but we have a thing later…"

"It's a small category," she said. "You'd only have to be here for around thirty minutes," she added. "And then another round of thirty minutes sometime later. It could go to three rounds, but you'll probably be done at two."

"I wouldn't mind," Zeus said. "We'd still make our thing."

"Are you sure?" I asked.

"It's perfect. Who would be a better judge than you?" he said, clearly pleased that my identity was gaining depth. My guys and their spy stuff. So nerdy.

The serious woman, who introduced herself as Mary Ann,

taught ag sciences at a nearby college, according to her badge. She lowered her voice and said, "We had a contestant who's being a problem with a two-judge panel when the rules stipulate a three-judge industry panel. You'd be perfect to make up our third. He wouldn't be able to raise objections with a third who's an educator."

"And the judges' gift baskets are mind-blowingly good this year," the man said. He introduced himself as Cal. "I'm a maker. Bovine."

I nodded. The cheese world is split into bovine and nonbovine. This entire festival was nonbovine; no doubt there were a lot of small-farm bovine cheese artisans working as judges. Small-farm nonbovine cheesemakers would probably be judging aplenty at his next bovine competition. It's a whole thing.

I confirmed with Mary Ann that my judging would end with this aged goat cheddar gig—the last thing I needed was to be judging my sisters' sheep cheese. Mary Ann assured me that it would just be this one small section. She wasn't even planning on spitting out the cheese after tasting—with just one section, she wasn't worried about palate fatigue. Naturally, I preferred not to spit out my cheese, either. Because, cheese!

A few minutes later I was wearing a white lab coat of my own.

"Report back here in an hour and we'll start gearing up for the first round," Mary Ann said.

"Will do," I said. "We're going to make a quick round and then I'll be back."

Zeus and I set off. "You're going to be an amazing judge," he said. "If there's one thing that you have no shortage of, it's opinions on cheese."

I punched him in his padded arm.

"Also, I like the doctor's coat." He lowered his voice. "A lot."

"I'll have you know that cheese judging is both an art and a science, and that this is a lab coat, not a doctor's coat, and it is most certainly not a prop for sexy games. I know that's what you're thinking. So I will ask you to get your mind out of the gutter, sir!"

Zeus snorted. I was kidding, of course. The gutter was one of my favorite places for his mind to go.

"Seriously, why the lab coat?" he asked. "What's so sterile about cheese?"

"I know! It should be a toga," I said. "Cheese is a pleasure."

We walked on, sampling cheeses here and there, but we paused when we got within five tables of my sisters. I pretended to talk with Zeus while watching them from afar.

Odin was still at their table, in an animated conversation with Candace from the looks of it.

Vanessa and Kaitlin were talking to people and sampling. Ice chests were stacked up behind the table—full of cheese to sell, no doubt. I was hoping that they'd brought enough. People loved Sunny Sisters cheese.

I continued to pretend to be talking to Zeus, who expertly maneuvered us around so I could see them better. They looked great, but they really were growing up fast. Vanessa had matured into a poised young woman. Candace, who would be in her second year of community college by now, had her red hair twisted into an elaborate design held together by something sparkly. Kaitlin would be graduating from high school soon. She'd added several wild pink streaks to her red hair. It looked nice. I wished that I could tell her that.

"Odin better buy a lot of their cheese," I said.

"Oh, I'm sure he will," Zeus assured me.

Good luck, I whispered to them, striving to send them all of the good luck vibes possible. Zeus grabbed my hand. Not good to linger. I didn't want to leave, but eventually I let him pull me away. We headed back to the opposite corner.

I sampled some soft goat cheese on a raisin cracker. "Heaven!" I exclaimed.

"Don't spoil your dinner," Zeus warned.

"So weird to be recognized." I snagged another goat cheese treat. I loved goat cheese a lot, but as animals, sheep had better personalities.

I was eager for Odin to come back with his report, but that would have to wait; it was time for me to judge.

We ambled over.

Mary Ann waved and pointed to the tasting station next to her, and I took up my post. The three of us stood there in our lab coats, ready to decide which aged goat cheddar would rule them all.

People crowded around to watch. Most of these people were probably the makers and their families and friends.

A festival volunteer rolled up a cart with twelve blocks of cheese on it. The cheeses were identified by numbers only, and it was our job to grade each one on appearance, flavor, body, and color. We would be grading them numerically, and the five highest-scoring cheeses would compete for ribbons in the final round.

We weren't supposed to discuss anything on this first round. We were just to grade, and then on the second round, that's when we'd have discussions about the merits of the different cheeses.

And yes, for the record, I have very extreme and specific opinions on cheeses.

The cheeses were presented one by one. The three of us examined the appearance and makeup of the blocks, looking at things like uniformity and deducting points for irregular finishes.

A volunteer then bored a hole into the cheese and pulled out three samples, one for each of us and we evaluate the firmness and color.

Then it was time to "flavor" the cheeses, which meant we were tasting each cheese as well as evaluating the odor, body, and texture of it, while participating in the sad transformation of nouns into verbs.

We cleansed our palates with crackers, apples, and soda between each round.

I had to admit, this was an excellent group of cheeses. Any one of them deserved a medal, but a few definitely stood out. When all the scores were finally tallied up, I was pleased to see that we all more or less agreed which cheeses were at the top of the cheese heap.

We wrote the final scores on flags and stuck them to their respective blocks of cheese.

With ceremonious solemnity, Cal opened a manila envelope and pulled out the key that showed which of the cheesemakers corresponded to which of the numbers. Cheers went up when he announced the five finalists, though there were also some very long faces.

I really felt for the makers who didn't get into the final round. A blue ribbon from a festival like this could get you onto store shelves and restaurant cheese trays.

There was a two-hour break between judging rounds.

Odin was still on the sheep side of things. I was glad he was gathering intel, but still!

I headed out the gate to the grassy parking area where the porta potties were for a preventative pee break. The guys had gone in search of manly food. Because apparently cheese and crackers is girl food. Fine with me. Please go ahead and leave all of the cheese and crackers to the girls!

The line at the porta potties was insane, but I got through it only to discover that the line to get back into the main showing area was even more insane. People were excited about fancy cheeses, and I could hardly blame them.

Of course, there were perks to being a judge, including the staff entrance I'd noticed earlier. I left the long line and headed behind the shady bleachers to use my badge to get in the staff entrance. That's when I heard the voice calling out to me—"Miss Newsome! Miss Newsome!"

I spun around to see a middle-aged man in a sweater vest barreling toward me with great determination. He had a lantern jaw and swept-back hair, slightly graying at the temples. "You heading back to the goat cheddar table?" he asked—or more, demanded.

I *was* heading back, but I didn't want to tell him. I didn't want anything to do with him. I didn't like how he was creepily beelining toward me.

My mind spun, remembering how Zeus and Odin had seemed overly focused on the rearview mirror this week. Even Thor had seemed weirdly cautious, like he was hiding something. Had they seen signs of ZOX? Was this creepy guy a part of ZOX? Was he planning on using me to get to my guys?

Also, we were basically alone in the empty back-of-festival area, alone in the gloomy expanse between the people entrance and the special staff entrance.

I gave him a tight smile, mumbled something, and turned to walk off at a fast clip, hoping he wouldn't catch up to me.

"Hold up!" he commanded. "A moment of your time!"

I didn't hold up, but he overtook me all the same, literally racing around to stop in front of me, blocking me.

"Quick question," he said. "Do you have any favorites? In the goat cheddar competition?"

I frowned. "Excuse me?"

"Which are your favorites?" he asked.

"You'll find out during the last round of judging," I said. "Now if you'll excuse me." I sidestepped him and made a beeline for the staff entrance, which was still too far away. My knees were trembling.

This was all wrong.

Again he came in front of me, this time extending his arms out to his sides, really blocking me. "No favorites?" he asked in his demanding way.

"I'm not at liberty to discuss this any further," I said.

Right then, he grabbed my lab coat-clad arm.

I tried to wrest my arm from his iron grip. "Let me go!"

He didn't. "Let's cut to the chase—I have an offer you can't refuse."

Alarm shot through me. In our world, *an offer you can't refuse* meant, *do this thing or I'll kill you.* Naturally I was thinking ZOX at this point. "Forget it," I said

"You haven't heard my offer," the man said.

"I'm going to scream if you don't let go!" I threatened, even though the last thing I wanted was to draw the attention of the police or any authorities of any kind.

"You're gonna want to hear this," he said.

"I won't betray them," I hissed.

He looked confused. "Won't betray who? Has somebody else gotten to you?"

I frowned. He wasn't making a lot of sense, but our enemies were ruthless and not above mind games.

He leaned in. "There is a pale yellow cheddar with notes of brioche bread, nutmeg, and black chocolate that is far and away the best of the five. It has the palest yellow hue of the final five, you understand?" he said. "That is the one that should win. It's objectively the best one, and I'm willing to make it worth your while to judge accordingly."

"W-what?" My gaze dropped to his badge. Merona Meadows Dairy. This guy was a cheesemaker. This was about the competition! "I haven't picked a winner," I said. "I don't take bribes. All five finalists have an equal shot."

"Then who won't you betray?" he demanded. "Do you have allegiance to one of the other contenders?"

"Of course not!"

He tightened his grip. "Was it Happy Dairy?"

I tried to pull my arm away from him, but he pulled me close to his side and repeated his bit: "Pale buttery yellow in color with brioche bread, nutmeg, and black chocolate notes."

Zeus had taught me a lot of self-defense techniques: head-butt. Knee to the groin. Knuckle punch the Adam's apple. But all of that would draw attention, possibly resulting in a police report.

"You're on your way to being disqualified," I threatened.

"I doubt that." He started fumbling with my pocket—creepily.

"Get away!" I tried to wriggle away, but he was weirdly strong.

"Calm down! I just put something into your pocket, that's all," he said, exasperated, like I should know what he was doing.

"I don't want anything from you!"

His grip turned steely. "Oh, yes you do," he said. "In your pocket is an envelope with five thousand dollars cash in it. There will be another envelope just like it in your pocket when the right cheese wins. Are we clear on that?"

"No. I don't want your money."

"It's five thousand," he said. "Not five hundred, not one thousand, but FIVE thousand." This like I was so stupid. "And another five after, to make ten thousand."

"I don't want it."

"Nobody will know."

"I don't take bribes."

"Consider it a gift, then."

"Forget it!"

"Come on, Sarah. You're an online nobody who can barely pull together enough students for one class a year. You live in an RV with your boyfriend, whose greatest accomplishment seems to be doing pushups by the Santa Monica Pier. You spend your time needlepointing inspirational cheese-themed art and you're obsessed with visiting Switzerland someday and touring the city of Gruyere. You could finally do that. Don't pretend that's not important to you. Ten grand can take you there in style."

I frowned. "I'm not open to bribes."

Also, needlepointing inspirational cheese-themed art? What the hell was Odin writing in our online bios?

"It's not as if you'd be elevating a substandard cheese—let's face it, the five finalists are all excellent cheeses, but you'd like to choose the very best cheese to be the winner, which is clearly the one with the buttery pale color and the notes of brioche bread, nutmeg, and black chocolate."

"I'll choose whatever cheese I want, and if you bother me about it anymore, I'm going to report you to the judges and have that cheese disqualified." I pulled the envelope from my pocket and slammed it into his belly, then I yanked my hand away and ran toward the gate.

Feet pounded behind me, and a viselike grip clamped onto my arm, stopping me short with a jerk that nearly gave me whiplash. He pulled me close, shoving his lips to my ear like it was a microphone. "It would be a shame if somebody shut down your online course with armies of sock puppets," he said in a menacing tone. "It would be a shame if somebody complained to some kind of authority about you not having a business license to teach that class. It would be a shame if somebody tracked down that RV of yours and slashed the tires...or worse."

"Are you threatening me?" I asked, heart racing. Sort of a dorky question because, hello?

"I'm just saying it would be a crying shame," he continued, "it would be a *crying* shame if that happened, just like it would be a crying shame for the wrong cheese to win. Just like it would be a crying shame for you to lose this money."

My pulse pounded. It was disturbing that he was putting so much emphasis on crying.

"I see that you're thinking about it," he said. "Good girl. You know that you have to protect your livelihood, don't you?"

I sucked in a breath. I was not a fan of his threats, especially ones that involved the phrase *good girl*. A freak with a vendetta could definitely make trouble for us. Best-case scenario: we could never use the Newsome identity again. Worst case: he could lead ZOX to us.

My gaze lowered to his Adam's apple, which was starting to

look knuckle-punchable, attention or not. But he was a lot bigger than me, and something seemed off about him. Dangerous-off. And we were all alone back here.

He gave me a weird smile, like he was just realizing that, too. My skin began to crawl.

"And let's face it," he continued, "this is merely a regional cheese competition—is it really worth passing up thousands of dollars? Enduring a *crying* shame with somebody who'd go after you with every weapon he can muster? Is it really worth all of that trouble?" He stepped in closer, using his size. "When you know that the pale yellow one with nutmeg notes is the best anyway?"

A deafening chorus of alarm bells clanged in my head. It was his manner, and the fact that he'd added crying to every instance of shame. What exactly was his understanding of the phrase *crying shame*?

Just then, I noticed movement over his shoulder.

Three man-sized blurs racing toward us.

Three man-sized blurs in the form of Thor and Odin and Zeus.

"Well?" the man asked, oblivious to the trouble coming at him.

"I have a question," I said. "Would it be a crying shame for you to shove that buttery pale cheese right up your ass?"

"Excuse me?"

"Would that be a *crying* shame? Or just a plain shame?"

Before he could respond to my wee question, two strong hands clamped over the man's shoulders and ripped him away from me.

Zeus.

Zeus held him by the collar, practically lifting him up in the air. It was almost like in a cartoon when a character is hoisted up or goes off a cliff or something, and their legs are still paddling.

Zeus knew he shouldn't make a scene, but he wasn't hugely rational when he thought I was in danger.

"What the fuck do you think you're doing?" Zeus demanded.

"Nothing!" the guy said.

"Are you okay?" Thor asked, coming up, touching me gently.

"I'm fine," I said. "Just..." I handed him the envelope. "H-he..." I was losing my voice. I hadn't realized how terrified I was.

"Bribing you?" Thor asked gently. "Was he bribing you?"

I nodded mutely.

"Is this true?" Zeus growled.

"Who are you, the cheese police?" the man demanded.

In a flash, Zeus had a gun pressed up under the man's chin. His eyes widened like saucers. "That's right, we're the cheese police, aka your worst nightmare."

I could see people approaching. This was bad. There were cops and security personnel inside the festival grounds, and if we somehow attracted too much attention, it wouldn't just be ourselves in danger, we'd be putting my sisters in danger. This was why I'd forced myself to stay away from them this whole time—to avoid dragging them into the circle of danger that was ZOX.

"Seems you dropped this." Odin had the man's wallet. How did he get it? He took out his driver's license and read the man's name aloud—"Jasper Tolverson"—and then he read out Jasper's address. "Now we know who you are and where to find you."

"Who are you?" he asked.

"I told you," Zeus said, "we're the cheese police, and let's just say we're making sure this will be a fair cheese competition."

"You work for the festival?" Jasper asked, bewildered. I suppose it was weird that a small cheese festival would have this kind of undercover muscle.

"If you threaten this judge or any of the judges ever again," Zeus began, "at this or any future cheese competition, we will fuck you up so hard, you'll be lucky to be mistaken for a Picasso painting."

"A Picasso painting from the Cubist Period, motherfucker, not Blue Period," Thor added. "And if you don't know what Picasso's Cubist paintings look like, let's just say the facial features are in the wrong fucking places."

"I know what the fuck Picasso's Cubist paintings look like," Jasper said.

Thor nodded. "Good."

A pair of security guys were coming our way from the direction of the gate. Would the guy say something? Zeus put away his gun.

Thor smiled breezily, like everything was fine.

Odin looped an arm around Jasper's shoulders, drew him near, and whispered something into his ear. Jasper turned white as a sheet, stumbled backwards, and then turned and ran the other direction toward the porta potties.

The security guards reached us. It was two burly guys. The older one stared after the sweater vest guy. "What's going on? Was that guy giving you trouble?"

"We're good," I said.

"You sure?"

"Too many nutty notes in his brie," I said.

The guards seemed to like this. "We'll keep an eye on him," the one said, and they ambled toward the porta potties.

"You sure you're okay?" Zeus asked.

"I'm fine. I just wasn't expecting anything like that here," I said, though deep down, I was still shaking. "Maybe I should have just done what he asked. He could make a lot of trouble for us."

"Goddess," Odin said, "we may have doomed you to a life of crime, a life as a fugitive, always looking over her shoulder, but we would never want you to have to lie about something you love as much as cheese." His voice had morphed into a growl at this point. "Not ever!"

"Thank you, baby," I said. "So, what did you whisper in his ear that got him so upset?"

Odin shook his head.

"Oh, come on, tell me what you said to him!" I shoved Odin playfully. "Please?"

"Whatever it was, you don't want to know," Zeus said to me.

"Do *you* know?" I asked Zeus.

"I've got a guess," Zeus said.

"You don't have the first clue," Odin said.

"I know I don't," Thor said.

I turned to Thor. "And you stayed in character, making a threat that involved knowledge of fine arts," I said. "Amazing."

Thor grinned. "I am amazing, it's true."

"You are."

I turned to Odin, wanting to get every detail he gleaned from my sisters table, but right then, my phone buzzed. It was my fellow judges, warning me that I had ten minutes to return to the table.

"Were you out doing the fifty-yard dash or something?" Mary Ann asked me when I arrived, breathless.

"Might as well have been," I said, smoothing my hair back.

I centered myself and sat down just as the five cheddars were brought out on a platter.

The crowd around our table fell silent as judging officially began. We sniffed and inspected the different cheeses. We smooshed them, evaluating texture. I didn't see the guy who had threatened me anywhere, but there was a pale, buttery-yellow cheddar, one that was paler than the rest, and I found, once we got to the tasting part, that it did have delightful brioche bread, nutmeg, and black chocolate notes. It wasn't as good as the cheese that we ended up awarding a blue ribbon to, but it did win third—mostly because Cal had rated it with near-perfect marks. Had he taken money, or did he just love that cheese? I suspected the former; it was very extreme to have such high marks.

I hated the idea that a cheese competition could be corrupt. Not just because my sisters had cheeses competing out in the world, but because I wanted to know that these competitions were pure and true. Maybe it's ironic, coming from somebody involved in a life of crime. Or maybe being involved in a life of crime makes you appreciate when people follow rules.

At any rate, the cheddar we picked was really amazing and

absolutely deserved to win. Mary Ann would be presenting the blue ribbon at the final event.

But what I was really interested in was what happened over at the small-farm sheep gouda table. How were my How had Sunny Sisters' cheese fared? Would they be awarded best in class?

As soon as I could, I thanked my fellow judges, promising to keep in touch, then worked my way through the crowd to Zeus.

"Where are…"

"We're saving a place for you, goddess. Come on," he said, leading me down the length of the football field, past all of the goat cheese tables, and around to the bleachers, making a wide berth around my sisters' table and the whole sheep judging area, which was definitely more unruly than the goat judging area.

Thor and Odin waved from a spot at the corner of the bleachers. Thor had binoculars. We went up and sat with them.

"Well?" I said to Odin. "Tell all!"

"Your sisters seem great," he said. "Happy. They tell little stories about the sheep to people. I heard Vanessa tease Kaitlin about a boyfriend."

"No!' I made him repeat everything he'd overheard. He'd asked questions about the farm. He'd taken some discreet photos, too. I pressed him for every last detail.

"Someday you'll ask them these things for yourself," Zeus said.

I sighed. It was a nice dream. But was it just that?

The award portion started up. The cheeses were announced and awarded one by one with the makers coming up to the table to stand behind their respective rounds of cheese. I kept an iron grip on the binoculars when my sisters' category came up.

"The blue ribbon for small-farm sheep gouda goes to…" An envelope was brought to the podium—it was just like the Oscars! —"Sunny Sisters sheep gouda!"

I screamed, and my guys hooted and whooped. My grin nearly cracked my face in half as I watched my little sisters file up to stand behind the winners' table as their round of cheese was set in front of them with a giant blue ribbon affixed to it. I stood and hugged Zeus, and then I hugged Odin and Thor. "They won! They did it!"

We were massively thrilled. It was almost like our win.

I watched them as long as I could. People congratulated them. Their table got mobbed. My sisters wouldn't stop smiling.

My heart couldn't have been fuller by the time we drove out of there.

We headed up the coast and celebrated at a little out-of-the-way restaurant that had dim lighting—ideal because I was getting tired of wearing my chipmunk cheek implants, and I definitely didn't love eating with them in—and then we headed back.

❧

Our proprietress, Sue, was in front of our Airbnb trimming hedges when we pulled up.

"I do not like this one bit," Odin mumbled.

"I'm just glad I didn't pull off my eyebrows yet," I said, shoving my cheeks back in.

"So nosy," Thor grumbled. "You know she wants to see what art we bought. She's totally trying to get a scoop on our hot lead."

"Good. Let her nose around. There's nothing for her to see," Zeus said. "Nothing in the place that's not one hundred percent Newsome. She can look all she wants, and she'll see that we are who we are."

"And if she wants to talk about art, I'm ready with my research on Picasso," Thor said, pretending to brush something from his sleeve.

We got out. I waved at her. "A little yardwork?" I asked her.

"Yes," she said. "I'm sorry, I don't mean to intrude, but we meant to get to these before you came. I'll be out of your hair," she said, seeming a little sheepish.

I took a small round of cheese from the gift basket that I was awarded for being a judge and handed it to her.

"What is this?" she asked.

"We spent the day at the artisanal cheese festival," I said. "I was serving as guest judge, and they gave me all kinds of cheeses. That one was awarded best in show—it's a pecorino that will be amazing on pasta."

"Wow, are you sure?" she asked.

"I want you to have it. Thank you for letting us stay in your beautiful place." I smiled over at Zeus. Judging at an artisanal cheese competition—that was some next-level Newsome shit right there.

She finally took off. We barbecued out that night, making delicious burgers topped with the fanciest cheese on the planet.

I acted bored of hot tubs all through dinner and soon found myself naked in the hot tub with three growling guys making me take back my assertions in exciting and fun ways.

The next morning I put in some very serious time on the hammock with my book and a glass of iced coffee, which fit perfectly into the handy hammock drink holder. Zeus came over and gave me a foot rub. "Are you sure you should be in a hammock with that vertigo?" he asked.

Riiiight, the vertigo.

"It's all better," I said.

"But what if lying in the hammock makes it come back?" he asked, moving deft fingers over my pinky toe.

"I really don't think it's going to come back," I said. The whole vertigo ruse wasn't necessary anymore, considering that Zeus's surprise was the cheese festival and not the romantic balloon ride.

I read out there for hours, until I was drawn inside by the scent of fresh honey popovers. We sat around the ultra-California sunken living room feasting on warm, gooey pastries. There were also mimosas—one of my favorite drinks—and I had two giant ones. I will admit to feeling a bit tipsy.

We had really underestimated Zeus with the balloon ride stuff. Yes, he always got that crazy bee in his bonnet when it came to fighting for our foursome. And yes, there had been times when he freaked out when businesses offered romantic packages for two for things that he wished the four of us could do, but we all had our quirks.

"That was an amazing day yesterday," I said. "The Sunny Sisters' gouda is going to be getting so many orders now. And did you see how happy they looked?" I snuggled into Odin's lap.

It was only the third time I'd said that.

Odin brushed my hair from my forehead with gentle fingertips. "They looked happy, goddess."

"Don't get me wrong—I'm happy that they're finding success and all that," I said. "It makes me happy, but weirdly, it also makes me sad. I guess because I'm not there."

"I wish you could celebrate this win with them," Odin said.

"I guess I'm celebrating now," I said.

"Someday we'll clear our names, and you'll celebrate with them properly," Zeus said. "Someday we'll get the truth out, and the truth will crush ZOX into little smithereens, and Denko and all of his people will be in jail, and you'll be able to see your sisters again. And we'll be granted total immunity, and we'll live wild and free."

"Well, that's a rosy *fucking-g* prediction," Odin said.

"What's wrong with rosy? It's not impossible," Zeus said. "Nothing is impossible if you work hard enough at it."

"Technically, time travel is not impossible," Odin said. "But I'm not holding my breath."

Zeus glared at Odin. Thor frowned into his coffee like he was feeling really stung by this exchange. What was up with him?

"I might need another," I said, holding out my glass to Thor, who filled it up.

"Is there any way we could send them a congratulations gift?" he asked, setting down the pitcher. "Maybe anonymously?"

"Risky," Odin said, and Zeus grumbled in agreement.

I sighed. "Yeah. And it would probably just upset them. Like if it was a nice gift, they'd wonder who it was from and it would be weird. And if Vanessa figured out that it was from me and us, she'd have to playact that she didn't know, and that would be awkward. It would be a gift of weirdness and awkwardness."

"Nobody likes a gift of weirdness and awkwardness," Thor said.

"Nope!" I grinned at Zeus. "Your surprise was the opposite of weirdness and awkwardness," I said. "Especially compared to what we thought you were gonna spring on us."

Zeus tilted his head, eyes sparkling. "What did you think it was going to be?"

I snorted. "Omigod, it's sort of funny…" I scanned the area for the brochure, then I remembered Thor hiding it under a stack of travel magazines. I leaned over, rooting around for it. Maybe I should have paid more attention to Odin holding me too tightly, almost like he was trying to pull me back, like he didn't want me to get the brochure or something, but I had two and a half mimosas in me—I was feeling jolly!—and I broke away and grabbed the thing.

"This madness." I tossed it at him, laughing.

Zeus studied the picture, frowning at the happy couple riding in a balloon basket high in the sky, clinking glasses against the backdrop of a brilliant sunset. The hills below them were lush with stripes of greenery mixed with orange and brown rock, glowing deeply in the light. The small inset picture showed Harley sitting unobtrusively on the business end of the hot air balloon basket, wearing a gray jumpsuit and gray cap, diligently working the controls. Across the top it said, "romantic balloon rides for two."

"Romantic balloon rides for two? What the fuck?" he said. "Why just two?"

Dread shot through me. "Anyone want to play gin rummy?" Gin rummy was one of Zeus's favorite card games, second only to poker.

"Don't change the subject," Zeus said. "You've always dreamed of going up in a hot air balloon. Remember in New Mexico how you were like, 'it would be so amazing, floating through the clouds. Perfect silence.'"

"Um...I said that?" I was sobering up, needless to say.

Zeus frowned, studying the brochure. "Who is this man to rob you of your dream of a romantic balloon ride with your three men?"

"That's not really my dream—"

"I'm sure he'd let us four on," Zeus continued. "I'm sure I could get him to be flexible."

Odin whisper-groaned behind me.

"I noticed that they had Pictionary, too!" I suggested enthusiastically. "That is my current dream."

"I'm good with Pictionary or gin rummy!" Thor said. "I wouldn't recommend a balloon ride, what with Isis's vertigo."

"Her vertigo is gone," Zeus said. "She said so an hour ago."

"It could come back," Odin said.

"It feels like it might," I said.

"One vertigo-free day doesn't mean she's out of the woods," Thor pointed out.

"Exactly," I said. "It could definitely come back."

Zeus frowned at the pictures. "I think you're just saying that because this brochure makes you feel like you can't have a romantic ride in the balloon with three men. You said it was your dream, don't you remember? You can't un-say that. Once we explain that we are a romantic unit, I'm sure he'll see reason." With that, Zeus began to scroll and tap his phone.

"What are you doing?" Odin asked.

"Looking at the schedule of availability. This guy's got walk-in availability this afternoon. We could do it this afternoon!"

"But...gin rummy..." Thor said.

"Fuck that," Zeus said. "Isis is gonna have her dream balloon ride, goddammit."

"There might not be enough space in the balloon," I tried. "It looks small."

"I'm sure there's a weight limit, but it's probably pretty high for a balloon of that size. I bet the four of us are well within tolerances. This man would have no reason to object. I'm sure he'll be thrilled to accommodate us."

Inwardly I winced. I was no gambler, but I definitely would've bet that Harley would not be thrilled to accommodate us.

"Is it really the wisest thing?" Thor said. "Floating up there like helpless fools?"

"Helpless foolish sitting ducks," Odin added. "Talk about no escape routes. A seven-hundred-foot plummet is *not* a viable escape route. Ridiculous."

"It's not ridiculous if Ice wants it," Zeus said. "Nothing is ridiculous if it's what Ice wants."

"But I *wouldn't* want it," I insisted.

"You're just saying that, Ice," Zeus said. "We make enough compromises in this life. You shouldn't have to settle on the small things, on a simple dream." Just like that, he was on his feet, car keys in hand. "I'll go talk to this guy myself and suggest a special romantic package for four. I'm sure he'll be good with it, especially if we offer him double the price. Come or don't. Up to you. I am doing this."

With that, he headed out the door.

"Noooo," Thor whispered.

Odin ejected me from his lap.

"Erp!" I said. "Why did I show him the brochure?"

"Should we just let him go?" Thor asked.

"Let him go? Do you love the idea of Zeus telling Harley he needs a new kind of balloon romance package?" Odin asked. "Does Harley strike you as a flexible guy? Do you think that conversation will go well?"

None of us thought that conversation would go well.

Chapter Seven

Zeus parked the car on the dusty field that was Harley's Balloon Emporium. He seemed really excited. "If you have to pee, you'd better do it now!"

I was starting to think that maybe going up in a hot air balloon was just as much of a dream of his as it was of mine.

"Their online scheduling tool might not be up to date," Thor warned.

"I'm feeling lucky," Zeus said, getting out. We all followed suit.

Harley came over, grinning. "Well, looky who's here!"

"Hey," Zeus said. "I don't have a reservation, but I was wondering if I could book a balloon for one of your romantic balloon rides today."

Behind him, Odin was vigorously shaking his head.

Thor was shaking his head and waving in a baseball *you're out!* style.

I went with the ol' finger drawn across the neck.

Harley gave us an arrogant smile. "As a matter of fact, I do have an opening for you. I'm not booked until four. Pay the fee, and I'll take you and your lady up, no problem." He gazed triumphantly over Zeus's shoulder at us. "I can't think of anything I'd rather do than take this man and his lady up for a romantic balloon ride."

"Wow...well, great," Zeus said, surprised at Harley's weird enthusiasm.

"Partner and payment, that's all we'll need," Harley said. "Ride runs just over an hour. Could give you a noon, one, or two o'clock slot."

"Well, it's all four of us," Zeus said. "Obviously you'll need to charge us double since we're double."

Harley looked confused. "Only one couple at a time," he said. "These are romantic balloon ride packages for two. Romantic rides for couples. Says right on the sign."

Zeus cleared his throat. "Here's the thing, we four *are* a couple."

Harley squinted at Zeus. "Four people can't be a couple."

"Here we go," Thor mumbled beside me.

"They can," Zeus said. "In fact, the word 'couple' comes from the Latin *copula*, meaning bond, and a bond can be four people."

"Romantic couple means two," Harley barked.

"Here's the thing," Zeus said. "We four are a romantic unit, and we would like our romantic balloon ride. Don't worry, we're not gonna fuck up there, we just want the four of us together. To celebrate our romance. Like I said, we'll make it worth your while."

Harley did that move where you put your hands on your hips in a way that lets people see that you have a holster with a gun under your jacket. Not the best idea, ever.

"Here's the thing," Harley said. "I make the rules here, and you wanna know what one of my rules is?"

"Why don't you go on and tell me," Zeus said.

"No perverts allowed," Harley said.

In a blur of motion, Zeus was on him; one more blur and Zeus had the gun.

"Easy as taking gun candy from a gun baby," Odin said.

Zeus put on the safety and nestled it into his pocket.

"How about now? Will you make a new rule now?" Zeus asked. "We want our romantic balloon ride for four and to make a champagne toast to our love against the backdrop of the Pacific Ocean as we soar high above the trees. We will pay you fairly to take us up on this romantic balloon ride—double, in fact, because there are two extra people, and then when it's over and after everybody's had a very nice time, we'll return your party favor." He patted the gun. "How does that sound?"

Harley gave Odin a pleading look.

Odin usually stepped in when off-the-chain Zeus appeared, but Odin just shrugged. Clearly, off-the-chain Zeus was working for Odin.

Harley glanced at Thor. So, Harley decided to defer to us suddenly?

Getting no help from Thor, Harley finally decided to consult my breasts. Eventually, he managed to drag his eyes up to my actual face. I raised my eyebrows in an *I told you so* way.

Having our warning come true in such a spectacular fashion was satisfying for sure, but it would've been a lot more satisfying if the situation had never come to pass.

"Even if I wanted to do this, there's a limit of three people," Harley tried.

"Actually, the model of balloon that you fly has a thousand-pound passenger limit. The five of us come in well under that." As a super-spy, Zeus always did his homework. "It's a beautiful day for a balloon ride, so let's start this thing up."

"Not going to happen," Harley said. "Go ahead and shoot me. I'm not taking you up."

"Would you mind if we take the balloon up ourselves, then?" Zeus asked.

Harley sized him up. "You wanna die? Be my guest."

"I assure you, we can fly one of these things just fine," Zeus said. "It might be more fun that way."

"That doesn't sound fun at all," I said.

"This is what you wanted," Zeus said. "And now you'll get it."

"But I don't want it now," I said.

Zeus looked incredulous. "You always dreamed of riding in a balloon with us."

"Riding in a balloon! Not balloon-jacking a balloon!" I said, feeling the tears coming on. My fun mimosa buzz had definitely worn off.

"Baby," Zeus said. "I can fly one of these things like a boss."

"While he calls the cops?" I said.

Zeus snorted like that was so ridic. "Nobody's calling the cops. We'll tie him up, and when we get back, we'll do some threats."

"Do some threats? Do you even hear yourself?" I demanded. "Don't you see that being with you guys is romance enough? When you go around freaking out on people who don't bend to your every whim, it's not sexy!" I said. "It's not hot!"

"I think it's a little bit hot," Zeus said.

"Not hot," Thor said.

Zeus turned his angry gaze on Thor. God, were Zeus and Thor gonna fight now?

"Uhh!" I spun around and stomped toward the far end of the giant area. I couldn't take any more of this interpersonal stress!

I didn't have a destination, I just wanted to get away from the whole situation. I headed on past our car, past fuel tanks, out to where the shuttered popcorn wagon truck stood, sides painted with bright yellow and white popcorn puffs, long since faded in the California sun.

The group of them were arguing back there, all growls and raised voices. Zeus was being obstinate. Harley wanted his gun back. Odin was trying to make everybody be rational. Thor sounded upset, even guilty, like the whole thing was his fault in some way.

I stomped onward, eyes clouded with tears. I suppose that's

why I didn't see the figure separate from the shadowed side of the shuttered popcorn truck way off to the side.

By the time I heard the crunch of gravel, it was too late to do anything sly or defensive. A hand gripped my arm. The nose of a gun touched my temple. A split second later I was staring into the angry gray eyes of our mortal enemy.

Agent Denko. From ZOX.

Time slowed. Fingers of cold sweat traveled up my spine.

We'd been so careful! How did he find us? I tried to yank away, but he tightened his grip.

"Behave," he warned. "You're just as good to me with a shot foot."

My mind whirled. Was this really happening?

Over across the dusty field, all arguing had ceased. Four faces turned to me and Agent Denko.

"Let's go," he said, marching me across the field toward Harley and my guys. "I'm not looking to hurt anyone."

"Fire up the balloon!" I yelled. "Get away! He has nothing if you're not here!"

"I'll shoot that thing down so fast," Denko yelled. "So fast."

"Wait, what?" Harley said, looking ashen.

"Do it! Get away!" I pleaded. "He won't shoot it down—he doesn't want you dead!"

"I just want to talk," Denko said.

We were just a few yards away now.

My guys appeared to be motionless, but the opposite would be true. They'd be talking in low tones, working up a plan, arranging weaponry between themselves. They'd do anything they could to keep me safe, even if it meant giving themselves up to face imprisonment, torture, and ultimately death.

Which was why this was such a nightmare scenario.

My legs were shaking so hard, I could barely walk. I could never live with myself if they gave their freedom for mine—I wouldn't survive it. I wouldn't even want to.

"No way are we talking to you when you have that thing pointed at her," Zeus said. "Take one of us instead."

"And give up this pretty little high-value hostage?" Denko said.

My guys were slowly fanning out now, with the intent to surround us. They'd provoke Denko to take one of them out, but whoever was behind Denko would take him out.

Harley backed away.

"Do I look like a dipshit to you? Back together," Denko said. "I want you all where I can see you. I can shoot her without killing her."

When the guys didn't comply, he pressed the gun under my chin. My pulse raced. The ground seemed to tilt.

My guys pulled back together.

Denko reached the testosterone-heavy little gathering and produced a bag from his satchel, tossing it on the ground. "Weapons in the bag. Now."

Zeus pulled Harley's handgun from the back of his belt and tossed it in.

Odin and Thor pulled guns from ankle holsters.

A puff of wind blew across the field, kicking up a ghostly tower of dust.

"Keep going," Denko commanded.

Harley's eyes widened as Thor pulled another gun from a side holster and a knife from his jacket pocket. Zeus pulled a knife from a hidden thigh pocket and a garrote from yet another pocket.

Denko pointed at Harley. "Phone on the ground and sit over there where I can see you. Go."

Harley threw down his phone and backed up, hands raised, practically running backwards toward the far fence Denko had indicated. Maybe next time when somebody warned him not to take a certain passenger in his balloon, he would heed that warning.

My guys said nothing as Harley settled himself down out of earshot.

Denko still had the gun stuck into the fleshy part of my chin, and I kept imagining him pulling the trigger. Which is exactly the opposite of what positive visualization gurus tell you to do—you're not supposed to visualize the thing you don't want!

I tried to imagine Denko realizing how wrong it was to work for such an evil organization as ZOX. I tried to picture the expression of horror that would come over his face as he really thought about how many lives he'd ruined, and how heartless he had been. I tried to picture him throwing down his gun and dedicating his life to helping my guys clear their names and then taking up flower arranging. And my guys and I would be free to do silly things like go up in balloons.

But my mind wasn't buying it. My mind was all, *um, gun to chin aiming at the back of your brain! Finger about to pull trigger! Alarm! Alarm!*

"I want to talk," Denko was saying now. "I want to make a deal."

"We don't make deals with people who threaten Ice," Zeus said, though he had exactly zero leverage, and everybody there knew it.

"Then you'll listen," Denko said, gun pressing harder. "I need you to do something for me. I'll make it worth your while."

My guys said nothing. They were in listening mode. Info-absorbing mode. Rabid-tiger-craving-an-opportunity-to-rip-some-body's-face-off mode.

Chapter Eight

"I NEED YOU TO FIND SOMETHING FOR ME," DENKO SAID.

I felt like he'd had the gun poking into my chin forever.

"Oh yeah?" Odin asked casually. "What would that be?"

His seeming nonchalance was a tiny nick in my heart, until I realized that he was playing a part—the unstable guy who didn't care about anything and could go crazy at any moment. This was one of my favorite sexy personas of his; I could see now that it was equally effective in a standoff.

He brushed a bit of imaginary lint off his shoulder. "What do you want us to find for you?"

"A German shepherd," Denko said.

There was this long silence where I suppose we were all trying to make sense of this request. It seemed like he was going through a lot of trouble if that's what he wanted.

"Um...j-just any German shepherd?" I asked. "Because you didn't have to go through all of this trouble if you just wanted to find a German shepherd. I mean, they're not that rare—"

"No, not *just any German shepherd*," he bit out. "*My* German shepherd. My dog. Doris."

"You want us to find your lost dog?" Zeus asked. I could see the worry in his eyes. Maybe he was right to worry. There were a lot better resources to turn to for a lost dog than, oh, your mortal enemies who wanted to kill you and who you definitely wanted to kill in return.

Had Denko lost his mind?

Not the best development ever. Because if there was one thing that was worse than having a gun pressed up in your chin, it was having a gun pressed to your chin by a madman.

Also, he named his dog Doris?

"We're listening," Zeus said simply.

"Doris was stolen, and I'm ninety percent sure I know who has her," Denko continued. "You'd have a week to locate her and get her back to me."

"If you're imagining we'd let you hold Isis for a week while we look for your dog, you are *fucking-g* bananas," Odin said. "Isis doesn't leave our sight; that's a nonnegotiable."

"It's fine," I insisted. Them having to find a stolen dog was better than imprisonment, torture, and death. To be honest, finding a stolen dog was something that I would do for free.

Thor shot me a look. "There might not even *be* a dog."

"Oh." I hadn't thought of that angle.

"This is real," Denko insisted.

"You take Ice away over our dead bodies," Zeus growled.

They argued more, negotiated more. Every time Denko spoke in any kind of a heated way, the gun smushed into my chin and totally freaked me out—and not just me; my guys were vibrating with tension.

Also, Denko had to know that if he were to hold me hostage, my guys would go crazy and spend all their time looking for me.

"Okay, I can be flexible. Let's talk about something else," Denko said. "You get me Doris back—alive—by Friday of next week, and I'll give you the one thing that you most want in this world, and I'm not talking about Isis."

"There isn't anything we want more in this world than Isis," Zeus said.

"What you want most in the world *besides* Isis," he clarified, like that was so obvious. This pleased me a bunch, but let's just say it would have pleased me a lot more if there weren't a gun to my chin *that smushed around every time he spoke!*

"What would that be?" Odin asked disinterestedly. He was definitely playing the guy who might go wild at any moment.

"Evidence that clears your names," Denko said. "All collected nice and neat in a tackle bag."

Evidence to clear their names? What?

Shivers skittered over my skin. My guys kept their faces neutral, but the idea that such evidence even existed? It was huge.

Though as far as bargaining chips went, I preferred something other than the splatterment of my brain.

Odin snorted.

"I could give you the location of a tackle bag of clips and recordings of what really happened in that valley. Documentation. Names, locations, affidavits, copies of marching orders, email trails. The real culprits behind what you saw, Christian," he said, using Thor's real name.

Thor stared at Denko with strange intensity. "Are you fucking with us?"

"Something like that exists?" Odin said. "And it's in a *tackle bag*?"

"A yellow and white Big Bill tackle bag, to be precise. It's somebody's insurance policy," Denko said. "They don't know that I know about it. But I do. What do you say?"

"We can't have this discussion while you have her," Thor said.

"He's right. We might be open to your proposition, but…" Zeus waved a hand. He was going for a calm vibe, but I could also hear the strain in his voice. Could Denko hear it? The whole gun-to-chin thing was getting to all of us.

Denko was taking his time deciding to release me. I waited. *Release me!* I thought. *Go for plan B!*

If a tackle bag like that existed, it was a game-changer—my guys would totally play detective for a tackle bag that would clear our names.

Or at least it sounded like the tackle bag would clear Zeus, Odin, and Thor of the initial crime that they were wrongfully accused of. Hopefully the clearing would extend to me and all the crimes we had committed since. It was a vast list, unfortunately, but getting a nine-to-five job isn't exactly a recommended fugitive activity.

Finally, Denko took the gun off my chin and gave me a shove toward my guys.

I stumbled into Zeus's arms. He pulled me to his chest for a quick, fierce hug, then pushed me behind his back. Odin crowded in next to me, holding my right arm with both hands like he needed to know I was really, really there. Thor was on the other side of me, rubbing my shoulder.

It was only then that I relaxed. I was safe in my manwich.

"We're okay," I said softly. *"We're together. We're okay."*

Thor clamped a hand over my shoulder. Odin squeezed my arm harder. Odin had had a lot taken away from him in his life. We all had, but with Odin it was more extreme.

"So lemme get something straight here," Thor began, dark rage rumbling through his every word. "Assuming this bag exists, you want us to believe that while you've been chasing us all this time, you had proof we were innocent? You knew what happened back there, and you continued to chase us?" I hadn't heard Thor so angry in ages, possibly ever. "While the real perpetrators walk free?"

"A job is a job," Denko said, keeping his gun trained on us.

Odin muttered darkly under his breath in one of the many languages he spoke.

I could feel the anger radiating from Zeus. He had no words.

It was truly messed up that Denko knew we were innocent all this time. They all knew they were pursuing innocent people who'd only tried to do the right thing...in the beginning, anyways.

Zeus swallowed, straightening. "How do we know you'll actually give us the location of the tackle bag? How do we know it even exists?"

"You don't," Denko said. "But I let Ice go, didn't I? Be thankful I'm not taking you in right now."

"As if," Odin said. Now that Denko didn't have me, there was no way. But Denko could've used me to get them. All of us knew it.

"Let's do this," Zeus said. "We'll find your dog, and you'll get her back when we decide your intel is worth it. Who do you think has her?"

"Don Pedro," Denko said.

I knew enough not to make a face or cringe or react in any way, but we knew Don Pedro. He was a massive crime boss.

"Why would Don Pedro want your dog?" Zeus asked.

"I'm sitting on evidence that will help put Don Pedro and his crew away for a very long time," Denko said. "It's a ledger—names, dates, facts, and figures. It ties him to a lot of crimes, and I've got somebody in custody who would be willing to back up that ledger. We had him by the balls—"

"Until he stole something that was more valuable to you than his conviction," Zeus said.

"I want my dog back, *and* I want the conviction," Denko said.

Zeus snorted. "And you assume that just because we're part of the criminal underworld, we have a relationship with Don Pedro, and that we would be able to figure out where among his properties and people he was keeping your dog stashed? Is that how it goes? You think all of us just know each other and hang out together?"

"You don't know him?" Denko asked.

Zeus's gaze was hard. "We'll get your dog. You better hold up your end, though."

"I'll hold up my end," Denko promised.

My guys exchanged looks, expressions unreadable, but I'm sure they were thinking twelve chess moves ahead.

"We'll need the full download," Odin said. "How they grabbed Doris, how they communicated with you, and everything else."

Denko launched into the story, pulling out his phone and forwarding the text message he received. It was instructions to drop the ledger at a certain place at a certain time or else Doris would die.

It was weird even to be talking to Denko in an almost normal way, considering what happened the last time we were together. Were my guys thinking about it?

"The number's a burner," Denko said, pocketing his phone. "It doesn't exist anymore. It blinked out minutes after the message got sent."

Zeus asked more questions about the case. I'd heard that Don Pedro was a careful criminal—it was weird that he'd be in trouble. You didn't get to be a big crime boss by making mistakes.

Denko's witness against Don Pedro was an expert violin appraiser named Wilson Brockmeier who was currently hidden in a safe house. The whole thing was about money laundering. Denko had this complex explanation about cheap violins being appraised for hundreds of thousands of dollars, then being sold and resold through shady violin dealers and overseas collectors controlled by Don Pedro. There were Panamanian bank accounts and auctions involved.

The basic idea was that Don Pedro bought and sold himself the same worthless violin over and over until the money looked legit, and Wilson Brockmeier helped him. Wilson Brockmeier could explain and verify the incriminating ledger.

I suppose that, in a way, it was sweet that Denko was making these deals and putting his career in jeopardy to save his dog, but it would have been a lot sweeter if he hadn't been pursuing us knowing that we were freaking innocent the whole time.

"This will be the last communication between us," Denko said. "If you need anything more, you'll talk to my second-in-command, Agent Alfred. He'll be our go-between. He'll be responsible for getting you any kind of information that you need. All Alfred knows is that I've hired you to find Doris."

Denko handed Odin a photo. "She has a distinctive white marking on her right ear. You can see it there."

Odin nodded.

"How do we know that we can trust your guy Agent Alfred?" Thor asked. "What if ol' Agent Alfred decides to take us in?"

"I've got Alfred by the balls, too," Denko assured us. "Don't worry, there's nobody I don't have by the balls."

"I don't like this," Odin said.

"Fine, I'll hire different private investigators," Denko snapped. "Is that what you want? To lose your chance at getting this exculpatory tackle bag?"

There was this silence where I could feel my guys thinking of alternate ways to get the exculpatory tackle bag o' proof—if it truly existed. Denko was definitely taking a chance telling us of its existence. I suppose it just showed how badly he wanted his dog.

"No other *fucking-g* private investigator would be able to find your dog, and you know it. Not if Don Pedro has him," Odin said.

"And I'm the only one who could tell you the whereabouts of the tackle bag."

Never was there such a weird alliance. We needed Denko, and Denko needed us.

The feeling in the car ride back was heavy—heavier than I could ever recall. As a group, we tended to roll with the punches, but this was bad.

. . .

"He freaking *knew* we were innocent all this time?" Thor asked, tone grave. "He and his people knew? They thought they'd let us take the fall for everything that happened back there? What the hell is that?"

"There are no words," Odin said.

Zeus just looked murderous.

"I always thought if they knew the truth, they would stop chasing us," I said.

"Me, too," Zeus grumbled.

I leaned up from the back seat and put a hand on his shoulder. Deep down, Zeus was an idealist. There had been a time when he'd believed in right and wrong, and had wanted to be a hero more than anything.

"Well, we know there's proof now," I said, trying to look at the bright side.

"But is there proof? Does it truly exist?" Odin asked. "Or has Denko discovered a new way to mess with our heads?"

"Seriously," Thor bit out, "they had proof we didn't do it all this time? This is organization-wide knowledge?"

Zeus let out a hissing breath. "When you go into law enforcement, you should have at least some passing respect for the law." I knew he was thinking about his past as an intelligence agent. He had wanted to make the world safe and had worked with integrity —of that I had no doubt. Bank robbers or not, my guys had integrity—a moral compass and a genuine code of honor. I wouldn't have loved them like I did if they hadn't had those things.

More silence.

"All this time," Zeus said. "Not giving a shit that we're innocent."

"To be fair, we've committed many spectacular crimes since then," I said, trying to lighten the mood. "A totally badass array of crimes."

"Our crime spree is vaster and more glorious than the Sahara, unimaginable in its devastating *fucking-g* beauty."

"Yeah, that!" I agreed.

"We need to make him pay," Zeus growled.

"And if he thinks we're gonna tie him up and fuck in front of him again, he's got another think coming!" I said.

Zeus gave me a dark look.

Tying up Denko and having group sex in front of him was one of our weirder escapades, but I had enjoyed it. What could be hotter than to be fucked in front of a stern and dangerous stranger who is tied up, angry, and unable to move? And none are sterner or more dangerous than ZOX Agent Denko. The man wanted to kill us and very well might succeed. Can you get sterner than that?

It was a combination of the sternness and the way that it was so wrong, not to mention being the ultimate fuck you. The ultimate way to say, *look at us being wild and free, asshole! We're living our best lives!*

However, it seemed like not the best time to be getting into that.

"We should have taken him out," Thor said.

We all came to attention at this.

It was a shocking thing for Thor to say, even offhandedly, being that he'd been such a dedicated doctor. Still was a dedicated doctor.

Thor had been forced to kill a man one time, and it had shaken him to the core. No way would he be okay with any kind of killing ever again. That's not who he was, not who we were.

"I get it," Zeus said to Thor. "I hate that motherfucker, too, but we're gonna find his dog. This is what's in front of us now."

"Well, it shouldn't be in front of us; a normal life should have been in front of us," Thor said. "They knew all along?"

"I know," Zeus said softly. "But now we have this chance to reverse things. What if?"

Thor glared out the window. "If this exculpatory evidence does exist—evidence that clears our names once and for all—why the hell do they continue to pursue us? Who are they protecting?"

There it was: the zillion-dollar question.

Back when Thor was a volunteer doctor in a war zone, he'd witnessed some sort of atrocity—they would never tell me what —and he had tried to bring it to light. Odin, and then Zeus, were sent to kill Thor, but they quickly realized he was innocent and had refused to kill him, thereby turning from hunters to hunted.

They had known they needed to disappear. During their escape, Thor had been forced to step up and shoot a man who was about to kill Zeus and Odin. The act of shooting and killing a fellow human being had shaken Thor to the core.

"ZOX is protecting somebody more powerful," Odin suggested. "Whoever they're protecting, that's who's behind it." Meaning, that's who was behind the atrocity Thor had witnessed —the atrocity that they would never tell me about.

"If the tackle bag exists, we have to get it," Thor said grimly. "We need to do what it takes. Whatever it takes. We end this. One way or another, this has to end."

There was an urgency to his statement I didn't like, and I settled my head onto his shoulder. "Is this so bad, though?" I said. "I feel like we have things nobody else in the world has. A normal life wouldn't give those things to us. We'd never have found each other if not for all of what happened."

Thor just grumbled in his sexy Thor way.

"It's wild that Denko would be willing to blow his whole career to find his dog," I said. "He doesn't seem like the type. But I guess we run with it."

"Screw that," Zeus said, turning to Odin. "You up on him?"

Odin had his phone out. "He's heading back to his office, it looks like. This window is not gonna last. We up for a road trip?"

"Wait, are we talking about Denko?" I asked. "Denko's heading back to the office? You're tracking him?"

"I put a little something in his pocket when he gave us the picture of his dog," Odin said. "It's only a matter of time until he figures it out, so we need to move on it. He's got a condo on Waring."

"Wait, what?" I exclaimed. "You're not saying what I think you're saying, are you?" Was he suggesting we ransack Denko's home?

Odin turned back and smiled at me.

"If you need to pee, you better do it now," Zeus said.

"Oh my god, you have to stop saying that!" I said.

Chapter Nine

Agent Denko had a first-floor condo in a very modern building made out of huge slabs of concrete with wrought-iron accents. There were tons of windows all around, and lots of state-of-the-art security too, which was probably why it took Odin a full two minutes to crack into the basement door's digital lock.

"Did you know his apartment was here this whole time?" I asked.

"Know thine enemy, isn't that one of the commandments?" Zeus muttered as we slipped along the hallway and let ourselves into Agent Denko's condo. "But we've never actually been inside." He shot Thor a pointed look. "No trashing the place."

Riiiiight. Because Thor was still in that wild-card mood.

"We'll see," Thor said.

I went over and linked my arm in his. I loved him in his crazy moods, but it was obvious that he was hurting.

"I'm fine," he said.

I kissed his cheek, and then we stole in, silent as the bandits we were.

I don't know what I expected in Denko's apartment—something along the lines of a tidy furniture showroom, I suppose. And yes, there were some showroom-looking pieces, like a boxy red couch, but he also had a lot of framed vintage French movie posters and a buffet that looked like it was partly made out of old machinery.

Thor pulled the photo Denko had given us from his pocket and held it up next to one on the bookshelf, a framed shot of Agent Denko with his arm around a sweet-looking German shepherd. "Same dog," he said. "Same white markings. Same everything."

Zeus came up after me.

"It's a start," Zeus said. "I'll be happier if I find more dog stuff, though. If he's doing what he's claiming to do, he's literally risking life in prison to rescue that dog."

I found a dog bed that looked used. There were some hairs on it. I called Zeus over to look.

"That's something," he said.

"What? You think he would have invented the dog and gotten these things to put around in his apartment?" I asked. "Seems a little elaborate."

"I just want to feel one hundred percent on this," Zeus said. "I want to know that he's actually trying to find her."

Odin had wandered off. "Laptop!" he called out from the direction of the den.

I headed into the kitchen with Thor. We found an open pack of dog treats in a drawer. Thor found a half-used bag of frozen dog food in the freezer. It was made from raw meat and contained lots of very fancy-sounding supplements.

"Definitely a respectable amount of dog food," Thor said.

I checked the refrigerator. There was a lot of chicken, some takeout containers of soup, a bag of carrots, a decent selection of cheeses, and a pie box. "Ooh. Pie from The Pie Hole."

"What kind?" Thor asked.

"Can't tell," I said.

Thor gave me a mischievous look. "Should we find out?"

"It's sealed shut."

Thor slid the box out of the refrigerator and set it on the counter. "Grab that knife," he said, motioning to a butcher block holder of knives.

"Omigod," I whispered. "We can't!"

"Don't you want to know what kind of pie it is?" he asked, plucking the knife from the holder himself.

I grabbed his arm. "We could just smell it!"

"But wouldn't you rather taste it?"

"But...it's Denko's pie!"

"I know." Thor grabbed two plates from the cupboards. "He's our worst and most dangerous enemy, and it's fucked up that we're in his home. And now we have his pie?"

"Oh. My. God." I wrapped my arms around Thor's back, pressing my face into his shoulder to muffle my laughter.

"Can you imagine a more delicious pie, goddess?" Thor asked.

"No!" I let him go.

"Me, either." Thor cut two giant slices and set one on each plate. "Looks like peach pie," he said, handing me a plate.

"Smells like peach pie." I pressed my fork into the tip of my slice, through flaky crust and peachy goodness. I popped a bite into my mouth. It was an explosion of bright flavor and sugary crust. "Mmm!"

Thor grinned, lips covered with crumbs. "Yum."

"It's really bad we're eating it," I said.

Thor gave me a beautiful smile, and I felt so much love for him, I thought my heart might burst.

I smiled back and took another bite. "Sorry, Denko, but this is what you get for being the star employee of an evil organization!"

"So delicious," Thor said, closing his eyes and blissing out. "I bet all of his food tastes delicious."

"I bet," I said, taking another bite. "Zeus and Odin would have a fit if they saw this."

"They would." Thor took his plate and headed out of the kitchen. I followed him with my own plate into the den where Zeus and Odin were hunched over a laptop, backs to us. On the screen was a lost-dog poster.

"This Doris thing looks legit," Odin said. "There are photos going years back—it would be hard to fake this. Denko's contacted the Humane Society, the pound, and he's got postings on every last dog-posting place."

"He even hired a few guys to be out looking for her," Zeus added. "And then the activity stops at the time that he got the text."

"Lotta dog pictures on his cloud, too," Odin said.

"Is going through his entire photo history really the best use of our time?" Thor asked, taking a bite of his pie, fork tines clinking against the plate.

"I just want to be sure..." Odin flipped through another set.

"Okay," Thor said in an impish tone.

Zeus spun around. "What the fuck are you eating?"

"Pie," Thor said.

I grinned. "Denko's pie. Quite delicious."

"You guys can't be helping yourselves to Denko's pie," Zeus said.

"We're outlaws," Thor said. "Breaking into the homes of our enemies and eating their pie is part of our job description."

"Or if it's not, it should be!" I added.

"He's gonna know we were here," Zeus grumbled.

"Gulp," I said.

Zeus snorted. "Get me a piece. With ice cream, if there's any."

"Ditto," Odin said, not looking up from the laptop.

"I want ice cream, too!" I called out to Thor as he headed out of the room.

"If he doesn't figure out we were here from the pie, I'm sure his nosy neighbors will say something." Odin nodded at the window. "They just opened their curtains. They've been very interested in watching what we're doing."

I peered out and, sure enough, there was another building across a small walkway with a window facing Denko's. You could see a man and a woman on a couch, faces flashing blue from the screen in front of them, but they weren't watching—it was totally obvious that they were watching us. I gave them a tentative smile and a wave, but they just frowned and directed their gazes at the TV.

"What if they call the police?" I asked.

"We're standing in Denko's house eating pie in broad daylight. They probably think we're his guests," Odin said.

"Nosy neighbors. Probably why he has the curtains right here," I said, looking at the curtains that were completely wide open at this point. "Too late now."

The four of us ate Denko's pie and went through his stuff under the stern and watchful gazes of his neighbors.

"He's gonna find that tracker any minute and disable it. We can't trust that he's not on his way back," Zeus warned, studying Denko's bookcase. He was on his second piece of pie by now, and there *was* ice cream.

"Anyone want beer?" Thor asked. "There's beer in there."

We all wanted beer, or at least, we wanted Denko's beer. Thor got beers. Odin was still busy on the laptop, probably planting a back door.

"This is fun," I said, surveying workout stuff on the far side of Denko's den. "I wonder what else we can do."

Thor's eyes sparkled. "I have an idea."

My belly tightened. I could tell from his tone what he was thinking. "Dude, I was imagining reprogramming his exercise bike, not..." I said, knees going slightly weak, because the idea of fucking in Denko's bed was very forbidden and wrong, and therefore very hot.

Thor took a step toward me. "What do you think?"

"That would be absolute madness." I backed up a step.

Thor kept coming. "Would it, though?"

My ass hit a table. "Yes," I breathed.

"Grab hold of the table, goddess," Thor rumbled, positioning my hands on either side of my hips. He lowered his voice. "Grab on nice and hard, and don't let go."

My pulse banged in my ears as wicked fingers began to undo one of my shirt buttons, and then another, and then another.

"So wrong," I said.

"Don't try to resist, goddess," Thor said. "You love how wrong it is."

"Is she wet?" Odin piped up from his seat at the laptop. "Check. I want to know. I want to know how wet and *fucking-g* depraved our goddess is that she wants to fuck in the home of our worst enemy."

Thor came flush to me, lips just a feather's breadth from mine. "Are you?" he whispered, toying with the snaps of my jeans.

"I'll never tell," I whispered back.

Thor jerked open my fly and pushed a rough hand down into my pants, sending tremors of desire all through me.

"Yes, she is," Thor rumbled.

"Yes," I gasped as thick fingers invaded my core.

Odin rose from the laptop with a dark look on his face. "I'm sorry, we can't let something like this go." He looked around the room and his gaze seemed to land on a wingback chair. He pulled it to the center of the space, positioning it right in front of the window. "Right here, goddess. I want you to bend over right here. Show your ass to Denko's neighbors. Show them what a beautiful ass you have."

"W-what? We can't!" I exclaimed, vibrating with dark anticipation.

"Thor, roll up that magazine, nice and tight."

"Oh my god," I said as every inch of my skin rose up with excited goose bumps.

"You've earned five strokes already. I believe I will have to add two for your refusal to comply with our orders." Odin came to me, finishing undoing the rest of my shirt buttons. "You're so *fucking-g* beautiful. I have to do this. And you know that it must be done."

"But those people..."

"They're stern, humorless assholes who wouldn't smile or wave back at you," Odin said. "Fucking in front of stern, humorless people is your jam, is it not?"

Of course he was right—I loved an audience! The sterner and angrier, the better. My sex was practically pulsing with warmth and excitement at this point. "Yes," I gasped. "But—"

"I'm sure Denko's been a boring neighbor up until now. This will give them a new perspective on him," Odin rumbled.

I was faint with arousal. The idea of fucking in front of Denko's stern and angry neighbors was almost as delicious as fucking in front of stern and angry Denko. "I don't know," I demurred.

"Such *fucking-g* bullshit. Eight strikes," Odin commanded. "Thor, take down her pants."

"Eep!" I said.

Thor came to me with one of his apologetic looks that wasn't all that apologetic and undid my pants while Odin pulled off the rest of my shirt. Soon I was completely naked, bent over the chair sideways, ass in the air for all to see.

Odin slid his warm, rough hand over the tender flesh of my ass. "So beautiful," he said. "Your body is ours to do whatever we want to with; best you remember it."

"And luckily I'll never see those people over there again," I said.

Suddenly the warm caressing hand was replaced with the swift sting of a rolled-up magazine. *Whack!*

"You know you love it, goddess," Odin said.

I gasped as the vibrations of the expertly angled magazine reverberated through my entire pussy. I gasped in something like pleasure. I did love it.

Thor pushed a hand into my hair. "I want to watch you while Odin punishes you. Keep your eyes open and watch me. Watch my eyes."

Odin whacked my ass again. It wasn't easy to keep my eyes on Thor, but it was definitely hot, what with him looking at me so grimly.

"Those people across the way are watching. They look incredibly stern. They are angry and humorless but they can't stop watching—" *Whack!* "They can't stop watching how depraved you are."

"Good—I *want* them to watch," I gasped as Odin hit me again, followed by a soft caress that left me breathless. Then—slowly, ever so slowly—one slick finger slid up past my asshole.

I shut my eyes, reveling in the feeling of it, up and down and up—

"Hey!" Thor said. My eyes flared open to meet his stern blue gaze. The finger was gone.

Whack! Odin hit me again.

I was panting now, pussy full of stars. I was about to come—any minute. *Any second.*

Thor wrapped my hair around his fist, holding my head so that we were face to face. "Don't you dare come."

Odin hit me again—*whack.*

"What the fuck is happening in here?" Zeus stood at the doorway holding four beers.

"Our goddess was being very naughty," Odin said. He spanked me again.

"Fuck," Zeus said, eyes seeming to go unfocused. "You know those people are watching."

"Of course she knows," Odin said. "She loves when things are wrong."

Thor stood, undoing his fly with the hand that wasn't fisting my hair. His thick pulsing cock sprung golden from his underwear. "Take me, suck me now," he gasped, pressing his cock to my lips.

"Mmm," I hummed, swirling my tongue around the tip of it like he liked, and then I grabbed him by the root and took him into my mouth.

Another wet finger began to probe my asshole as I sucked Thor's cock, seeming almost to move in rhythm with my own movements.

"Zeus, put those down and go see if our host has any kind of oil. Isis needs your cock in her asshole right now," Odin said, and he was right.

Zeus set the beers down and left the room, returning with a jar of coconut oil, maybe. I couldn't see it properly, and I didn't really care at that point.

Strong hands separated my butt cheeks.

Thick fingers oiled up my asshole, swirling around the oil, sure and slow.

Thor had withdrawn from the face-fucking portion of our festivities, leaving me to fully concentrate on the finger now pressing into my asshole.

One finger became two fingers, sliding in and out, spreading around oil. After a short hiatus, I felt the head of Zeus's cock pushing slowly in, filling me deliciously. I buried my face into the chair arm, fully getting into the pleasure-pain sensation of a cock pushing deep inside of me while unseen hands tweaked and squeezed my nipples.

Another hand—Zeus's?—stroked my vageen, stroking and stroking, ruthlessly stoking my pleasure and bringing on an explosive climax.

The whole world dropped away—my guys, Denko, the people across the alley who probably thought Denko was a sex freak now —all of it dropped away and there was just the pure pleasure of it all.

Vaguely I could hear Zeus's rumbly voice— *"Uh-uh-uh."*

Somewhere behind me, Thor was coming, and no doubt Odin, too.

I started laughing. I hadn't even come down from my orgasm but I was just laughing—I don't know why.

Eventually we were collapsed in a God Pack heap.

Zeus looked around at the mess we'd made of Denko's office. "That'll teach him to pursue innocent people and cover for murderers."

Odin kissed me. Thor handed me a towel, and I cleaned myself up.

"Best Three Bears re-enactment ever," I said.

Five minutes later we were speeding back toward our Airbnb, happy and sated from the afternoon's festivities, Zeus and Odin in the front seat, me in the back with Thor as usual. I spun around and sat sideways with my feet on Thor's lap. He grinned and settled his hands on my bootlaces.

"What if Denko had come back?" I asked.

"Would you have liked that?" Thor asked me.

"No way," I said. "I would never want him to be free to get involved, if you know what I mean. Uncomfortably tied up and forced to watch with a stern face, that was a good one-time thing, but bursting in and roaming around? No freaking way."

Thor's eyes sparkled. "Agree."

"I'd chop off his fucking-g hands if he ever roamed around on you," Odin said.

"So, what now?" I asked. "Obviously the dog is real. He genuinely wants his dog back."

"We'll find the dog," Zeus said.

"What if there really isn't any tackle bag? What if that's all fake, but he made it up because he thinks we're the only ones in the world who can find his dog?"

"I've got a call in to my contact in Washington, D.C.," Odin said. "Maybe my contact has heard of the tackle bag. If my contact hasn't heard of the tackle bag, it doesn't mean it doesn't exist, but it's a good place to start. We may not ever know if the tackle bag exists until the end."

"And then what?" I asked.

"If he can't produce the tackle bag, we'll keep Doris. And then we'll have leverage on Denko. Somewhat. It's not like we'd hurt a dog. But we could hang on to her for a while."

"I love dogs," I said.

"So do I," Zeus agreed.

I could practically feel our minds spinning on the subject as we sped down the road. What would it be like to have a dog? How awesome would it be? We really never could have one, considering the life that we led. A dog would make us vulnerable the way it made Denko vulnerable.

"I know we can never have a dog," I said. "It's not like I don't get that, but it would be fun to pretend. We could take her to the dog park and stuff."

Thor looked at me sadly.

"You have to admit it would be fun," I insisted.

"It would be fun, goddess."

"How well do you guys know Don Pedro?" I asked.

"Not well," Zeus said. "But Don Galvano knows him. We'll start there."

Chapter Ten

WE PULLED UP TO THE ORNATE GATES OF DON GALVANO'S gorgeous art deco-style mansion in the Palisades. The same elderly guard was manning the booth just as he had been so many months ago when we were last here, but he was a lot friendlier this time around. Part of it was that we actually had an appointment this time, and also, we were on the Don's good side these days, thanks to the fact that we'd solved the mystery of his stolen Corvette. Some guy had tried to frame Don Galvano's future son-in-law for the crime, and let's just say we saved a lot of Galvano family strife by uncovering the true culprit.

We parked and walked up the marble steps to his mansion. I'd worn one of my favorite green maxi skirts with a cute white top. My guys looked amazing: Thor wore a fine white linen sports coat and slacks, Zeus was in all black, and Odin was in an ugly, too-small, piece-of-shit suit, part of his quest for people to take him seriously as a tough guy instead of mooning over his runway model looks.

As usual when Odin wore an ill-fitting, piece-of-shit suit, all it did was make women think, *wow, maybe I like guys who wear ill-fitting piece-of-shit suits after all.* And you could see the guys thinking, *I should try to wear an ill-fitting piece-of-shit suit—who knew they looked so good.*

We were to wait in Don Galvano's super-masculine study with its black globe and ornamental wall sword.

A few minutes later, the Don trundled in with his big belly and big bald head on prominent display. His usual sour expression softened as he regarded us, like maybe we'd graduated to friends status. "Still doing the PI shit?" he barked.

"You know it," Zeus said, taking the man's outstretched hand in a warm grasp. We all shook hands.

"Check this out." The Don pulled out his phone and showed us pictures of his son-in-law, Herk, and his daughter, Maria, at their Mafia destination wedding in Sicily. "This family will always be grateful to you," he said. "Though I'm guessing that might be part of why you're here. Visit out of the blue…"

"We have reason to believe that Don Pedro kidnapped a dog," Zeus said, cutting right to the chase. "He'd be holding this dog as leverage regarding an upcoming case."

Don Galvano nodded. "I know what case. Man's in some trouble."

"Have you heard anything about him nabbing one of the feds' pet dog? We're interested in finding that dog."

"Really," the Don said, eyeing us with interest, but not a whole lot of surprise. Don Galvano was a man of a thousand deals, a man who did what it took to get what he wanted.

"Any light you could shed on it would be extremely appreciated," Zeus said. "Where Don Pedro might be keeping such a dog, what his plans might be, which of his people might be guarding such a dog."

"I haven't heard anything about him having someone's dog. But then again, it's not as if Don Pedro tells me what he's doing. You know he and I are not friends, right?"

"We know you're not friends," Odin said.

"I'll have to reach inside his organization to get this kind of information," the Don said.

Zeus looked solemn. "We understand it's a big ask. We'd be extremely grateful."

The Don seemed to think about this for a bit. "Let me reach in, then," he said. "I'll call you."

We thanked him and got out of there.

"Do you think he has an informant inside Don Pedro's gang?" I asked once we were rambling down the road in our shiny Jag.

Odin said, "I'm thinking he probably has a guy in there, like his own guy. Is that what it feels like to you?" he asked Zeus.

"That's what it feels like to me," Zeus said.

"Agreed," Thor said. "He's got a guy in there. And he'll consider us even after he does this favor."

"Can't imagine a more worthy reason to cash in," Odin said.

As usual, I was amazed at how well my guys read between the lines, how much unsaid information they heard. Like wolves, they operated on instinct and emotion, moving as a pack, paying more attention to how things smelled—metaphorically, anyway—than how things appeared.

We got back to our place and ate. I spent a nice afternoon in the hammock with a book while my guys buzzed around town, running errands. It had been a while since we'd been in the Los Angeles area, and they had people to see. I enjoyed having the afternoon to myself. Later I did yoga off a YouTube tutorial on the fluffy rug, tidied up the place with '80s music cranked up to ten, and then I messaged my jewel-thieving galpals, the Gigis, to come over.

"The sheep farmer's back!" screamed the Gigis' leader, Macy, when I flung open the front door.

We all hugged each other.

"Did you bring your suits like I told you?" I asked.

It turned out that they had, and they had real diamond tiaras to wear with their suits, too—spoils from one of their latest jobs.

"We even brought one for you!" exclaimed second-in-command, Angel Gigi.

We spent the afternoon in the pool on giant flotation devices, floating lazily around like slow-motion bumper cars while making a sizable dent in the liquor collection that my guys had built up. My galpals told me about their latest jewel-thieving escapades, and I told them about our gang's bank-thieving escapades, minus the very X-rated parts.

It was great to see them—beyond great!

One of the hardest things about being on the run was that you never got to see people that you had history with. Everybody was a stranger in every new town. But not these girls. They were my friends, and there was a standing invitation to join their gang, not that I would.

I told them about the case we were working on, and they were surprisingly opinionated on it, especially Angel.

"That is fishy," she declared, tossing her platinum and pink hair.

"How so?" I asked.

"Kind of a big gamble!" she said. "How many people would be willing to destroy their career and possibly go to prison for the life of a pet?"

"I would," Macy said.

"I would," I agreed.

"But not a ton of people would when it really comes down to it," Angel continued. "A kidnapped baby, yes, most anyone would destroy their career for a kid, especially if it was their own kid, but a dog? Even a person who loves their dog might not make that decision. From the point of view of Don Pedro, that's just a long shot, don't you think?"

"I never thought about it that way," I said.

"Don Pedro is betting that this Denko would be willing to risk not only his career but jail time to save his dog. I'm not saying there aren't people who would do anything to rescue their dog, but how do you know who those people are? How does Don Pedro know something so personal like that?"

"Yeah, that's the question you gotta be pondering," said Jenny Gigi.

"You think it's some kind of inside job?" I asked, sipping my bubbly pink drink while swishing my toes in the water. "You're thinking that somebody in Don Pedro's organization knew Agent Denko well enough to know that this would work?"

"Or maybe Don Pedro has his hooks into somebody close to Agent Denko. The guy's personal trainer or housecleaner or dog walker or whatever," Macy suggested from the back of a large duck. She was sipping something yellow because she had insisted on her drink going with her flotation device. She raised a gold-painted fingernail in the air. The fingernail had some jewels stuck onto it that probably weren't diamonds, but you never knew with the Gigis. Anything was possible with the Gigis. "Assuming it's not a trap, only somebody who knows him well could make this call."

I spun lazily around in the water and thought about the people in the apartment across the way, watching us so angrily. Could it be them? "That is some good insight," I said. "You are probably right."

"We're right a lot of the time," Macy boasted. "That manwich you got going isn't the only game in town, Ice." Here she pointed a golden fingernail at me. "If you ever get sick of them and their testosterone overload, you're welcome to be a getaway driver for us. We can always use a decent driver."

I grinned. I would never leave my guys, but I loved that they wanted me to join.

"Jewels, jewels, and more jewels, baby!" Angel said, splashing water through the air like diamonds.

We were still floating around when night fell, though we'd lit candles and we were playing music. It was awesome and utterly relaxing until my guys came back and did cannonballs, breaking the serenity into little bits. The Gigis were pretty angry, especially

Jenny, who had been successfully protecting her blowout the entire time.

They made up for it with an excellent cookout. Odin informed us that his contact in Washington, D.C., didn't know of any kind of tackle bag of evidence, but his D.C. contact thought it sounded "credible." That's all the guy would say. Credible.

We had to get that tackle bag!

I told my guys about Macy's ideas that somebody close to Agent Denko was probably on Don Pedro's payroll, and they liked that idea.

Naturally they were fine with my telling the Gigis what was going on. The God Pack had no secrets from the Gigis, and vice versa.

Odin was just laughing. "Ice, you and I are going to have to maybe canvass the nosy neighbors. What do you think about that?"

"I'd be happy to," I said defiantly. "I'm sure they'd love to meet me. They'll probably want my autograph because I'm clearly the girl with the mostest."

"Mostest *men*," Macy said.

Zeus pulled me into a hug, and Jenny threw a pickle at us, and we spent a long time arguing about whether Don Pedro should've changed his name so that he didn't remind people of Don Pablo's, the restaurant chain.

That was around the time that Thor and Angel disappeared. They came back a few minutes later with a large cardboard box. The handwriting looked familiar, and when I drew nearer, I recognized it as my sister Vanessa's handwriting.

"Did you order a Paris Hilton comforter?" I asked, confused. The Paris Hilton comforters were really expensive quilts from the farm. The gang and I ordered them as gifts when we felt like donating money to my sisters. But who was this one for? The Gigis had a few of them already.

"You'll see," Thor said mysteriously. "It's for later."

Even weirder!

After the Gigis left, he handed the mysterious package to Odin, who looked surprised at its weight. "What the hell? What the hell is in here? Too heavy for a wool comforter."

"Open it," Thor said.

Odin set it on the table, which creaked—that's how heavy the box was. Odin tore open the packaging materials. I recognized immediately the off-white cotton that we used for the sheep's wool comforters, but this one was three times as huge, and it was clearly far heavier.

Thor took it from Odin, hauled it into the bedroom, and unfurled it over the two queen-sized beds that we had pushed together earlier in the week. "This is a normal comforter except one end of it is weighted," he said.

"Like a weighted blanket?" Odin asked.

"Exactly. I commissioned it specifically for us four. Your end is heavy, with an amount of weight that is amazing for anxiety and sleep issues, but unlike the seat belts that made you feel like you were tied up, this is comfortable."

Odin looked skeptical.

"Just try it. See what you think," Zeus urged.

"It's not gonna work," Odin said.

"Please? For me?" I said.

"Just try it," Thor pleaded. "There's lavender woven into it for calming aromatherapy, and it's large enough that four people can sleep under it, but only you get the weighted area."

Odin shook his head.

"Think about it." I grabbed his arm. "We could sleep together almost like normal."

Odin yanked away his arm. "Stop trying to force this!" With that, he stormed out.

"Fuck," Thor groaned.

"It was a great idea," I said.

Thor gathered up the blanket and stormed out with it.

"Thor!" I called after him. I turned to Zeus. "He'd better not be throwing that out."

"It's not as if we can take something that heavy with us on the road if it's not being used," Zeus said, getting under the covers.

I climbed into bed next to him. "This needs to get resolved," I told him. "Odin can't go on like this."

"Or Thor," he said quietly.

I nodded. "Or Thor."

Chapter Eleven

HERK AND MARIA STOPPED BY THE NEXT MORNING while we were having our coffee out on the veranda. I sprung up from where I sat. "You guys—congratulations! We loved your wedding photos."

"We just wanted to thank you so much," Maria said. "For all that you did for us. Solving that mystery—there wouldn't have been a wedding without it."

"Well, it's our job," Thor said, "when we're not running for our lives."

"Yeah," I said. "Some people have nine-to-five jobs, but our work hours are anytime we are not running from our mortal enemy."

"Who damn well knows we're innocent," Zeus grumbled.

Herk and my guys spent the next hour exchanging gossip. The criminal element were the worst gossips ever, I'd found. I sat with Maria and made her show me more pictures of her dress, wishing we'd had proper pictures from our own wedding at Pastor Roger's Wee Chapel.

I told her that the Gigis had been over, and we speculated for way too long on whether they were gluing actual precious gems on to their fingernails. Maria felt sure that they were real, but I just couldn't imagine it. Then again, I'd grown up on a sheep farm.

So, I guess we were all gossiping.

Eventually, voices went low, and I could tell they were talking about the case. Had Don Galvano's guy already come through with the information that we needed? Was that part of why Herk and Maria had stopped by? To deliver the intel from Maria's dad?

Los Angeles was quite the freaking small town. Especially when you were in the criminal underworld.

"So it turns out that Don Pedro doesn't have Doris," Zeus informed me once Herk and Maria were gone.

"Wow, that was fast," I said. "They're sure about this?"

Odin and Zeus looked at each other like there was a really big secret in play.

"What?" I asked.

Zeus lowered his voice even though nobody could hear; this just showed what a big secret he was about to tell. "Looks like Don Galvano has somebody planted high up in Don Pedro's organization. That's how they know."

"Really high?"

"Top level. They told us that not only does Don Pedro *not* have Doris, but he's getting ready to leave the country for good. He's got a luxury mansion on an island off the coast of Brazil, and he's been waiting to retire there."

"No extradition treaty with Brazil," I said.

"Nope," Zeus said. "And Don Pedro is the only one on the hook for this crime. He's gonna turn the operations over to his second. They've been planning this ultra-luxury retirement escape for months. That is their entire plan for dealing with this court case. He doesn't give a shit about this violin appraiser guy or the ledger."

"So why would they kidnap Denko's dog and hold her hostage?" I asked.

"Exactly. They wouldn't," Thor said. "If Don Pedro can

successfully flee the country, why would he care if they have the ledger?"

"And trust me, he'll successfully flee the country," Odin said. "He's probably got a double on the job already."

"Which means somebody else kidnapped Doris," I said. "But who else would care enough about Don Pedro's court case to kidnap a dog and hold her hostage in order to get the ledger?"

"Wilson the violin appraiser would care about the ledger," Zeus pointed out. "I doubt he knows of Don Pedro's plans to skip town. He's probably sweating bullets worrying about what happens when he testifies against a powerful mob boss. And if he refuses to testify, he goes to jail. Remember how Agent Denko told us that without the ledger, Wilson's useless?"

"So Wilson would have a major incentive to make the ledger disappear," I said.

"Yuppers," Thor agreed. "And it's good news for us. I wasn't looking forward to going up against Don Pedro's people, but a violin appraiser's people? If they've got Doris, this job just got way easier."

"So it's somebody who wants Wilson to walk free," I said. "Does he have a wife? Kids? What's up with Wilson? We need to talk to him."

"We have to contact Agent Denko's assistant and get access to Wilson," Thor said. "That Agent Alfred guy."

"Which is a problem," Odin added. "What do we say about why we want to talk to Wilson? We can't let on what we know about Don Pedro's flight plans."

"Right," I said. "It's not like we can go, 'Hey, we ruled out Don Pedro. Don Pedro doesn't give a shit about the ledger, considering that he's headed to Brazil.'"

"Exactly," Odin said. "We also can't reveal that Don Galvano has an inside man."

"Absolutely not." Zeus was vehement. "These are big fucking

secrets that we need to keep. We gave Don Galvano our word on that."

"We have to pretend we don't know," I said. "We have to proceed with the investigation as if we don't know this information. Maybe we're having so much trouble finding Doris, we need to talk to Wilson the violin appraiser out of pure desperation. As though we're desperately throwing mud at the wall."

"Act *fucking-g* inept?" Odin growled.

I gave him a big fake frown. "Does it hurt your heart to have to act inept, baby?"

Odin sparkled at me. "You know it does."

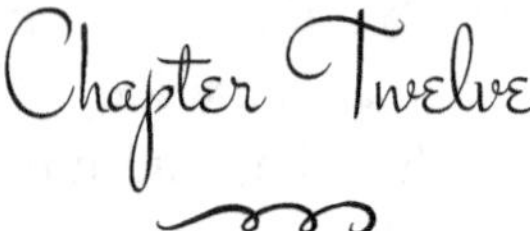

AGENT DENKO'S ASSISTANT, AGENT ALFRED, WANTED to meet in person. My guys were annoyed about that.

"Why would he insist on meeting in person?" I asked.

"It's smart of him," Zeus said. "The man wants to see our faces when we talk. You always want to see the faces. And not fucking Zoom, either."

"*Fucking-g* Zoom," Odin grumbled.

My guys chose the vast, empty parking lot of an abandoned big-box store as the meeting place. They liked it because it had lots of escape routes—just in case Alfred brought company.

Before we even told Alfred about it, we walked all around the perimeter of it, trying to figure out where the sightlines were and where somebody might want to hide for an ambush. It was decided that Thor and Zeus would hide in spots where they could watch all of the other possible hiding spots, basically staking out the stakeout spots.

"You're not going to put me anywhere?" I asked, feeling a little unhappy. I might not have been the kind of person you wanted in a gun battle, but I was good at watching places.

"You're meeting Agent Alfred with Odin," Zeus said.

"You want *me* to be in on the meeting with Alfred?" I asked, not sure whether I was hearing him correctly. "Me and Odin?"

"Why is that so surprising?" Zeus said. "You're very good with people. You're very perceptive. You and Odin make a good team. I want to know what you think."

I grinned. "Telling you what I think…I have skills in that area!"

"Oh, we know you have skills in that area, goddess," he said.

"I'd need to rustle up my beauty mark and my police sketch wig," I said excitedly. The beauty mark and blond wig was my look for most-wanted posters, stemming from the time I'd worn that particular getup to a bank robbery gone wrong where I had to kidnap a nurse from a Zip Clinic, though it was a humanitarian kidnapping.

Whenever we did anything that might get us seen by official people who knew who we were, we wore the disguises that matched the police sketches. Consistency was important when it came to choosing disguises.

The morning before the big meetup, Zeus popped the trunk where we kept our disguise essentials, and I grabbed the stuff I needed, did a quick change, and finished by tucking away stray hairs and donning the beauty mark.

You always wanted to count your blessings, especially when you were on the run. One blessing was that I didn't have the Sarah Newsome chipmunk-cheeks persona for my police sketch, but our police sketches were still unflattering. My guys said not to worry about it, but seriously, police sketches were like the *US Magazine* of our criminal set, and you wanted to be looking good.

Odin already had on his fake dead tooth, fake neck tattoos, and his wig of frizzy hair. Naturally, he looked amazing in spite of it all.

Odin and I drove to the spot a few minutes early, choosing a place in the middle of the mostly empty expanse of pavement, cross-hatched with faded white parking lines and littered with decrepit shopping carts.

We got up on the hood and sat there, waiting for Agent Alfred.

"Has Thor said anything about what's got him so twisted up?" Odin asked me.

"He hasn't said much of anything, no." I stared at the highway curlicue in the distance. "I'm wondering if he's just tiring of this on-the-run life. We all go through phases of that, you know?"

"Yeah," Odin said, somewhat mysteriously.

"Also, he hasn't been doctoring in a long time," I pointed out. "Being a doctor anchors him. It reminds him who he is."

Odin just looked thoughtful.

"But, on the bright side, now that we're back in L.A., it's only a matter of time before someone we know gets shot. Give Thor a scalpel and a guy with a few bullets in him..."

Odin scanned the horizon for trouble, saying nothing. Did he have extra thoughts on the subject?

"You and Zeus chose this life when you joined the intelligence agency," I prompted. "You always knew something like this was a possibility. Unlike Thor."

"You chose this life too, Ice. You wanted the excitement."

"I wanted us," I said. "I wanted our gang of four. But Thor had it thrust on him."

"Yes," Odin said.

I looked over at him. Was there something he wasn't saying? But then, when wasn't there? Odin always thought more than what he said out loud. "You have thoughts you want to share with the class? Because I think you have thoughts to share with the class!"

"I wish we could make it better for him," Odin said. "I don't know that we can."

I waited. Was that it?

"We can show him how much we value him. How much we love him," I said.

"Will that be enough?" Odin asked as a gray compact car turned into the parking lot and began rolling toward us.

"We're family. We protect each other. We'll do as much as it takes."

Odin turned to me with a warm sparkle in his dark amber eyes. "How we survived without you, goddess, I do not know. You help us remember our hearts."

I linked my arm in his, feeling indescribably happy.

Odin picked up his phone. "One visible," he said.

Indeed, one guy was visible, driving—Agent Alfred, presumably—but that didn't mean that was all the people in the car. I'd hung with my guys long enough to have that kind of thought cross my mind.

We hopped off the hood.

"He could have just done this by phone call," Odin grumbled, unsnapping his left shirt sleeve, the one that concealed his super-spy sleeve blade-holding compartment, though he always warned me not to call it that.

"Maybe Agent Alfred just wants to get to know us," I said, pulling my ladylike mother-of-pearl-handled Smith & Wesson from my purse. I held it loosely at my side. If things went hot, Thor and Zeus would be the ones shooting and we'd be the ones running, but you couldn't be too careful.

The car pulled up a few parking spaces over from us and stopped. Just the driver from what I could see—so far so good. I'd promised not to say anything about Wilson the violin guy or Doris the dog. I could chat, but Odin was to do the questioning about the case. Odin was the one with the skills in the interrogations area. I was to soak up the information that came of his questions.

A squat, muscle-bound man with dark, gray-flecked hair got out of the car and ambled over to us—Agent Alfred, no doubt, right-hand underling of Denko.

"Isis and Odin, I presume," he said. "Where's the rest of your crew? You all were supposed to be here."

"We occupy four of the ten-top slots on most-wanted posters

all across the nation," Odin said casually. "Rest assured, the whole crew is here."

I gave Alfred a sassy smile. *We occupy four of the ten-top slots on most-wanted posters all across the nation, bitches!* Being an outlaw definitely sucked, but at least you could say outlandish shit about yourselves.

I shoved my lady gun into my jeans' waistband and crossed my arms. "Though we do want to talk to somebody about those post office posters. We have complaints, like why are we not in the top-five most wanted? I get why the Mapleview Mangler is in the top position, being that he's a serial killer—we definitely don't want to challenge him on the notoriety level—but I feel that we should really have beat out that hacker that you have in the number two spot. What's up with that? Anybody can hack from their basement."

"Yeah, what we do is way more challenging," Odin echoed, trying his hardest not to smile.

"I mean, we have to go out there and do takeover robberies," I continued. "Sooooo much more challenging."

Alfred's lips thinned in annoyance.

Odin liked to say that annoyance was a window to the insides of people. Odin loved seeing that window get opened, so I was glad I could help with that.

"And another humble request, if you would be so kind," I said, thinking I could open that window a little wider. "If we were to supply you with better line drawings of our faces, could they be switched out for the ones that that sketch artist in Nevada did? Because honestly, unflattering much?"

"The most-wanted poster program is not a beauty pageant," Alfred said.

"Maybe not to *you*," I said.

Agent Alfred turned to Odin. "You had questions?"

"Yeah, we need a little more information," Odin said. "We're interested in talking to anybody who might benefit from Wilson

Brockmeier getting out of there, including Wilson and his people."

"You're looking at *Wilson* and *Wilson's people*?" Alfred said. "Wilson's a fine-instrument appraiser, not a criminal mastermind. The man's a pawn with no juice."

"We like to inspect all the angles," Odin said. "That is how we work."

Alfred looked at us like we'd lost our minds. "There's a ticking clock on this thing, and Don Pedro is the one who has the dog. Why would you waste your time on Wilson?"

"Don Pedro *allegedly* has the dog," Odin said. "We four sat down and made a list of all the people who would benefit from that ledger disappearing, and we realized Wilson would benefit."

Alfred blinked, stunned.

I tried to keep my expression neutral, but it was kind of funny. *Made a list. Realized Wilson would benefit.* I had no doubt it pained Odin to make us sound so dorky and incompetent.

"What is this, Detective 101?" Alfred said. "Why would you waste your time like that? You want to make lists instead of concentrating your energy on the most obvious suspect?" Of course, he had a point; it was pretty obviously Don Pedro unless you knew what we knew.

"So?" Odin said after a while.

"At our agency, we rule out the obvious suspects before we start pursuing baroque theories."

"We thought it would be good to speak with the person at the center of it," Odin said. "Who knows what he can tell us."

"Wilson's not at the center; Don Pedro is," Alfred said, exasperated. "This dognapping is a matter of Don Pedro trying to get leverage for his court case. Wilson knows nothing because he's a nobody."

Odin frowned. "Still. We would like to question Wilson. He is on the list that we made."

"If Wilson was the kind of guy who could engineer anything

like this, he wouldn't be in the situation that he's in. I don't understand the problem with the Don Pedro angle. You have motive, you have means, you have everything but a trail of breadcrumbs leading from Agent Denko's condo to Don Pedro's organization. Your assignment is to figure out who inside Don Pedro's network has the dog. Agent Denko thought you were good at finding things, but..."

"Denko said we could get whatever assistance we wanted," Odin reminded him.

"You're not getting to Wilson without something more than a ridiculous list," Alfred said.

Clearly, he wouldn't budge. Odin crossed his arms over his chest. "Okay, then, what about the people around Wilson? Friends, family, associates."

Alfred studied Odin's face and then looked over at me, studying my face. "So, your theory is that somebody in Wilson's life wants to crash the case? That's your line of thinking?"

I said, "We made a list—"

Alfred's mouth muscles tightened—just a little change in his lip shape. "Yeah, so you've said," he bit out, seeming to have reached peak annoyance. "You don't get paid if you don't find the dog in time. We're clear on that, right?"

"This is our process," Odin explained. "Are you instructed to prevent us from pursuing all other avenues that are not related to Don Pedro?"

"I'm not bringing you to Wilson," Alfred said. "The man is in deep WITSEC. But I can email you info on his people if that's how you want to waste your time. He's got a wife still living in their place in Culver City, and there's a brother in Mar Vista. Wilson played in some kind of music quartet with three friends; one of them is a particular friend, and we can get you that name and number."

"We'd like that," I put in.

"Yeah, because who knows?" Alfred said sarcastically. "Maybe

Wilson's hippie musician buddies are having trouble finding a new fiddler for their group and have decided to run a sophisticated dognapping operation in order to claw Wilson back from the clutches of the feds. You never know, right?"

Very funny, I thought, giving him a nice big fake smile.

Alfred promised to email all of the information on people associated with Wilson, and then he jumped into his car and sped off. We stood there waiting until he'd disappeared down the frontage road, heading toward more populous areas.

"What do you think?" Odin asked.

"I think he's annoyed with us, and I think his annoyance tell is a slight tightening of the mouth muscles," I announced, pleased that I'd noticed that.

Odin swung into our own car, and I got into the passenger seat and shut the door, buckling up.

"Anything else? What did he want?" Odin asked.

I sat back and set my feet up on the dashboard. Odin and Zeus were always in front, so this was a nice change. "Hmm."

"That's a very dangerous way to ride," Odin said. "You know what would happen to you if we got in an accident when your feet are on the dashboard like that?"

"Who cares, we're outlaws. We live for danger," I said.

"I think we are a bad influence on you," he said.

I grinned. "Thank goodness for that!"

Odin gave me a concerned look. "Please don't ride like that," he asked. "It really *is* dangerous."

I put my feet in their proper place, weirdly touched.

"What else?" Odin asked. "What else crossed your mind about Alfred?"

"Hmm..." I was enjoying our conversation. This was usually the kind of conversation he had with Zeus. "It's weird he needed to meet with us personally. He wasn't a huge amount of help."

"He wasn't, was he?" Odin said.

"He was super into us pursuing Don Pedro," I added.

"Micromanagement?" he asked.

"What do you think?"

"I don't know," he said.

&

The four of us met at a seaside place for a lavish lunch. Odin and I did the big download, which was mainly that Alfred was unhelpful and his mouth tightens when he's annoyed.

Our food came. I had ordered an appetizer plate of mini crab cakes for my entrée. They looked absolutely delicious. I pushed a fork sideways into a crusty shell, enjoying the fragrant steam. I smeared a bit of sauce on top.

"He also seems really invested in it being Don Pedro," I said.

"Well, I'd think it was Don Pedro, too, if I didn't know otherwise," Zeus said, checking his phone. "Here it is—Alfred's email with the names and addresses of Wilson's people. I say we start with the wife."

"Do you think Wilson's wife could have Doris?" I asked.

"Who knows," Zeus said. "Could that be why she chose not to go into witness protection with her husband?"

"Interesting," I said. "Though she could just be fed up with his criminal ways...not that I can imagine that myself," I quickly added.

Thor grinned. "You love our criminal ways."

"You know I do, baby!"

"She's unhappy with him, he's unhappy with her, or she's helping him," Zeus said.

"Yeah, maybe this was their plan all along," I mused. "Like they hatched the plan to grab Doris before Wilson went into witness protection, and they feel sure they can get that ledger, rendering Wilson no threat to Don Pedro."

Thor nodded. "A little Bonnie and Clyde action."

"She could be the clever and daring mastermind," I said. "She could be the one who encouraged him to go criminal, and when he got caught, she was like, 'I'll fix this, baby!'"

Odin grinned.

"What?" I shrugged. "I'd do it for you guys in a second."

Odin's grin softened. "I know you would. It makes me happy, that's all."

Chapter Thirteen

Before he had been taken in, Wilson and his wife, Clarice, lived in a cute little bungalow just inland from Venice Beach. Clarice didn't answer the door when we knocked, but her car was in the drive.

Zeus pounded harder. "Federal agents!"

This got an open.

Clarice was an attractive, petite woman in her fifties with a platinum pixie hairdo and healthy-looking freckled skin. The way she was dressed, she looked like she was ready for a jog. She even had a visor on.

"You're not the feds," she said.

"We're working with the feds," Zeus said.

"Well, that doesn't give you a right to say that you're the feds, does it?" she said.

"We're acting as an extension of the feds, so I think it does give us that right," Thor said. "Do you need us to come back with the agents we're coordinating with? Or are you going to talk to us now?"

She sighed. "I'm out of here in twenty." With that, she led us into her home. "You're wasting your time, though, because I don't know anything. I've been through this over and over. Wilson kept me completely in the dark."

"This shouldn't take long," Thor told her.

There were a lot of salmon-colored furnishings, beachy pastel pictures, and photos of buildings in Rome. In the corner, leaning against the wall, were pictures of Wilson and Clarice as a couple plus some very masculine shit—pictures of MMA fighters and bullfighters. I was guessing she had taken down all of Wilson's favorite stuff.

"What do you want to know?" she asked.

"Did you have any idea he was appraising things in a less than accurate way?" Odin asked.

"How would I?" she said. "How would I know that kind of thing?"

"Well, you worked at the shop together," Odin put in.

"And like I told the others, he was the one who knew about the instruments; I did the bookkeeping and clerked. I came out of a shopkeeping background, not a fine-instruments background. If Wilson said an instrument was worth a hundred thousand bucks, how was I to know it was worth more like a hundred? Those fine instruments, when they've gotten old enough, an expensive one doesn't look all that different from a piece of crap. You put a little polish on something and restring it..." She shrugged.

"When was the first time you noticed something wrong?" Odin asked.

She looked away, seeming to compose her thoughts. "He started acting nervous and upset several months ago. He said he had a stomachache, but if he did, it was obviously *because* he was nervous and upset, not the other way around. Because he was completely *lying* to me. He would stay out at night a lot..."

"Doing..."

"Doing what? Is that what you want to know?" She shrugged again. "That's what I keep asking myself."

I looked at Odin, biting back a smile, because *that's what I keep asking myself* was one of his top annoying answers. *Why would you keep asking yourself the same question over and over? Either you know or you don't,* he always said.

"You chose not to go into witness protection with him," Odin said. "Usually spouses go in together." He didn't ask it as a question, but it was a question.

"Why would I?" she asked. "It's not like I don't still love him, but he got into bed with the mob. He destroyed our livelihood. How would you feel if you found out that your husband of twenty years had turned your business that you built together into a money-laundering outlet for a dangerous mobster?" This question she directed at me.

"Not great," I granted her.

"Are you worried about being used as leverage against him?" Zeus said.

She sighed. "He put my life in danger, blew up our business, and got half our instruments seized. I'm left alone to run a shop that's going down the tubes now because our customers are going elsewhere. He's obviously not worried about what's gonna happen to me. I think that's probably clear to everybody, including his mobster friends."

I nodded, feeling sorry for her.

"People keep asking me if he stashed the money or whatever, but I don't know. Did he have a girlfriend? Did he have a gambling addiction? How bad did he throw me under the bus? I'm only just now figuring it out. So no, I won't be going into witness protection with him. Are we done here?"

"I guess I'd be mad, too," I said, just to keep her going. I could feel that's what we needed.

"Please don't get me wrong—I love him," she said to me. "But there's only so much a person can take."

I nodded.

"Is there anybody that might want to see him get out of this mess?" Zeus asked.

"Get out of this mess?" she asked, like the concept was somehow surprising.

"Besides you, who was closest to him?" he tried.

"Was I even close to him? That's what I keep asking myself." She gazed dolefully at the taken-down man art.

I bit my lip and looked over at Odin who narrowed his eyes at me.

"He played gigs with his friend Ferdinand a lot. That's his best friend, or *was* his best friend. He has a brother, Harold, and they were close. I know he's taking all this pretty hard. Harold had no idea of any of this, and he's absolutely shocked." She paused to think. "And there were a few customers that he had close relationships with."

Zeus got their names and then thanked her warmly. "We really appreciate your time."

She ushered us back to the foyer.

"Was Wilson into the UFC?" Thor asked, nodding at the giant autographed photo of two men wrestling in skimpy shorts hanging in a place of prominence.

Clarice rolled her eyes. "Very. He was obsessed with it. He followed the fighters on social media. He never missed their fights."

"Do you think that he could have been gambling on the fighters?" Zeus asked.

Clarice shrugged. "It's possible," she said. "Aside from stringed instruments, the UFC was definitely his thing. Do you think that's where the money went? To gambling?" She looked at us like she thought we had the answer.

I gave her a sympathetic smile, and we got out of there.

We headed up the Pacific Coast Highway on our way to see Wilson's brother's shop. The ocean shone bright gray out the window, and the sky looked huge.

"So, Clarice's list of Wilson's people isn't really that different than the list Alfred gave to us. With one exception," Zeus said. "I've got one more person to add to the list of people that might have Doris."

"You do?" I asked, surprised. "I didn't hear her mention anybody new."

"Can I guess?" Thor grinned at Zeus. "I'm going to go with Wilson's bookie."

"Ding ding ding," Zeus said.

"Wait, so you think she's right about a possible gambling addiction?" I asked.

"It would explain a few things," Zeus said. "You don't turn to crime for the fun of it."

"You think Wilson's bookie would dognap Doris?" I asked.

"If Wilson has a gambling problem, he might owe his bookie a lot of money. The bookie can't exactly get paid if Wilson disappears into a witness protection life, right? Also, don't forget—nobody knows where all of that money went. You heard Clarice say so herself. Maybe her husband lost it all gambling. Or maybe he hid some, knowing he'd be starting over. Wilson's bookie would want to get at that."

"Oh, I see," I said. "Like once Wilson's in his new witness protection life, he plans to retrieve it. And not bother to pay his bookie, because he's a new person."

"It's worth checking out," Zeus said. "Unless she's working with him and she's just a good liar."

"She *was* taking the couples pictures down and all of the dude pictures and dude art, too," I said. "It suggests she's pissed at him." It seemed like there was something about that... But Zeus was already calling around, and two minutes later we had the name of Wilson's bookie.

Stan the Man.

"Stan the Man. Ugh," Thor grumbled.

"I know, but better Stan the Man than Handsome Jack," Zeus

reminded us. We'd gotten Handsome Jack in a lot of trouble some months back.

"Stan the Man," I said. "Is that the kind of nickname you make up for yourself?"

Thor just grumbled. "Too early for Stan the Man. He doesn't come out until dark."

"What is he?" I asked. "A vole?"

"A vole would be better," Odin said.

Zeus caught my eye in the rearview mirror. "Did you notice anything else about Clarice?" he asked.

"Not sure," I said. "Though I don't think she's sad that he's gone. She wasn't lying about that."

"If anything, she might be glad he's gone—more so than she let on," Odin said. "That was my sense."

"Agree," I said. "Her whole 'don't get me wrong, I love him' bit felt off. Something about that whole scene back there felt off."

"Now that you say that, I agree," Thor said.

I narrowed my eyes, looking at the scenery as we went—or more, as we crawled; the traffic was insane. "Maybe she doesn't wanna dance on his grave, but Wilson definitely sounds like a jerk."

"We need to talk to him and get a sense of other people in his life," Zeus said. "It's not good enough that Denko and Alfred interviewed him, because they interviewed him with a mind to Don Pedro having taken the dog. There would be questions that they didn't think to ask Wilson."

"Does that gray Buick look familiar?" Odin suddenly asked. "Back two lengths. Shaded windows. I feel like I keep seeing it."

Whenever anybody was following us, Odin was usually the first to notice. He was brilliant and sensitive and highly attuned to the outside world. He had an uncanny knack for feeling when we were being watched, stretching back to the time he'd been sent to a terrible prison.

Zeus grumbled a yes. "Fed car if I ever saw one."

"Is this more *fucking-g* micromanagement from Alfred? Because no, just no," Odin said. "See if you can sneak in over there," he said, pointing at the next lane over. Traffic was thick, but Zeus managed to maneuver over, earning angry gestures from a few people. He maneuvered over yet again, straight onto a side street and back in the direction from where we came, efficiently losing the Buick.

"What the hell," Zeus complained. "Alfred? Did he guess we'd go see Wilson's wife? It's the obvious place."

"Piggybacking on our investigation?" Odin bit out.

"We lost him," I said. "But does it matter? I'm sure he can figure out that we'd go to see Wilson's people. We told him as much."

"I don't care," Zeus said. "I don't like him on our ass."

Such a Zeus thing to say. I beamed at him, feeling all the love in the world for him.

Chapter Fourteen

HAROLD'S AND WILSON'S SHOPS WERE A TALE OF TWO cities.

Whereas Wilson's fine-instruments center was apparently a huge, brightly lit, gleaming wooden-floored showroom in a glam part of town, Harold's violin repair shop was a little hole-in-the-wall in a modest part of town known for pawnshops and dollar stores. Dusty instruments hung in crooked rows along the walls, and the place smelled of wood stain and resin and strange seed oils.

We rang the bell on the counter. A tall bald man with bushy brows came out from a back room, wiping his hands on a stained brown cloth. His rubbery-looking apron was also stained brown.

"I already talked to your other guys," Harold said after Odin made introductions and told him that we had questions.

"We need to go over a few things," Odin said.

He frowned. "Is everything okay with Wilson? Things are okay with him, right?"

"No change," Zeus said.

Harold nodded.

I could barely concentrate on anything because of Harold's wildly bushy eyebrows. I desperately wanted to ask him to smooth down those brows, maybe with a dab of that seed oil or something, or at least get them even, but that was probably not the kind of question my guys wanted to lead with.

"Just a bit of background clarification," Thor began, "did you and your brother go into the stringed-instrument business at the same time?"

"In a way, yes," Harold said. "I mean we both attended music conservatory. We were both interested in classical music—something of a family tradition, really, though Wilson was more on the performance end of things. Wilson is a brilliant musician—a lot of people don't know that. He wanted to be a concert violinist, and he could have done it, too, but competition at the highest levels is really fierce, and auditioning was never his strong suit. But being involved with the instruments, it keeps you close to the music."

"Was that hard for him?" Thor asked. "Being close to the music but not as a performer?"

"Oh, he still played around. He did a lot of gigging, and he had his quartet," Harold said.

"How often did you see each other? Did you do business together?" Thor asked.

"I wouldn't say we saw each other a lot. Life gets busy, and I have grown children and grandbabies, the shop. But we always knew what was happening in each other's lives…" Harold's brows knit in confusion, which made them look even more wildly unkempt. "Or I thought we knew, anyway. We would text about family matters and funny shit, business stuff—missing instruments, that sort of thing. He was a great uncle to my kids, and that might be the biggest loss. My three boys are grown now. They don't know what's happened—you all have kept it out of the papers, so they have no idea what's up with Uncle Wilson. They think he's on a buying trip. They're going to need to know the truth eventually."

"Did you have any ideas that he was up to anything?" Zeus asked him.

"Absolutely not!" Harold said, lifting his brows of madness halfway up his forehead.

Wildly I looked over at Thor—was he seeing this? Thor quirked his head at me as if to say, *what's up?* Zeus and Odin didn't seem to notice anything, either.

Harold went on and on. "I had no idea what he'd gotten involved in, or I would have tried to help him. I've been going over it in my head, over and over. If only I had taken the time to visit his shop and taken a look at the instruments he was valuing in the six figures, I could have told you something was wrong."

"You ran very different establishments," Thor pursued, delicately.

"If you mean the success of his shop, I want you to know that was all elbow grease. Yes, I know what they're saying about him in terms of the inflated appraisals, but I can't imagine it was anything that he'd been doing on the regular. He must have gotten into trouble, that's all I can think. He's a good man, Wilson is, and a fine businessperson. He enjoyed taking risks on fixer-upper instruments. He loved being the center of attention, but I guess somewhere along the line..." He shook his head sadly, brows lowered in consternation, trembling slightly. Oh my god, the eyebrows! Was he *trying* to distract us?

He did this for a long time, shaking his head and making his brows tremble.

"What happened, do you think?" Thor asked.

"That's what I keep asking myself," he said.

"You've been asking yourself that?" I repeated, trying not to look at his brows.

"Yes, a lot," Harold said.

Odin gave me a dark look. "Can you think of why he might have needed all that extra money when his store was doing so well?"

Harold sighed and gazed out the window. "When he'd go on

his buying trips to Europe, he did tend to go in style. He liked nice hotels. But that was him. He lived life to the fullest."

"Buying trips?"

"Taking a chance on worn-out or damaged instruments from lesser-known makers and refurbishing them was a big part of his business."

"People do that?" Thor asked. "They speculate on violins?"

"Absolutely," Harold said. "Fine-instrument makers can go in and out of fashion in the same way that clothes designers or car brands can. Sometimes you go to auction and see something special in an instrument. You think maybe you can bring out that special something with a little know-how, or maybe that maker will get hot. Just like flipping homes."

"So, he did a lot of this sort of speculation?" Odin asked.

"Yes, and he was excellent at it. He invested in the occasional boondoggle, don't get me wrong, but he could usually pick a winner. He enjoyed the thrill of that. Maybe it became an addiction with him. They say that people can get addicted to taking risks with their money."

"You think he might have been into other forms of gambling?" Thor asked.

Harold glanced at me, brows raised almost supernaturally high.

I swallowed, struggling to act chill.

"Did you ever hear him talking about speculating on other things?" Thor continued. "Cards, ponies..."

"Do you think that's why he got into bed with that mobster?" Harold asked, shocked.

"We're asking you," Odin said softly. "What do you think?"

"It would explain the situation. He wasn't the type to turn to crime, and it breaks my heart, because we were very close. And it confounds me on another level, too. The lack of ethics in what he was doing, considering that we grew up surrounded by music and a love of instruments. To think he was out there literally claiming that worthless instruments were worth so much…" More head-shaking and brow movement. I stared at a violin display on the wall, unable to take any more of his brows. "I refuse to believe he would lie about the value of an instrument. Instruments, they have souls. They are the beating heart of life."

"Did he ever say anything to you about money problems?" Thor asked.

"No, but he must have had debts, right? Where did all of that money go? Maybe he speculated on the wrong instrument. Maybe he was under some sort of pressure."

"Was he into any sports of any kind? Or possibly any sports betting?" Odin asked.

"Come to think of it, he loved that fighting sport—not boxing, but the other one—the more violent one," Harold said, perking up. "He would play videos for me now and then, but it wasn't my thing. Maybe he speculated on that, too." Harold and his brows took on a somber mood suddenly. "I'm sorry that I'm not more help to you."

I was thinking about that UFC picture in Wilson and Clarice's home. Had sports betting sent him into a life of crime?

"One last question," Odin suddenly popped in. "Do *you* buy instruments on a speculative basis? Thinking that they would rise in value or that you could fix them up and flip them?"

"Me?" Harold asked.

"Yes. Is it a practice that's common in the fine-instrument business or was it more something that Wilson did?"

"Well, of course, we all do that from time to time, but…" Harold waved his hand. "I wish I had more answers for you."

"No, you've been very helpful," Odin said.

We thanked him and left. After a quick check of the area and we were back in the car

"Omigod, the brows!" I practically screamed, unable to contain myself any longer.

"What about them?" Thor asked as we got on the road.

I slugged him in the shoulder.

"What?" Thor complained, rubbing the area.

"That's all you got, goddess? The brows?" Odin asked. "You're so good at reading people. You can't let yourself be distracted."

"Well, one thing I noticed—he seems to care about his brother, but is he secretly a bit superior, maybe? Something about how he kept on about the whole speculative and gambling end of things."

Odin was nodding energetically, like he was glad I said that. "I thought so, too. Possibly even a bit eager for us to follow the bread-crumb trail of gambling?"

"Right? Like he wanted to direct our minds!" I said. "When he wasn't clouding our minds with his brows, that is."

"But here's the question," Odin said. "Is that man capable of stealing Denko's dog and blackmailing him for the ledger? Was that a man who would do that kind of thing to get his brother out?"

"I don't know," I admitted. "I'm still hung up on how intense he was on the speculative information."

"He could be just grabbing for an explanation," Thor suggested. "People like to create stories to explain behavior they don't like. Maybe that's his story and he wants everybody to think it."

"He seems a little bit like a control freak that way," Odin said. "But there's something more. Something hidden. Is he maybe less upset about this whole thing than he's letting on? Have the brothers always been in competition, and he's thrilled to have finally won, but he doesn't want to come out and act like that? He's holding something back for sure, but we need to concentrate on the main question—is this a man who breaks into a federal agent's high-security condo, kidnaps a large dog, and then runs a sophisticated blackmailing operation?"

"I'm thinking not," I said.

"Same," Odin sighed. "And even if he did have the guts and the smarts to do it, is this a man who'd put it all on the line to protect his brother?"

"If anything, I'd imagine he's looking forward to grabbing some of the business his brother's shop had," Zeus pointed out.

"Either way, we need to get the story on Wilson's gambling habit," Odin said. "Let's see if Harold called it. Was it gambling that caused Wilson to turn to the mob? And did he gamble enough that somebody wants him out of witness protection? Walking free where they can get access to him and his money?"

"The brother did seem cagey," I said, "just like Clarice. Is everybody just up to something?"

"Listen to you all sad and jaded," Thor said, giving me shit as only he could. "What is happening with the world? Everybody's up to something!" he teased.

"What?" I protested. "It's sad."

"We *are* up to something," Thor said. "We're up to way the hell more than Harold and Clarice will ever be up to."

"That's for sure," I said proudly, relaxing into the comfy Jag seating array.

"We need to keep an open mind about everybody," Odin said. "It's all just words so far. Stories people have spun that may or may not be true."

Zeus kept looking in the rearview mirror. "I don't like this. I feel like I keep seeing the same cars. I feel like we've had a tail for a while now."

"Hmm," Odin said, checking the side mirror. "Agent Alfred?"

Zeus grumbled. He didn't like that at all. "We'll ditch this car and take an Uber back to the Airbnb and figure it out."

The next twenty minutes was an odyssey of slipping the tail, which involved fake-evasive driving, then parking in the lot of a motel, breaking into an empty motel room, and slipping out the back. We crossed a road and headed into a gas station to call an Uber.

After a stop to pick up stone-fired pizzas, we arrived back at the Newsomes' Malibu home away from home for a relaxing evening on the outdoor patio. We had our disguises on in a half-assed way, just being vigilant in case people peeped, though Zeus and Thor both wore hats instead of dealing with that part.

Everything was relaxing and fun, until Odin's phone started buzzing like crazy.

My guys sat up, staring at the phone, and just like that, they had guns in their hands. I should've been used to it, but it was still a little weird to be hanging out on the patio cooking food and loafing around, and suddenly you find out your companions are heavily armed.

"If you don't want to talk to anybody, just send it to voice-mail," I joked feebly.

"That's my perimeter alarm," Odin said ominously. "Some-body's here, Ice. Somebody's inside."

I sat up. Damn! Had we not lost our tail after all? Thor grabbed my hand and pulled me to the edge of the property behind a boulder. "Stay here," he whispered, handing me his gun.

My pulse whooshed in my ears. "You keep it."

"Don't argue." He was picking stones off the ground and filling his pockets. "Damn. If somebody knows where we're stay-ing, this'll be bad."

"Dude, seriously? Stones?" I hissed, trying to hand him the gun.

"I'm gonna be distracting whoever it is with these, drawing them out." With that, he disappeared.

I waited. The moments drew out long. Wind whistled. Surf crashed in the distance. And then I heard laughter—a woman's laughter. Sue's laughter.

What was Sue laughing about? Was she dangerous?

I snuck toward the house, gun in hand with a towel draped over it. Stealthily I peeped in the window.

Sue was standing in the middle of the living room with a fresh stack of towels talking to the guys. Zeus caught my eye and shook his head. What did that mean? No danger? Or stay away?

But Thor seemed to be laughing now, too. Then Sue saw me and waved. "Sarah!" she said. "Hello!"

I adjusted my wig, stood up, and came in the porch door with the towel fully wrapped around the gun. "Hi, Sue," I said.

"Fresh towels, piping hot from the laundry," she said cheerfully. "I think I startled your Theo here." She turned to Zeus. "I'm so sorry—I didn't see your car, and I figured I could drop these off."

Zeus grunted, and I could see that it had been awkward that she'd come like that.

"Like I said, I was just going to set these on the doorstep, but the raccoons have been active lately," she said.

"Thank you!" I chirped.

Sue made a big show of taking them to the linen closet and putting them in. "I'm sorry; I didn't mean to intrude," she said, coming back out.

"We can always use more fresh towels," I said.

"You want me to take that one?" she asked, holding her hand out for mine.

"Oh, no, I'm using it."

"You sure?" she asked.

"Yes."

"We'll let you know if we need anything." Zeus's tone was distinctly unfriendly.

"Sorry again to bother you." With that she left.

"Are Airbnb people even supposed to do that? Just show up without warning?" I asked.

"No," Odin grumbled. "And we had an entire *fucking-g* closet full of clean towels already. It's not okay that she's coming over like that."

"You think she knows who we are?" I asked.

"She wants to know if we've made a discovery for our gallery," Thor said.

"If I'd looked into her more closely, I would've never used this cover story, goddamnit," Zeus said. "And, Ice, don't be so freaking friendly to her. She's supposed to give us warning before she comes over. I don't want her to think it's okay not to give warning."

"Well, it was just a little awkward," I said.

"We *wanted* it to be awkward," Odin pointed out.

Men. I handed Thor his gun back.

Chapter Fifteen

STAN THE MAN'S SPORTS BAR WAS A LARGE WINDOWLESS building between a strip joint and a liquor store, a sort of one-stop vice destination.

The place was dark and heavily air-conditioned inside; unsurprisingly, it smelled of stale booze. Everywhere you looked there were giant screens showing sports of every kind, with people gathered in little clusters watching them. Low-hanging lamps illuminated row upon row of busy pool tables at the far end.

"You really think it's possible this guy could have the dog?" I asked.

"Assuming Wilson's debts are extreme enough, and assuming this guy believes the rumor that Wilson has buried money somewhere, it's more than possible."

We went up to a clean-cut, sporty-looking bartender at the center bar.

"We're looking for Stan," Zeus said.

"Who's asking?" the sporty bartender asked. Another one sidled up next to him, this guy also clean cut, but a little older. "God Pack," the older one said. "Go let him know."

The young one looked at us like we were aliens and then scurried off.

That's right, we're the God Pack! I thought, feeling super notorious.

"What can I get you?" the older bartender asked. "On the house."

"Thank you," I said. "I would love a wine spritzer." The guys ordered tap beer, and Odin tipped him a fifty. We got our beers and then Thor tapped my shoulder and pointed at the pool tables. There had to be twenty of them. People were probably gambling on the games.

"That's a lot of pool tables," I said.

"No, look at the walls." Thor pulled me nearer to him, and that's when I saw them—paintings of dogs playing pool stretching all along one wall. "Isn't that your favorite kind of art?"

My heart was just pounding. "I've never seen so many different ones in one place!"

"You think they're painted on velvet?" he asked.

"They'd better be," I said, dragging him over to get a closer look. It really was an amazing collection, with a beautiful bulldog-and-collie one that I'd never seen before. "Okay, I like this place a lot better now. Maybe this Stan the Man is okay."

Thor slung an arm around my shoulders. "Not a chance."

"What is it?" Odin came up, swigging his beer, with Zeus next to him.

"The dogs." Thor pointed.

"When we have a place someday, we're going to decorate it with those kinds of pictures," Zeus rumbled.

"Oh, we don't have to. I just think they're fun and funny, that's all." It was painful to think in terms of someday like that. "I wouldn't inflict this art on you guys," I said wistfully.

"No, it's settled," Zeus said. "When we get a place, it has to reflect all of our tastes. We all pick art we love."

"And maybe we could have a flying toilet," Thor said. "And a robot butler too. Because why not?"

"What's that supposed to mean?" Odin asked.

"It's just stupid to talk about it like it'll actually happen," Thor said with uncharacteristic negativity.

"We could have a home someday," Odin said.

Thor snorted.

"Maybe we'll go to Jerba," I said.

My guys all groaned. Jerba was a vacation island I'd identified off the coast of Tunisia. My guys were not keen on living in a tropical paradise, but I'd go for it. Best of all, Jerba had no extradition treaty.

"What? Maybe Don Pedro has the right idea," I said.

"We're not going to *fucking-g* Jerba," Odin muttered. Of course, like many people with PTSD, vacations were the worst times for Odin. Peace left him alone with his thoughts.

The young bartender approached and nervously waved us to follow him. We went down a dark hallway, stopping at a gray steel door that definitely looked reinforced. The young bartender knocked twice and then scurried off.

The door was opened by a wiry man with wire-rimmed glasses and a very nice suit, but most notable was his troll-style beard in which everything around the mouth was shaved clean.

"The notorious God Pack," he said, inviting us into his surprisingly bland-looking office. I don't know what I expected from a big-time bookie, but not a desk setup that looked like it came straight off of the showroom floor of a big-box office center.

He watched us take a seat with an air of expectancy, like we were about to do something wild.

Being on the run and never knowing anybody could feel lonely at times—always a stranger in a strange place.

However, having people recognize you when there were zillions of outrageous rumors circulating about you also had its downsides. Imagine walking into a place and everyone expects you to start dancing on the desk while your guys trash the furniture.

Which, to be fair, had happened.

"To what do I owe the honor?" he asked.

"Have you ever heard of Wilson Brockmeier?" Zeus asked, getting right down to business.

Stan the Man leaned back on the front of his desk with a strange grin on his face. "The name does sound familiar," he said, crossing his ankles.

"How familiar?" Zeus asked.

"I don't like to kiss and tell," he said, looking at me a little too long. "Generally."

Zeus rose from his seat and stood in front of me, cutting off Stan's sightline. "How about you tell it anyway," he said. "We're not asking you anything we can't get from the customers out there."

"Then why not ask them?" Stan said.

"Because we're asking you. If you weren't interested in talking to us, you shouldn't have invited us back and wasted our time," Zeus said, words laced with threat.

Stan regarded us for a long time, weighing Zeus's words. "Yeah, Wilson Brockmeier came in. Placed bets. Fights, mostly. I wish he'd never darkened that door; I can tell you that. Nothing I can do about it now."

"How much has he got outstanding with you?" Zeus asked.

Stan made a strange face. "You really don't know, do you?" he asked. "But then again, not a lot of people know."

"Know what?" Odin barked.

"What he was up to," Stan said.

"You mean the appraisals?" I asked.

Stan snorted. "No, beyond that. I'm talking about something far more interesting, in fact. You could see why he'd want to keep it quiet of course."

Odin stood now. "You gonna fill us in at some point here?"

"I'd be happy to," Stan said. "I actually have some very interesting fucking information about Wilson if that sort of thing might be useful to you."

"We'll make it worth your while," Odin said. "If it's good information that we can't get elsewhere, we'd *more* than make it worth your while." Odin pulled out a wad of bills.

"Oh no, that's not what I had in mind," Stan said. "I was thinking about a little taste." Here he jerked his chin at me. "A round with this one."

I gasped.

My guys stiffened. The temperature in the room dropped by about thirty degrees.

Uh-oh.

Odin's voice came out ominously low. "*What* did you just say?"

"You boys can watch or not, Stan the Man isn't picky," Stan continued, oblivious to my guys' outrage, oblivious to the very real danger he was now in with his sexual ask. "I just need to get a taste...maybe a little poke—"

Zeus was a blur of motion, surging up to grab Stan's shirt front and pin him up to the wall. Whatever was left of Stan the Man's sentence became unintelligible chortling-choking.

Probably for the best.

"What the fuck did you just say?" Odin demanded again.

Stan attempted words without success, also probably for the best. The way Zeus held him, by his shirt's front and collar, Stan's feet were barely touching the ground. He was like one of those cartoons where the person is suspended in midair with their legs still running.

"What did you just say?" Thor demanded, not that any of us wanted it repeated, and it most definitely wouldn't have behooved Stan, who was doing more chortle-choking.

"Ice is not for sale," Zeus growled. "Ice is not a bargaining chip. She is our amazing wife, and you will respect and honor her."

"I don't need him to honor me," I said, because what would that even look like?

"He will honor you or pay the price," Odin said.

I winced. I really just wanted to get the intel and go, but unfortunately, Stan the Man had officially flipped the God Pack's crazy switch.

"Please..." Stan the Man squeezed out. "Please...I'll take the...money..."

"Fuck that," Odin said. "We have a new offer now. You will tell us what we want to know, and I mean you will tell us everything, and in exchange we will not put you in the *fucking-g* hospital for insulting our goddess."

"But first you'll apologize," Thor said.

"No, you will *fucking-g* grovel, and then you will tell us everything, and after that, we might find it in our hearts to forget what you just said," Odin added.

"But we might not forget," Zeus put in, clearly in one of his irrational moods. "We probably won't."

"Umm..." Stan said.

"Now apologize. And make it good," Odin said.

"He doesn't have to," I said.

"*Au contraire*," Zeus said.

My pulse raced. "It's not an apology if a person is forced to make it. Let's get the info and leave."

"If we make him sorry enough, the apology will be real." Zeus changed his grip on Stan, maybe letting up, finally, because Stan began to make sense.

"I didn't mean it!" he choked out. "I know you are a perfect lady."

I snorted.

"That's not convincing," Thor informed him. "Ice is not convinced. Make it more convincing."

"How?" Stan complained.

"For starters, you can get on your hands and knees." Zeus

released his grip, and Stan crumpled to the floor.

Thor nudged him with his foot, partly being badass, though partly, I was thinking, making sure he didn't need medical attention. My guys were full-service outlaws.

"I'm so sorry for how I insulted you," Stan grumbled up at me.

"Fine," I said. "Let's get on with it."

"Why do you wish that he hadn't darkened your door?" Odin demanded, sitting back down. "Did he lose that much money? What kind of marker does he have out with you?"

"Nah, you have it all wrong," Stan grumbled, still cringing there on the floor.

"What do we have wrong?" Thor asked.

"The problem with Wilson was that he was winning too much. At first, I thought he was just lucky. But I think he was getting tips from his friends in the Don Pedro organization. I had him roughed up and thrown out."

"How did you know he was getting tips from the Don Pedro people?"

"He was winning big, but then he'd be all secretive and low-key about it. Think about it—who doesn't scream and shout when they've just won ten large? Twenty large? Who doesn't make a big deal out of that? I'll tell you who—a man who's using inside information and doesn't want people to know."

"Makes sense," Zeus said.

Warily, Stan started getting up. Odin clamped a hand on his shoulder and pushed him back down.

"I think Don Pedro had somebody fixing fights," Stan said. "People were never able to prove it because unlike Wilson, Don Pedro's people aren't so fucking obvious about everything. They don't go fix fights and then bet a shitload of money on those fights, you know? They play an incremental game, a sustainable game. But Wilson comes in here betting the farm on underdogs, winning big, and then acting all subdued? I wasn't born yesterday."

"He didn't want people to know," I said.

"The man was ripping off the mob—not money, but information. Definitely not something you want to publicize. I hope Wilson gets the shittiest WITSEC gig ever. Maybe see if there's any openings for a butthole spurge taste-tester."

My guys just glared at him, not in the mood for jokes.

"Seriously, it wasn't enough that the man was making bank on that fake appraisal gig with Don Pedro? He had to bilk a hard-working businessman like myself?"

"Did any of his people ever come in here?" Thor asked. "His wife, his brother, any of his friends?"

"Nah," Stan said. "Always alone."

"Did you ever get a sense for if he hid his winnings from his wife, his brother, any of his people?"

"Nah. He did sometimes make reference to a rainy day fund. And a rainy-day fund is usually a secret. But I really don't know."

"This is good information," Odin said.

"We're good?" Stan asked.

"Go on and get up," Zeus said.

Stan stood. His eyes slid again over my body. Zeus grabbed his cheeks and turned his face back toward him.

"Now we're not good again," Zeus barked.

"I'm sorry!" Stan said. "How am I supposed to control my reactions when she looks like that? A man can't control his actions when a woman looks like her!"

"Ugh! What the hell!" I groaned. He sounded like a sexual predator, talking like that.

"Yeah, what the hell!" Zeus was back in action, pinning Stan the Man to the wall. "Maybe I can't control my actions, either. When I hear you talking like that, how am I not ripping off your face right now? How can it be?"

"What?" Stan protested. "It's just nature."

"Does Isis's hotness have a *fucking-g* remote control on you?" Odin asked.

Zeus sputtered angrily and lifted him higher.

"Okay, okay," Stan the Man whined.

"Answer the question. How is Zeus currently controlling his reactions when your words are making him want to rip off your face?"

Stan the Man looked worried. "Motor control?"

"Very good. Zeus is a human being with a brain and motor control, and that's why you're alive right now, just like you have motor control. You're gonna remember that the next time you see a hot woman. And now you're going to use your motor control of your mouth to apologize to Ice."

"Sorry," he grunted out.

"Apologize better!" Odin bit out. "Or you'll be taste-testing the butthole spurge!"

"I don't want him to apologize again," I said. "His apologies are bad. Let's just go."

Zeus let him down. "Ice will now receive a parting gift." He spun around and led the way out.

We all followed.

Chapter Sixteen

"I DON'T WANT A GIFT," I SAID, CATCHING UP TO ZEUS

Chapter Seventeen

. "I just want to be out of here."

Zeus kept walking. He went to where the pool tables were and pointed to the wall of paintings of dogs playing pool. "Which is the best one?"

"Zeus, we can't..." I said.

"People need to learn to respect you. Now, tell me which is the best one?" he commanded.

"Do it, tell us!" Thor cajoled, always interested in a hint of mayhem.

Of course, I knew the best one; it was the bulldog-and-collie one. The bulldog was getting ready to take a shot as a bunch of collies wearing matching green visors looked on, with a German shepherd hoisting a mug of beer.

"I can tell you like this one." Zeus yanked it off the wall. Maybe it was something about his sense of command, I don't know, but everybody was watching him, and nobody said anything or tried to stop him. He headed out the door into the cool night, out to the parking lot, carrying the giant painting.

"Uber's coming in five minutes," Odin said, arms crossed.

"What are we going to do with that?" I asked.

"Don't you like it?" Zeus asked.

"Of course I like it, but we can't take something like that with us. Especially if we go on a plane somewhere, which we probably will soon."

"We'll figure it out," Thor said. "Stan owes you, talking to you like that. We'll enjoy it as long as we have it, even if it's just for a night."

"Thank you," I said, admiring the glowy brushstrokes in the early evening light as we waited for the Uber. It *was* amazing.

"Question," Zeus said. "Think this through with me."

"What is butthole spurge?" I asked.

Thor snickered.

I waited. I actually did want somebody to explain it!

"Focus, people," Zeus said. "Number one, we know that Wilson was getting inside information from the mob somehow and using it to win his bets. Number two, it seemed like his brother was dropping a lot of hints about gambling, like maybe Harold *wanted* to turn our attention this way."

"It did seem like that, didn't it?" Odin said.

"I agree," I said. "Harold *wanted* us looking this way."

"So here's the question, then," Zeus continued. "If Harold knew about Wilson's gambling, did he think Wilson was losing like the rest of the world thought? Or did he know that Wilson was quietly winning? In other words, did Harold think his brother was broke, or did he think his brother was rich with a stash of money?"

"And furthermore," Thor said, "what kind of parent names their kids Wilson and Harold?"

"My head hurts," I said.

"Guys," Zeus said. "This is important. Does Harold have motive to steal Doris and free his brother or not? That is the question."

Our Uber came right then, and we all got in, crowding in the back with the paint-on-velvet picture.

Zeus turned on his phone to a text from Agent Alfred. "Alfred wants to meet at the parking lot again. *Now*. He says we can ask Wilson some questions."

"That would be helpful," I said.

"No doubt," Thor said. "But if he thinks we'll meet at that parking lot again, he's a fool."

"Right?" Odin said. "Does Agent Alfred think we've gotten lobotomies since we saw him last?"

I supposed it *was* suspicious for Alfred to call a surprise meeting, enticing us there with the thing we'd wanted, which he'd previously refused to give us.

We stopped for dinner and my guys put their heads together and studied some satellite images trying to find a better place to meet. We called another Uber to drop us off at a bustling outdoor brewpub called Calamity Joe's.

The place was stuffed to the gills with a crowd of people busy drinking and yelling under colorful lights strung overhead.

"Are there enough escape routes at this place?" I asked, looking around.

"Technically, there are three," Thor said. "But in a crowd like this, there are really unlimited escape routes." Odin texted Alfred to let him know we were willing to meet now, but at Calamity Joe's. Alfred agreed to be there in an hour, at nine, just enough time for us to install Thor in a perch from where he could monitor the busy street and valet parking situation and hide Zeus among the patrons at the bar.

Needless to say, they couldn't be carrying my dog picture around, so Odin and I lugged it to a table for four. We set it on one of the chairs and took our seats across from it to wait for Agent Alfred.

I ordered another wine spritzer. Odin ordered a scotch.

"Dogs playing pool," he said.

"I know you probably think it's stupid. It reminds me of home, though," I said. "There was a bar that my high school friends and I did a lot of underage drinking at that had these kinds of pictures. And then Vanessa and I found some at a garage sale and put them in our rec room. I always just really liked them. I don't know why."

Odin grinned at me. "I wouldn't expect anything less from a woman who loves cartoon porn," he said.

I narrowed my eyes. "Are you making fun of me?"

"Most people, when you ask their favorite painting, they'll say the Mona Lisa or some such shit. That's not you."

"So you *are* making fun of me," I said.

"No, goddess, the opposite. Loving the dog art—it's the best. You march to your own drummer and make decisions from your heart. You go for dogs playing pool. You took up with a band of outlaws. You're more badass than the Gigis will ever be."

I grinned. Odin was famously down on the Gigis. He was jokey about it, but not all the time.

"Sometimes I have this feeling as if you found us in the wilderness," he continued. "Do you know what it's like to be found by you? To be chosen by you? It's everything, goddess."

"You're gonna give me a swelled head," I said. "It's everything for me, too." I set my hand on his arm. "Can I ask you something?"

"I'm not discussing butthole spurge with you," he said.

"Couldn't you just try Thor's blanket?"

"It won't do anything."

"How do you know if you don't try it?" I said.

Odin gave me a dark look. "You don't see what's going on here, do you?"

"What?" I said.

"The blanket's not about me."

"What are you talking about? Of course it's about you. He had it made for you specifically. To be able to sleep with us. All four together."

"No, right, in that way it's a little bit about me, but it's mostly about Thor," Odin said.

"What do you mean?"

"It's about him shooting that man, killing that man, Isis. He's not over it. He thinks fixing other people will undo what happened, but he's wrong. I think that's why he becomes so reckless and unpredictable when he's not doctoring."

"Wait. I always thought it was just that...like he hated when he couldn't be a doctor because that's his passion," I said. "He's bereft when he can't help others."

"Well, sure, on the surface, that's true," Odin said. "But what other dedicated and driven doctor turns into Mad Max the second they go on vacation or retire? Have you ever heard of such a thing?"

"I guess not."

"Of course not. It's not a doctor thing, it's a Thor thing. It's too much for him to sit still," Odin said. "He needs to keep healing or being otherwise distracted. Making up for something he can never fix. Trying to erase the guilt. But he never can."

"But it was kill or be killed!" I said, feeling upset on Thor's behalf. "Thor saved both of your lives, not to mention his own. It was self-defense and defense of you two! Why should he feel guilty?"

"You're preaching to the choir, sister," Odin said. "He had no choice, but deep down inside him, it doesn't matter. You cannot reason with those deep-down parts of a man. Thor took a life, and it sits with him hard. If he stops moving, stops healing, he's forced to remember. Forced to come face-to-face with the reality that he took a life. So now he turns to me to meet that need. Like healing me would heal him. I won't be used by him. I won't be that for him." He swirled the ice in his drink. "I can't be that for him."

This stunned me, but it had the ring of truth. Thor's reckless wild-card phases—they never truly did make sense.

"You think there's anything we can do?" I asked.

"I don't know," Odin said. "He needs to stop running from it. For starters."

I wanted to talk more about it, but Alfred was making his way through the crowd toward us, looking extra squat and bulky in a plaid sports jacket. He took the empty seat. "What's this for?" he asked, nodding at the dogs on velvet.

"None of your business," Odin said. "Let's talk about Wilson. We're eager to meet with him."

"First things first," Alfred said. "I need some indication that you've ruled out Don Pedro. I'm not just going to have you talking to Wilson for no reason."

"You need to stop telling us how to do our jobs and give us access to all the clues that exist. That includes meeting with Wilson. Tomorrow, if possible," Odin said.

"I said you could ask him questions, not meet with him," Alfred said.

"We want to see him. You know it's more effective to question a person when you can actually see that person," Odin said.

"I can't let you meet with him. You'll give me your questions, and I will relay them to Wilson."

"What? We can't even Zoom? At the very least we'd want to Zoom," Odin said.

"This is the best we can do," Alfred said.

"Why are we having this conversation, then?" Odin asked.

"Yeah, this could've happened via text," I said.

Alfred was looking at the dogs-playing-pool painting again. "Why are you carrying that thing around?"

"None of your business," I said.

Alfred frowned. "You carrying it around in relation to the case?"

I shrugged. "That's proprietary."

He frowned even harder. "There's a German shepherd in the picture."

"Our methods are our methods," Odin said. "We want to see Wilson."

Alfred kept staring at the picture. What was he thinking?

"You want us to solve this?" Odin asked.

"Look, even I don't get to talk directly to Wilson," Alfred said. "This is one of the most sensitive cases my office has conducted in a long time. We're talking in person because of that sensitivity."

I sighed. Evasion much?

Odin drained his scotch, set down the glass, and stood. "We're outta here," he announced. I slammed my wine spritzer and grabbed the picture.

"I don't see why you need to talk directly to Wilson," Alfred said.

"You need to stop questioning our methods and stop wasting our *fucking-g* time." He headed out toward the back exit. I followed close behind him.

"Wait!" The idea hit me as soon as we were out on the sidewalk.

"What?" Odin asked, pulling out his phone.

"Does Alfred think we're showing this painting to people to help them know what a German shepherd looks like? It would be so hilarious if he thought that."

Odin frowned. "I can't imagine it."

"He asked if it was related to the investigation!" I was just laughing now. "Sir, have you seen a dog that looks like the German shepherd in this painting? You have to picture her not hoisting a beer mug, and not wearing a visor."

Odin called an Uber while I texted Thor and Zeus that we were done with the meeting. "No way."

"He asked," I said.

We took an Uber to a midway point, and then slipped through a crowd, careful not to be followed, and caught another Uber, heading back to our Airbnb.

Chapter Eighteen

We walked in to find Thor and Zeus at the kitchen counter, tearing through bags of chips like a pair of locusts.

"Get anything?" Zeus asked.

"Yeah, we got that Alfred likes to waste our time, find out what we know, and get a tail back on us," Odin said, grabbing the sour cream Ruffles from Zeus. "Fucking-g bullshit."

I set the picture against the wall. "But on the upside, there's a chance that he thinks the dogs-playing-pool picture is part of our quest to find Doris," I said.

"Are you shitting me?" Zeus Looked from me to Odin and back to me.

Odin shrugged.

I grinned.

"This fucking case," Zeus continued. "All I can say is that exculpatory tackle bag had better exist."

We all sat there munching on chips, dreaming of a tackle bag containing proof that would clear Zeus, Odin, and Thor of that atrocity they were framed for...and hopefully we'd be pardoned for the crimes we'd done since then, being that we had so little choice.

The idea of living free, of not being pursued, of never having to look over our shoulders, of having a place to call home—it felt like a dangerous thing to hope for.

Our next stop was the home of Wilson's musician friend, Ferdinand. My guys wanted to get a sense of him. What did he think of Harold? Was there anyone else who could've taken Doris? Maybe Ferdinand himself?

Ferdinand lived in a 1970s apartment building on a sleepy dead-end street across from a large homeless encampment.

Zeus stabbed the button on the decrepit intercom, and I was shocked when it actually worked. Zeus spoke into the speaker area and introduced us in the very official way that he had that made us sound official without actually saying we were official.

The door was buzzed open, and we climbed some rickety stairs to the top floor.

Ferdinand was tall and wiry with unusually large hands and gray hair cut in a bangs-and-bowl style that looked very last century if not downright 75 BC.

"It takes four of you to do follow-up questions?" Ferdinand said.

"You should see how many of us it takes to screw in a light bulb," Zeus joked as we filed into what was basically a giant studio. There was a little eating nook on one side of the big open expanse and a music-playing area on the other side with a collection of instruments, a music stand, and what looked like recording equipment.

He offered us a couple of stools from the music area, but Zeus stayed standing.

"How long have you been playing music with Wilson?" Thor asked, even though we already had that information from Alfred.

"We've been jamming together since high school," Ferdinand

said. "An electronica string quartet type of deal. Wilson went off to conservatory after that, but we played summers when he came back. We played a lot of weddings."

"Weddings?" I asked.

"Yeah, I played the oboe, and he would do cello and we'd pull in a flute now and then. Classical standards. We've been in a lot of different groups. Sometimes it just depends on who's available."

"You're an industrial designer?" Zeus asked, more intel courtesy of Agent Alfred. There was no end of the useless information Alfred was willing to give us.

"Yes, freelance," Ferdinand said. "Mostly kitchen products. Pays a bit better than music."

"When did you first hear that Wilson was involved in this appraisal racket?" Odin asked.

"A mutual friend called and told me when it came out," he said. "It ripped through the gigging community grapevine like wildfire. It's not a large community."

"Were you surprised?" Odin asked.

"I was shocked," Ferdinand said. "Wilson liked nice things. I knew that about him. He liked to travel in style. He always used to say, 'it doesn't take much more to go first class.' So I guess in hindsight, with the sort of money he threw around, maybe I should have put it together, but I assumed the store was doing great. Being mixed up with the mob and all that..." Ferdinand shook his head with a baffled look.

"He's in witness protection now, as you probably know," Zeus said. "Likely never to be seen again. How do people feel about that?"

"People are mostly bummed," Ferdinand said. "Wilson was a good citizen in the gigging scene—lots of talent, always up for playing—but people are mad, too. I mean, this whole scam he was running—the whole stain of criminality on the world of fine instruments, it's just sad."

"What about his wife?" I asked. "You think she's sad?"

"I didn't feel like they were close. She never came to hear us play. She wasn't interested in his music. When he went on his nice buying trips, he would never bring her along. He brought other people—even me, once. He said it wouldn't be fun if she came along. There were other shopkeepers that he'd go with."

"He was friendly with other shopkeepers?" Odin asked, sounding interested. "Any in particular?"

"There were a few he'd mention that he'd travel with."

"Is it possible to get the names of shopkeepers he traveled with? Especially more recently?"

"I could look through my texts. He always texted pictures from his trips."

"Could you look?" Odin asked. "That would be helpful."

Ferdinand pulled out his phone and started scrolling. "This could take a while—we text a lot around the quartet."

"Let me put my number into your phone," Odin said holding out his hand. "Then you can round up the names and just text me or call me."

You could tell that Ferdinand didn't want to hand over his phone, but he did, and Odin used it to place a call to himself and then he handed it back. "If you could get it to us ASAP, we'd be really grateful."

"Did he ever go overseas with his brother?" Thor asked.

"No way," Ferdinand said.

"Why no way?"

"They weren't close. Harold was five or six years older than us." Ferdinand looked up from his phone. "So when we were hanging out in high school, Harold was already at conservatory. I mostly saw him at social gatherings and now and then he'd sit in our main quartet—if we were desperate. You have to be desperate to invite Harold to play."

I felt my guys perk up. "Why was that?" Thor asked. "Not as good a player?"

"He could play the music, but he's a jerk and a spotlight hog.

A quartet is musical voices weaving together, but when Harold would sit in, he wanted to be the star. Massively obnoxious."

What? Harold was the spotlight hog? Harold had said that exact same thing about Wilson. This whole thing was getting weird.

"A spotlight hog," Odin said.

"Completely," Ferdinand said. "Nobody liked playing with Harold, including Wilson. The man's a blowhard, but Wilson was kind to Harold, even when Harold was being a jerk during a gig or acting like an asshole at Wilson's shop."

"So Harold would stop by Wilson's shop and be an asshole?" Odin asked casually.

"Now and then. There was this one time—it was a couple of months ago, and we were going to be playing a cocktail party at the Getty, and Harold came by 'cause we were all going to ride out there together. And Harold is poking around, and he goes behind the counter, which really isn't okay, and started getting in Wilson's face about a Stradivarius he'd appraised. I stayed out of it. I was just sitting there noodling, but Harold was definitely calling the instrument a piece of shit, making jokes about it, and I didn't feel like it was the first time it had happened. I didn't think anything of it at the time—I figured Harold was being an asshole—but I definitely remembered it when I heard about Wilson's arrest."

This was interesting! Harold had definitely pretended that he didn't know about Wilson's fake appraisals! I tried to have a poker face, though.

"So do you think that Harold knew what Wilson was up to with the appraisals?" Zeus asked. "Do you think he suspected?"

"He had to suspect, judging from his reaction to seeing that violin with such a high price tag," Ferdinand said.

"So their relationship was strained?" Zeus asked.

"They weren't really close. On paper, they had a lot in common. Similar stores, both violinists, they both gravitated toward the early Romantics. But they were seriously different people. It's not like they did holidays together. Harold had his kids and their families. Wilson and Clarice tended to do friend holidays."

We headed out.

"That was weird," I said as soon as we were out the main door. "Which brother is the blowhard? Experts cannot agree!"

Zeus put out a hand, stopping us. Across the street was a car that hadn't been there before. Empty from the looks of it.

Odin swore under his breath.

"Ice, if you see me press my palms together, I want you to look excited. You know when you brighten up, like you have a secret that you're having trouble keeping?"

"What are you talking about?" I demanded.

"Or like, when we're playing poker and you have all aces, but you don't want anybody to know. Make a face like that," Zeus added.

"Wait, what?" I protested. "Should I be insulted right now?"

"No, it's cute," Odin said. "You're the most transparent person when you are excited about a secret."

"Oh my god!" I complained, following them over.

It turned out the car wasn't empty. Alfred stepped out of it.

Zeus leaned against it. "Checking up on us?" Zeus asked. Thor and Odin and I came up beside him.

"This is an important investigation that I'm in charge of. I'll do what I want. How'd it go in there?"

"Do you know what I think?" Zeus said. "I think you want to find that dog first."

"My interest is in the results," Agent Alfred said.

"Same as us," Zeus said.

"I think your interest is in cashing Denko's checks." Alfred squinted at Ferdinand's building. "Seriously? The musician friend? You do know that you only have a few days, right?"

"All you need to know is that we're making headway. We're gonna find that dog." Zeus sounded incredibly confident.

I kept my face blank, waiting to see whether Zeus was going to give the signal. Meanwhile, I was definitely thinking that it was a good sign that Alfred thought we were working for money instead of the elusive exculpatory tackle bag o' evidence. I don't know why; maybe it showed that the tackle bag might really be real. Something Denko needed to keep a secret.

"So what happened in there?" Alfred asked.

Here, Zeus pressed his palms together. I knew what he was doing. I imagined that I had an amazing secret, and I made the face.

"What happened is us working the angles," Zeus said.

"But Ferdinand?" Alfred asked, looking at each of us. It's here he noticed the face.

"Just our process," Zeus said. "We like to be thorough, even when there is a ticking clock. That's all you need to know." With that, he turned and walked off toward out Uber. I followed him, as did Thor and Odin.

"Very good," Odin mumbled under his breath. "Definitely worth letting you know about that tell of yours."

"Omigod. I sense a new era coming in the era of me not losing at poker with you guys anymore."

"Goddess," Thor said. "You have many tells."

"So were you trying to misdirect Agent Alfred? To make him think Ferdinand is involved?"

"I want him off our ass," Zeus said.

"So interesting," Thor said, watching Alfred drive off. "Harold lied about being shocked about his brother's scam. Harold saw a wrongly appraised violin. He knew what his brother was doing. And he lied."

"Why would Harold lie about knowing about the scam?" I asked. "Could Harold have taken Doris? Could the ledger implicate him in some way? Is that what's going on here?"

Zeus paused at the front of the Uber. "We need more information on Harold. We need to pay another visit to him. It's business hours. He should be in his shop."

"Or maybe we make sure he's in his shop and then we pay a visit to his home," Odin said. "We might get more from his home than from him."

"Possibly even a dog," I said hopefully. "What if we actually found Doris? What if Denko is good for his word? Can you imagine?"

Thor looked at me sadly.

"What?" I protested. "Things could work out finally!"

"We need our own car," Odin said. "What IDs do you guys have?"

I rolled my eyes. Maybe my guys didn't dare hope for a regular life of peace and love, but I had enough for all of us.

The guys compared IDs that they were carrying around and it was decided that Thor would rent us a car, just to mix things up a little.

Chapter Nineteen

Two hours later, after a quick confirmation that Harold was still stuck in his shop, we were slipping in through the sliding doors in the back of Harold's first-floor condo in Mar Vista.

The place was dark, gloomy, and even a bit musty.

"Does he never open his windows, ever?" I asked as we fanned out for a quick search.

"It does smell stale, doesn't it?" Thor said, opening a living room cabinet. "Don't think we're gonna find Doris in here."

Magazines about Los Angeles had been arranged in a careful fan on the coffee table. "Who keeps magazines about their city on their coffee table?" I asked.

"Maybe some people like decorating like that," Odin said.

"Like who?" I looked around the kitchen. There were no dishes in the sink—not even a coffee cup. The garbage was empty, too. "Too clean," I said.

"Some people are clean freaks," Thor said.

Odin settled into the couch with a laptop. "This laptop hasn't been used for months. However, that could just mean that he has a newer one that he uses more often."

"Or maybe he doesn't even live here." I headed over to the refrigerator and flung it open. The shelves were empty. The door was mostly empty, too, aside from some condiments. "Correction: he for sure doesn't live here."

Thor came over and stood next to me, peering in. "You might be onto something."

"Might?" I snorted. "No 'might' about it. I knew from the coffee table magazines, but this proves it."

Zeus wandered in. "Nothing interesting in the bedroom."

"Sometimes nothing interesting is something interesting." I stepped aside so he could see into the refrigerator. "Harold doesn't live here."

He nodded slowly. "Interesting."

I tried to act nonchalant, but I was thrilled to have been the one to catch on to that first.

"So where *does* he live?" Zeus asked. "And is that where Doris is living?" He checked his watch. "See if he left the shop. If not, we could double back and follow him."

Odin got on the phone to call Harold's shop. He asked whoever it was on the other end if they could give him a quote for repairing his violin. After a brief conversation, he hung up. "Harold's not at his store. He went home for the day."

"Damn," Zeus said. "I really want to search his place—his real place."

Odin sunk into the couch. "Is it possible he was in on the instrument appraisal scam?"

"But he wasn't in on it from the start," I reminded him. "Ferdinand said that when Harold found a wrongly appraised instrument at Wilson's shop, he got in Wilson's face."

"Did he make Wilson cut him in?" Odin asked. "And now is he worried about being exposed? That would be a motive for him to dognap Doris."

"Sure would," Zeus said.

"Don't forget, he wanted to direct our mind to the gambling," Thor said. "Maybe to throw us off the scent."

"Wait," I said, mind reeling. "I just realized something that's super weird!"

My guys all turned to me. I smiled and held up my pointer finger. "Remember how Clarice seemed to have packed up all of Wilson's stuff? And she had a stack of pictures in the corner, and she gestured to them when she talked about Wilson, as if to suggest that those pictures belonged to him?"

"Yeah, I definitely got that sense," Odin said. "And those bags of men's clothes on the stairway. His stuff was outta there."

"Exactly. She was totes through with him and cleaning out his stuff. But what picture did she keep on the wall? Did you notice anything in her house that she left up that was very distinctly his?"

"The UFC picture in the foyer," Thor said.

I nodded. "Right. No way was that hers."

"She left up that one picture in a place of prominence," Thor said. "Like she wanted us to see it."

"And you asked about it," Odin said. "Would she have said something about it if we hadn't asked? I'm thinking yeah. She wanted to talk about it."

"Right?" I said. "Seriously, if you're dumping a guy and erasing him from the home, the first thing that goes is the biggest and most prominent picture of a sport he loves that you don't care about."

"Nice work," Odin said. "She leaves that one picture. She was quick to supply all of those details about his obsession with the UFC. And she's the one who mentioned gambling first. She was like, 'does he have a girlfriend? A gambling addiction?'"

I smiled at Odin. Things were getting interesting.

"Question," I said, because I was on a roll! "Why would both Harold and Clarice be so interested in making sure we know Wilson's a big gambler?"

Odin beamed at me. "I say we ask Clarice." Everybody agreed.

We headed to Wilson's shop, thinking to surprise Clarice. Zeus parked across the street. You could see her inside, standing behind the counter with an employee.

"Who's going in?" Thor asked.

"Hold up. Got an idea." Odin pulled out his phone and called Clarice on her cell. After a bit of chat where she was obviously asking about the case—always something a guilty party does—he asked whether we could come into the shop and ask a few more questions.

"I can't," she said. "I'm in my car on my way to the dentist." She agreed to speak tomorrow at the shop, and they hung up.

"Super-spy sleuth skills, activate!" I teased Odin.

Moments later, she hurried out the door and got into her car.

We pulled out and followed her at a discreet distance. She got onto the expressway, heading west and then down the coast.

"Quite a ways to go for a dentist," Odin said after we'd been driving for what seemed like forever. Finally she pulled into the driveway of a beautiful, well-kept Craftsman in an extra-swanky part of Manhattan Beach. It had grand french windows and a perfectly manicured lawn.

We pulled to the side of the road just down from the house, keeping it in view.

"Visiting a friend?" Zeus speculated. "Who could it be?"

We watched her take keys from her jacket and unlock the door. "A very good friend," Thor said.

"Man friend, maybe," I mused. "And this is their love nest?"

"Is anybody else thinking we might find Harold and Doris inside here?" Zeus asked.

"Excuse me?" I perked up right there. "What?"

"Just a hunch," he said.

"That would be amazing," I said.

Zeus was on his phone. "This place is a rental. It's managed by a rental company." Zeus tucked his phone away. "Odin. You and me."

Zeus and Odin slipped out of the car. I watched them disappear up the side of the house, using bushes as cover.

"What if this is it?" Thor asked. "What if the dog is in there? Can you imagine?"

"That would be amazing," I said, leaning back and smiling over at him. "We get the dog. We make the trade for the tackle bag. Clear your names. Get pardoned. Being on the run ends."

"It has to be the end," he said. He sounded almost desperate.

"Well, if it's not the end, we'll figure it out," I said. "Like we always do."

"We're not figuring it out, though, that's the problem," Thor said. "Nothing's changing. Nothing's letting up. We can't go on like this forever—you know that, right?"

I couldn't help but think about what Odin had said. That Thor was desperate for the distraction of doctoring. That he'd never gotten over killing that man way back when. "We're a family. We're always home when we're together."

"It's not right that we live like this," he said.

"I love our life," I said. "We're here for each other. To have a family who is behind you no matter what—not everybody has that." I don't know, I was hoping maybe he'd open up.

He shook his head.

"We help each other—that's what we're about. You especially."

He sniffed in a way that suggested I was being full of shit or something.

"Don't even," I said. "You're a healer. It's your whole thing."

"I guess."

"When did you know that was your thing?" I asked him.

He sighed, faraway gaze out the windshield. "As long as I can remember, I guess."

"That long?" I prompted.

He simply nodded.

"My first memory is feeling shy in a sandbox," I said, hoping that would encourage him to share. I know he grew up rough, but he rarely talked about it. Medical school, yes, but not his boyhood.

"My first memory is saving a spider," he said. "Or more like, crying and utterly freaking out when I realized my mom was about to kill it. She had to take it outside in a Tupperware to get me to stop crying."

"Oh my god," I whispered, grinning.

He snorted softly. "Right?" He was still staring out at the neat row of homes up the street, palm trees shooting up randomly here and there. "Drove my mom crazy. I wouldn't let her kill anything. God, I'd put up such a fuss. And where we were living, we had doors open all of the time."

I smiled, imagining him as a little blond cherub ruling the household with his tiny little iron fist.

"Later it was me rescuing them. I'd rescue everything I could. One year my neighbor's dog got sick, and their family didn't have the money for a vet. It was the middle of nowhere, and people barely had money for food. I wouldn't let them kill her—I took the dog and googled the shit out of her symptoms. I got her back. It was allergies. After that, people were bringing me pets. I would google things. I'd do splints from YouTube videos."

"Wow!" I'd known he'd always wanted to be a doctor, but not this. "That's amazing."

"It wasn't ideal. Those animals deserved better, but I was all they had." He paused, slid a finger over the steering wheel. "People thought I had this gift, but if you observe any animal really closely, you learn things. You don't need to ask them questions. I mean, it would be handy, but..."

I brushed a lock of hair behind his ear. "Yeah."

"People are easier in that you can talk to them," he continued. "Though they're so much more complicated. But to heal a person. To make a person's life worth living. Or save their life. There's nothing like it, Ice. Nothing."

He went silent, and I worried he was thinking about the man he killed. Of course, he was thinking about that!

"You have saved so many lives," I said, kicking myself for pulling him down this path.

No response.

Maybe Odin was right—that Thor was still haunted by the life he took. Really, how could he not be? I wanted to say more, but there was movement around the corner of the house—Zeus and Odin coming out from the side.

"Not at their stealthiest," I said, trying for a joke. Zeus waved us over to the front door. "Really, really, *really* not stealthy."

"Let's see what's up," Thor sighed, getting out.

We joined Zeus and Odin at the front door.

"Change of plans?" Thor asked.

"Roger that," Zeus said, knocking loudly.

"Time to have a talk," Odin said.

Zeus knocked again.

"She's in there?" I asked.

"Yup," Zeus said.

"And Doris?" I asked.

"We're gonna find out." Zeus pounded on the door this time. No sound from inside the home.

Odin pulled out his little lock-picking tool.

"Erp!" I said.

"What? It's rude to not open the door," Odin said, breaking through the lock with ease and pushing the door open to a lavish living room, tastefully appointed with the latest home fashions, including a plush and curvy white couch upon which Clarice and Harold and Harold's bushy brows were huddled.

After a long beat of them adjusting to the outrageous new reality of us in their place, Harold stood up. "What are you doing? You can't just come in here!"

"I'm going to call the police," Clarice said.

"Are you, though?" Thor said as Odin kicked the door shut behind us and, more significantly, three guns came out.

"We don't care what you've been doing," Zeus said. "We're here for the dog. You give us the dog, and nothing has to happen."

Harold and Clarice looked confused. "What are you talking about?" Harold asked.

Maybe they were good actors, but their confusion seemed genuine.

Odin stalked over and grabbed their phones from the coffee table in front of them. "Do I get your passwords the easy way or the hard way?"

Thor frowned. Zeus tipped his head at us. "You two. Search the place."

Thor and I went to work, heading first down the stairs into the basement. No dog visible.

"You think they seemed surprised?" Thor asked, opening a closet that turned out to be full of old windows.

"They seemed surprised to me," I said. "But hey, everybody's an actor out here, huh?"

We came to a padlocked storage room. Thor backed up and kicked it open with a big manly bang. Just a bunch of old furniture. Thor turned around, eyeing me. He knew I loved when he acted badass.

"Mm-hmm, Thor!" I said.

He came to me and smoothed a hand over my hair. "Is something wrong?"

"I'm sad that you're feeling so bad," I whispered, inches from his lips.

"I'll be fine." Thor turned away, continuing our search. We headed back up the stairs, up to the upper level, checking every room.

Thor kicked open another locked door. A bedroom door.

"You are definitely running a surplus in the hotness bank account," I said, trying to lighten his mood.

"Don't you worry, I'll be cashing in," he said.

We got back to the living room to find Odin and Zeus looking bored. They didn't even have their guns out anymore.

"It's not them," Odin said, sounding pissed off.

"What were you doing up there?" Harold demanded.

"It's not them?" Thor asked Odin, ignoring Harold.

"They've been blackmailing Wilson," Odin said. "They know where the money is. Getting Wilson sprung is the last thing they want. They want to keep the money and never see Wilson again."

I sighed.

"You can't come in here and detain us and go around wrecking things," Harold said. "You've broken at least five laws, just in the space of these last fifteen minutes."

"We could break some more," Zeus said. "Right now. Whaddya think? Should we go for it? Get creative?"

"We can get pretty *fucking-g* creative," Odin said.

"You're gonna be sorry," Harold said.

"And we *will* be calling the police," Clarice warned, though I highly doubted it, since Clarice and Harold were being shady in their own way.

"Oh, you do that," I said, trying to sound like a badass. "We laugh in the face of the police."

Odin grinned at me. He liked when I talked tough—almost as much as I did.

I put my hands on my hips. "We'll enjoy laughing in their faces," I added.

❧

We stopped for lunch at an outdoor place near Venice Beach. The clock was ticking down, and we still didn't have any good leads. Nobody seemed to want to spring Wilson badly enough to kidnap a dog. Nobody seemed to want to spring Wilson at all.

So who had Doris?

"What the hell?" Odin said, swiping and tapping furiously at the screen of his phone. "I can't get this text to Ferdinand to deliver. Ice, I'm texting you. See if you get it."

My phone dinged with a text from Odin. "Got it."

"So it's not my phone," Odin said.

"You're texting Ferdinand?" I asked.

"I'm trying to follow up with him. Remember the list he was supposed to pull together of the people Wilson traveled to Italy with? Maybe there's a lead on that list."

Zeus tried texting Ferdinand on his phone, and eventually they gave up and just called the guy.

"No longer in service," Zeus said.

We all perked up.

In my mind, I thought *dum-da-dum,* but I didn't say it out loud. I just stuffed the last of my fries in my mouth because we were going to be leaving this restaurant very soon. Zeus threw a few big bills onto the table and signaled the waiter.

Minutes later we were on the road, palm trees and pastel buildings flying by.

"Ferdinand," Thor said. "What are you up to?"

"Maybe his phone is broken," I said.

"No, it's out of service," Odin said. "He gave up the number, or it was disconnected by the carrier. It's what you do when you go on the run."

"It's what a newbie does when he goes on the run," Zeus said. "Freaking overkill. All he'd have to do is turn his phone off."

"Damn," I said.

"How could we have been so wrong?" Odin seemed mystified. "Does Ferdinand want Wilson out of witness protection after all? Could Ferdinand have the dog?"

"Or does he know where she is?" I added.

"I was so sure he had nothing to do with anything," Odin said. "Is Ferdinand more of an operator than I'd guessed?"

We drove on in silence, all trying to make sense out of the idea of Ferdinand fooling us so thoroughly.

"It seemed like such a good idea to put Alfred onto Ferdinand, to distract him that way," Zeus said. "Did Alfred question him and spook him?"

"I still don't understand how it could be Ferdinand," Odin said.

We didn't bother buzzing this time; we went right in and up the stairs. Nobody answered when we knocked, so Odin let us in.

Ferdinand's apartment was messy, but it was more someone-packed-in-a-hurry messy than ransacked messy—kitchen cupboards stood open. Coats were draped on the couch back. Bedroom drawers were open. Zeus decided that Odin would go through the place for clues about where Doris might be or where Ferdinand might have gone while he and Thor and I went to question the neighbors about a dog.

"Yeah, I heard a dog in there," said the woman who lived next door to Ferdinand. "Barking its head off."

"How long?" I asked.

She figured it had been there for around a week or so. Which exactly fit the time frame of Doris's kidnapping.

"Did you ever see the dog?" I asked.

"Nah," she said. "Someone said it was a German shepherd."

"Ferdinand took off," Thor said. "We really want to talk to him. Did he say anything about where he's going?"

"No idea," she said. "We didn't really talk much aside from when we had a problem neighbor a year back."

We went across the hall and knocked. A guy in a track suit opened up. "We're looking for Ferdinand across the hall," Thor said. "You know where he is?"

"Nope," the guy said. "I didn't see much of him. Got a new dog, I can tell you that. Thing was barking its head off."

We asked at one more door and got exactly the same story.

Zeus was standing outside of Ferdinand's door when we

finished with the last neighbor on our side. "Anything?" I asked Zeus.

Zeus shook his head. "I spoke to five people. They all heard a dog barking, but nothing about where he went. The timeline lines up."

"Chatty group," I said. "I was shocked that they all opened their doors. I guess they all really wanted to talk about the barking dog."

"That *was* weird," Thor said. "Who answers a random knock on the door these days?"

"Right?" I said.

Back at Ferdinand's, Odin hadn't turned up anything. We filled him in on what the neighbors said.

Odin seemed to ponder it for a long time. "He had a dog here for over a week, so where is the dog hair? I suppose it's possible he kept her in a kennel in the bedroom, and she was quiet when we were here. Or is he working with someone?"

There was a kid on the stoop when we got out. He was on his phone, tapping away. "You the ones asking about the music guy and his dog?" he asked, not looking up.

"Yeah, you know him? You see them leave?"

The kid put his phone in his lap and gave us a long look. "I might have something interesting to say. For two hundred bucks."

"You got something interesting to say for two hundred bucks?" Thor asked. "How do we know it's interesting?" He was talking tough, but I could tell he liked the kid.

"I just know. And I know that's the going price."

"What do you mean, the going price?" Thor asked.

The kid smiled and put out his hand.

Odin snorted and slapped four fifties into the kid's hand. "Give us something good and we'll give you more."

"There was no dog," the boy said. "There never was a dog in there."

"You didn't hear a dog?" Thor asked.

"No, I'm saying there was never a dog in there. My dad and I live across the hall from the guy. We never heard a peep."

"Your dad wear a red track suit?" I asked.

"Yup," the kid said.

"So why did you dad hear the dog? All of your neighbors said they heard a dog barking," I said.

"That's because some guy gave us all a hundred bucks to say we heard a dog, and he said he'd come back later and give us another hundred if we convinced you. We're supposed to say it was barking its head off for over a week, and that's all we know."

Wow, I thought.

Odin peeled off what looked like a few hundreds and set them in the boy's hand. "Can you tell me what the guy looked like?"

"Kinda like a short version of The Rock, but with dark and gray hair. An old gym-rat type. Brown coat."

We all exchanged glances. Alfred.

"He say anything else?" Zeus asked.

"Yeah, he said you four would come around asking about the dog, and that you're bad news."

I grinned. "What made you decide to tell us?" I asked.

"My dad's an asshole and I don't want him to get the rest of the money."

Odin grinned. "Works for me." He gave the kid another hundred. "We never had this conversation."

"Works for me," the kid said.

We headed out.

"I believe the kid," Thor said.

We all believed the kid.

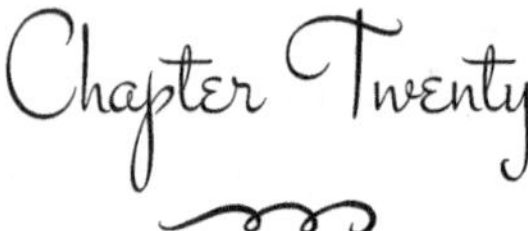

Chapter Twenty

THE SUN WAS JUST SETTING OVER THE PACIFIC AS I pushed the edge of a fork into a juicy grilled scallop. I took a bite, savoring its salty, buttery goodness. We were all falling over ourselves complimenting Thor on his cooking of scallops when Odin got the call back from his intelligence connections.

He took it out on the lawn, pacing up and down in front of the blazing sunset. Some ten minutes later, he came back and sat down, crossing his legs, looking like the cat who swallowed the canary.

I loved when he looked like that. "What?" I said. "What did you find out?"

"Our dear Agent Alfred has been passed over for several promotions," Odin said, gazing at me in that glittery way of his. "But here's the interesting part—the reason is Denko. Denko refuses to recommend him. Denko has been saying that Alfred's not ready to move up, that he needs to work on his skills."

"Denko's hurting Alfred's career," I said.

"So it seems," Odin said.

"Are you thinking that Alfred found out Denko is nixing his

promotions and decided to make him look bad? A little payback? Is that what is going on here?"

Zeus was nodding vigorously. "Makes sense. So Agent Alfred steals Doris, knowing Denko will do anything to get her back. He wants to force Denko to trade the ledger for Doris, and he'll make sure the authorities are on hand to arrest Denko when the trade happens."

"No wonder Alfred was so interested in our progress!" Thor said.

"Right?" I said. "So what about Ferdinand? Why try to frame Ferdinand?"

"I think he's pointing us at Ferdinand as a way of running out the clock," Zeus said. "He doesn't want Doris to be found, and he knows that we ruled out Don Pedro, so it's best if he gives us another suspect."

"I say we play along and take the bait," Zeus said.

We all liked that.

Zeus texted Alfred with a request for more information on Ferdinand—where Ferdinand liked to vacation, the names of Ferdinand's extended family, places Ferdinand had lived. Basically, we all but told Alfred outright that Ferdinand was now our main suspect.

"Okay," he said, putting down his phone.

"Thank you, Facebook," Odin said, putting down his own phone. "Alfred runs every morning at five. Tomorrow is his six-mile run. He's hoping to shave his time down to thirty-nine minutes. How very convenient."

"So we get in there and see what we can see. Doris may not be there, but there's got to be some clue as to where he stashed her. If not..." Zeus looked over at Odin.

"If not, then we'll find out the hard way," Odin said.

Odin could make Alfred talk. We'd bring Doris to Denko. The tackle bag was as good as ours!

"We are gonna find this dog," I said, hugging Zeus.

Zeus beamed at me. "Could be."

I looped my arms around Odin and Thor. "You guys!"

"It hasn't happened yet," Thor warned.

"What's the first thing you wanna do when our name is cleared?" I asked Zeus.

"Buy the house I grew up in. Fix it up and make it beautiful," he said.

"But what about our hills hideaway?" I asked.

"The hideaway would be our main home, but the other house could be like a cabin—a home away from home. My father had all these dreams about things he'd do to make the house beautiful, and I want to do them."

"I want to set up that westernmost room in our hills hideaway as an art studio," Odin said. "And I want to buy the hugest blank canvas that they'll sell me—ten by ten, maybe even bigger. I've been drawing these tiny drawings in my notebook for all this time, but I like to work on large canvases. I never appreciated what a luxury it is. A man on the run can't work on a large canvas."

"And you could get art books again," I said, remembering the Rembrandt book that he so loved at that secondhand store in Baylortown.

"What about you?" Zeus asked.

"The first thing I'd do is go back and see my sisters," I said. "I'd go sit at that kitchen table and we'd drink apple cider and I'd make them tell me every dorky little thing about their lives." I turned to Thor. "What would be your first thing?"

Thor gazed out at the horizon where the setting sun had left behind a bright glow. "We shouldn't be talking like this unless it's gonna happen," he said.

"If you want something, what's the harm in dreaming of it?" I asked him.

"Remember when you desperately wanted to see your sisters from afar, but you also didn't, because it would be too painful? To see them and not be able to hug them?" he said. "You wanted it too much."

I nodded. I remembered that well.

"That's how I feel about this whole exercise. What will we do when we're free? It's bullshit."

"Because you want it too much," I said.

"We all do, don't we?" Thor said.

I reached out and grabbed his hand, squeezed it tight.

Another ping on Zeus's phone. He picked it up and groaned. "Sue. Asking what we're doing," he said.

Odin rolled his eyes.

"Tell her we're eating," I said. "The truth for once. What a concept!"

Zeus texted her back. His phone pinged again, and again he groaned. "She's swinging by to drop a gift off."

"Tell her to fuck off," Odin said.

"We can't get a shitty guest rating," I warned. "She just wants to give us a gift. Let her."

"She's the one who should get a shitty rating. She shouldn't be bothering us. And now we have to put on our Newsome disguises?"

"At least she's telling us when she's coming over instead of popping in. This is behavior that I want to encourage," I said. "And maybe, after this week, we won't have to worry about our guest rating anymore."

I was tucking the last wisps of hair into my Sarah Newsome wig when Sue knocked. Thor and Odin were playing chess out on the porch, both in their proper disguises; Zeus was at the kitchen island with his phone and bald head. Glaring—not at anything specific so much as the situation.

I opened up the door. "Hi, Sue!" I said.

"Greetings and salutations!" Sue held out a white bakery box. "I'm really sorry that I barged in here without your permission the other day. I want to offer you this gift. It's a German chocolate cake. The best in all of California."

"Thank you!" I took it from her. "You didn't have to—"

"No, I did," she said.

"Dessert, guys!" I set it on the kitchen island and turned to her. "Would you like a piece? Come on in!"

"You sure?" she asked.

"Please do," I said. Because hey, we already had on our disguises. I lifted out the cake. It smelled unbelievably rich and delicious.

Zeus managed a smile from his seat at the island. "Very thoughtful. Thank you," he said.

He could be charming when he needed to be, and I suspected he was getting excited about the cake.

Sue's eyes roved all around the room.

Zeus gave me a triumphant look, like, *do you see how nosy she is?*

"What's this?" Sue wandered to the corner where I'd left the dogs-playing-pool picture.

"Oh, nothing," I said.

She spun around with a humorously suspicious expression, searching my face and then Zeus's, like she wasn't sure whether she believed us.

Zeus came to me and slung an arm around my shoulders, deciding to put more energy into his part as my man. "Sarah has a childhood love of these pictures. We saw it, and we knew she had to have it."

Sue had turned back to the painting. She was studying it closely.

I looked up at him—I could read the question all over his face: did she think that we were collecting these as serious collectors? Who would collect dogs-playing-pool art?

"I remember seeing these around when I was growing up," she

said brightly. She picked up the painting and turned it over, studying the back of it. "Just a dime a dozen at the time." She turned it back over, scrutinizing the front of it once again.

"They remind me of where I grew up," I said. "There's no value."

"Sure." Sue set it back against the wall, looking like the cat who ate the canary.

"Seriously," I said.

Sue grinned. "Of course." With that, she headed out and drove off.

"Oh my god, she completely thinks we're hunting for these paintings!" I said.

"Oh, you know it. Ten bucks says she's on the phone right now rounding up those paintings. That's why she came. You know that, don't you?"

"I really believed her, that she just wanted to apologize for her intrusions," I said.

"I like that you think the best of people," Zeus said, undoing my buttons.

"I don't think the best of you right now," I joked. "I think you're up to something right now." I grabbed his waistband and pulled him closer. "I think you're up to no good."

Zeus peeled off my shirt. "You think I'm up to no good? Is that what you think? Do you think that I'm going to throw you in the hot tub?"

"What about the cake?" I said. "I think I'd rather have cake. Cake's better than hot tub sex, don't you think?"

He stilled for a moment.

I snickered because this was like a red flag to a bull.

A split second later, I was hoisted up and ferried through the air, screaming and laughing. Out the door we went. It didn't take long before I found myself in the hot tub, Sarah Newsome wig and all, with my three fabulous husbands.

Chapter Twenty-One

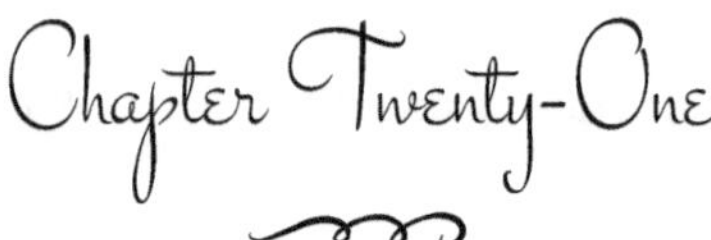

It was 4:45 a.m.—not yet dawn. We waited down the block from Alfred's place, one of a series of boxlike homes set in a row; Alfred's was painted a pale blue, and it had heavily manicured trees out front. In the darkness, they looked like blobs on sticks.

"There's some mad gardening techniques right there," Odin said.

The front door opened. We all slid down our seats and waited except Thor, who was watching him through binoculars, shielded from view by one of those reflective things that keeps the sun from heating up your car. My guys found those extra handy for staking out places.

Footsteps sounded on the pavement, soft patters as he ran by.

We waited until he was out of sight and then quietly got out of the car and melted through the darkened lawns toward his house, or at least my guys melted; I more crept in the style of a not-very-stealthy cartoon character. Odin let me in the back sliding door. The guys were already searching. We didn't think Doris would actually be there, but hopefully a clue to her whereabouts would turn up.

Alfred's house was decorated in a Southwestern theme with lots of pastels, which didn't exactly say dognapping employee of a murderous agency, but then, what does?

I searched one side of the living room and then the foyer.

"Anything?" Odin asked me, passing by.

"Just that, based on these decorations, he's definitely the one that picked the exterior paint color."

Odin came to me. "Is that really the kind of detail we're looking for right now?"

"All information is important; don't you always say that?"

"Nothing in the basement," Thor said, coming upstairs with Zeus. A search of the bedrooms and bathroom yielded an equal amount of nothing.

"No computer, no phone," Odin said, coming out of the kitchen. He was eyeing the walls and the ceiling, looking for false panels. I sensed that our search would soon be entering the demolition phase.

Thor spoke right then. "He's back."

It hadn't been even twenty minutes! I ducked behind a salmon-colored couch, and Thor crouched behind a matching salmon-colored chair; Zeus and Odin took the closet.

Alfred walked in the front, panting. He toed off his shoes and set his phone on the counter. A few seconds later, the bathroom door opened and closed, and then the shower went on.

Odin popped out of his closet and crept over to nab Alfred's phone. He made a hand motion that meant for us to stay in our places. I crouched back down.

He whipped an iPad and some cables out of his jacket and sat down in the corner. He hooked the stuff together and got busy tapping and swiping. I was glad I had a view of him; it really was a marvel to watch him work, the ultimate in competence porn.

A satisfied smile soon played across his handsome face—our techie was in, probably reviewing recent calls and text messages.

His smile soon turned upside down, however. Finding nothing, I guessed.

He stood and pulled out his gun. "Hard way it is," he said, not bothering to be quiet.

Thor stood and stretched his legs. Zeus strolled out of the closet with a huge sigh.

"You guys!" I whispered.

"He'll know soon enough." Zeus went into the kitchen and came back with a bag of Cheetos and settled himself onto the couch. Thor sat down on the chair and crossed his legs, posed like the ultimate man of leisure.

Odin was the one to actually go in and extract Alfred. Odin was the best at getting a person off-balance. It could be really sexy in certain scenarios, though I doubted Alfred would appreciate that.

"So it's gonna be that kind of party," I said.

"What's that, goddess?" Zeus asked, popping a Cheeto into his mouth.

"Psychophysical," I said.

Psychophysical was their fancy way of saying *act as if.* They were especially into it when it came to bank robberies, always going in strong and wild no matter how worried they felt, behaving as if they were a mighty and unstoppable force.

Zeus snorted, but they were doing just that, acting confident and relaxed and in control, like they owned the place, like a sign to Alfred that he'd be a fool to oppose us because that's how sure we were.

A sign to Alfred, but also to the universe. We owned this place, this situation, this reality.

I grabbed a nice big handful of Cheetos and positioned myself on Thor's lap, crossing my legs, the perfect complement to his leisure picture. Everything under control. Doing my part.

Thor gave me a gun to hold.

There was a bang of metal in the bathroom, followed by a

crash. We heard Alfred say, "What the fuck!" Then Odin dragged him out, dripping wet, clutching a towel to himself. Odin sat him down on a hard wooden chair that Zeus had put in the middle of the living room.

"You people are going to pay for this," Alfred warned, staring down Odin and his gun. "You're gonna wanna stop this right now, because you're gonna pay for it and you're not going to like it."

"Pay how?" Zeus asked, one leg dangling over the couch arm. "You gonna hunt us? You gonna kill us?"

Odin grabbed a roll of duct tape from his pack and proceeded to tape Alfred to the chair. "Some six-mile run, Alfred. Do you always lie on social media?"

"I'm telling you, I don't have Doris, and I have no idea where she is. That's the point of this whole thing—to find her!"

I kept my piece trained on Alfred. It wasn't the best shooting position, being on Thor's lap—you always wanted to go from a stable foundation—but I felt it added to our badass unpredictability. "And if you have hurt that dog," I warned, "if you hurt one hair on that dog's head or anywhere else, you'll be the one to pay. Spoiler alert: it will involve Odin ripping your intestines out like unraveling a ball of yarn from my grandmother's knitting basket!"

"Like unraveling rope," Odin amended, ripping off another piece of tape and securing Alfred's arm. Odin had made that threat before, and he preferred the idea of rope, but I preferred the folksiness of knitting yarn.

"We'll go with really thick yarn from the basket of a very disturbed grandmother," I said.

Odin continued on his work, growling, and he also seemed to be watching Alfred's face really carefully. "We're gonna finish up here and then ask you a few questions."

"Is this one stern?" Zeus asked. "Stern enough…you know."

"No!" I said. "Definitely not."

"You sure? He wants to kill us," Zeus said. "That's pretty stern."

I shook my head. "Forget it."

"Suit yourself," Thor said.

"Oh, I always do, boys," I said, all witchy. "I always do."

Alfred frowned. "What is this?"

"Shut up," Odin said, finishing up on the other arm.

"Denko is going to be so pissed when he finds out you have his dog," Thor rumbled.

"If you tell us now," Zeus began, "before we have to get it out of you, if you save us that trouble, we won't tell Denko you're the one who took her."

"I didn't take her!" Alfred said.

"Quite the offer," Thor said to Zeus, ignoring Alfred's protests.

"Yeah," I said with a big frown, like I was so disappointed. "I mean...what about..." I made a knitting motion, playing the crazy gang moll, which was fun, but I really, really wished he would just tell us.

Odin finished up and stood. "I'd settle for the location and combination to the safe."

"I don't have one," Alfred barked.

Odin went to the side of the room. He slid a picture aside. Nothing but bare wall. He pounded the area with his fist, then he toed the floorboard, then turned up a corner of the area rug. "Bingo," he said. "Zeus, you want to get me a blade?"

Zeus rose up with a heave and pulled a blade from the vicinity of his boot, gleaming silver in the light. He handed it to Odin, who pried up a square of parquet flooring to reveal the door to a safe that had been set in there, face up. He turned to Alfred. "You know I'll get in. Not like it's a Fenton Furst."

Alfred frowned.

"Have it your way." Odin went to his pack and pulled out some equipment that looked like an MP3 player from another decade, complete with earphones and a stethoscope.

"Okay, okay," Alfred said.

"Too late, you made me get the stuff out," Odin said, sitting cross-legged in front of the safe and going to work.

"I'll tell you where she is!" Alfred said.

"Like we trust you." Zeus slapped some duct tape over Alfred's mouth and headed into the kitchen for more snacks. I put in a request for chocolate. Thor asked for pie.

By the time he was out with a bag of Ruffles and a family-sized bag of plain M&M's, Odin had cracked the safe. He pulled out a phone. "Wonder what we'll find here."

"Where's the pie?" Thor asked.

"What is this, a restaurant?" Zeus threw the M&M's in our direction.

I popped M&M's into my mouth as Odin went to work on the phone like the sexy badass that he was.

"This isn't a good way to climb the corporate ladder," Thor said. "It would be the opposite of a good way to climb the ZOX corporate ladder."

"The exact opposite." I held the bag for Thor, and he took some.

"Here's an interesting number. You started calling there a few weeks back," Odin said. "And what is this on the search history? Pupper Palace in Inglewood."

Alfred looked distinctly unhappy.

"Got a PayPal linked up to Pupper Palace," Odin said. "Chris *Gallworthy*." He chuckled and looked up, seeming to like that name. "Gallworthy." He looked back down. "Chris Gallworthy is boarding his dog, Queenie, there. Very interesting."

Thor got on the phone and impersonated Alfred, letting them know he was sending an assistant to pick up Queenie and asking to settle the bill.

Alfred just glowered.

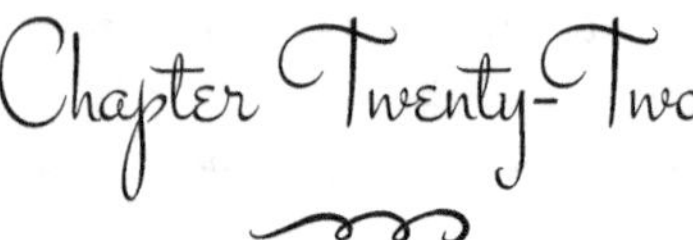

ZEUS AND I DROVE TO GET DORIS WHILE ODIN AND Thor babysat Alfred because, as Odin put it, "We're not going to be doing any *fucking-g* Batman shit, leaving a guy tied up so that he can take his time getting loose and come bite us in the ass."

I called Sue on the way to Pupper Palace and asked her about how she'd feel if we had a dog—just temporarily. "She was stolen, and we've been helping to locate her," I explained. I felt that had a better ring to it than the fuller explanation—that we were international fugitives planning to use the dog as a bargaining chip.

"How long are you thinking of keeping him there?" she asked, a good sign. It was always a good sign when the person was asking questions.

"Probably not that long. We have to contact her owner and arrange to meet him and get her back safely. We'd be completely fine paying an extra cleaning fee or any kind of pet deposit, and I promise, she's very well trained," I said.

Sue gave me her blessing. I hung up and grinned over at Zeus. "She's good with it!"

"She'd better be," he said. "She owes us."

We drove on silently for a bit. I'd learned to gauge my men's moods over our long travels, and Zeus was definitely in a reflective mood. Pondering. Having deep thoughts. He was such a man of action. I loved this side of him. I made sure not to bug him.

"It's hard to imagine this might be over," he said after a while.

"In what way?" I asked. "What's hardest to imagine about it for you?"

He watched the road, calm and silent. "Being on the run defines us so completely. And it has compressed us all together so intensely, I almost don't remember what it's like to be free. I'm looking forward to it, but there are things I'll miss about this. I'll miss the intensity of our group. I'll miss the way we're always together."

"I don't want that to change either," I confessed. "I'm not sure who I am out in the world not on the run. I'm a sister to my sisters for sure. But I would never live full-time on the farm again—that would feel like going backwards. But I don't know what forward is."

Zeus reached over and took my hand, warm and strong. "Whatever it is, we go together."

I stroked my thumb over his sturdy knuckle, over the rough tendons on the back of his hand, liking the sound of that. "It will take an enormous amount of weight off all of us."

Zeus nodded.

We grabbed Doris without incident. Not only without incident, but Zeus, being a brilliant person, brought along a sock that he'd nabbed out of Denko's laundry basket. He had me tie it around his wrist before we went into the dog hotel, and when they brought her out, he kneeled down and put his hands out for her, and she definitely warmed to him right away.

I gave her a bit of beef jerky we'd picked up along the way, and that really sealed the deal. We were friends.

Doris was even cuter than the photos showed, with a really fun smile, and while she didn't have the best breath in the world, her excitement made up for it.

I sat in the back with her on the way home, feeling happy, and not just about the fact that we'd get to pretend we had a dog for a while like an actual family; Doris was going to be the ticket to our freedom.

Thor and Odin were waiting on the stoop of the Airbnb when we pulled up. A gray sedan was parked nearby.

"What the hell? Where's Alfred?" Zeus asked as Doris bounded up to them.

"He's tied up in the trunk," Thor said, vigorously petting Doris's scruff.

Odin tipped his head at the sedan. "We wanted to stop at a pet store to get ready for Doris and we found Alfred's keys and realized we could just take Alfred with."

Zeus grumbled about that. Inwardly I winced—were we going to have another fight about rules? But Doris was racing around, jumping on us and happily licking our faces, and somehow it made everything okay.

Zeus checked the trunk to make sure Alfred was secure, and Odin showed him the alarm system he'd set up to make sure he stayed secure.

My heart warmed, seeing them get along like this.

We headed inside and I was just laughing when I saw the heap of dog toys on the table, along with several different types of leashes and treats and foods. "The proud papas went shopping!" I said.

Soon all of us were vying to pet and play with Doris, getting her excited about her new toys and giving her treats. Needless to say, she was in doggie heaven.

Zeus called Denko to let him know that we had her.

Denko wanted a picture of her.

"In due time," Zeus said, just to make him sweat. Denko wanted to know who'd her had, but Zeus held that back, too. Knowledge is power, after all.

We spent a glorious afternoon playing with Doris. Thor and

Zeus took her on a run down the beach. Odin taught her to shake hands.

"I can't believe Denko didn't teach her any tricks," Odin complained while we were hanging out in the back pool area. "Dogs love to be taught tricks."

I shifted in my hammock so that I was facing him. "I can't believe you taught her to shake hands so fast," I said. "I didn't know that you were the dog whisperer."

"Makes perfect sense to me," Thor said, setting down a bowl of chips and some dip, which Doris of course wanted and did not get, save for exactly one chip that Thor allowed her to have.

"How does that make sense?" I asked innocently. "Odin is trained to run psychological operations on men...but dogs?" I made a big show of looking around at my guys. "Oh, riiiiight," I teased.

"What is this insinuation, goddess?" Odin asked.

"Insinuation?" I asked innocently.

Zeus came over and tickled me. "You are going to take that back," he said.

"Not likely!" I squirmed and laughed. "Not likely at all!" I tried to tickle him back.

Doris barked like mad.

"Help, Doris! Get him! Bite him!" I cried.

"Stop traumatizing Doris!" Thor said.

Zeus and I were on the couch at this point, play wrestling. Doris was barking her head off. Normally things would have turned sexy, but Doris was flipped out enough as it was, so we broke it up.

"Come on over, Doris," I said. Zeus and I petted her, and then Thor and Odin petted her, too.

"You don't know how good you have it right now, Doris," Odin said.

"Eight hands petting. It's as if we've been practicing for this, somehow," I joked.

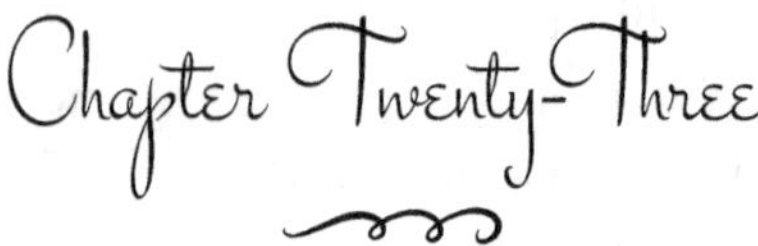

WE CALLED DENKO THE NEXT DAY. ODIN DEMANDED that it be a video chat.

"Took you long enough," Denko said, looking scowly. Was he worried? Angry? It was so hard to read him. "How is she?"

"Having the time of her *fucking-g* life," Odin said.

"Let's see her," Denko said.

"Do you have the tackle bag?" Odin asked.

"Of course I have it."

"Let's see it. Let's have a peek inside," Odin said.

"It's papers and a few thumb drives," Denko said.

"Let's see," Odin said. "If you want to see your girl, we get to see that bag."

Denko got up and went somewhere, returning with the tackle bag he'd described.

"Hold up one of the papers," Odin said.

"I'm not gonna start showing you everything," Denko said.

"One paper. Let's see."

Denko held up a paper—an email printout of some sort. Odin screenshotted it, needless to say. Thor let Doris out of the bedroom. She came bounding over, and we let Denko get a look at her, then Thor called her back into the bedroom.

"Let's do this now, then," Zeus said. He named a dog park that we'd scoped out. It had a lot of exits and a lot of sightlines—the perfect place to do the exchange.

Denko grumbled, not into it. "Too many people," he said.

"We won't start shooting the place up if you don't," Zeus said.

"I'm going to give you a different address," Denko said. We heard papers shuffle. He rattled off an address that was in an industrial area near the airport on West 102nd Street. "Ninety minutes."

Odin had a map pulled up. "Are you fucking kidding me?" He showed his phone to Zeus.

Zeus frowned. "Not loving it!"

"Work with me," Denko said. "It's a compromise."

"That evidence better be worth it," Zeus said.

"It's worth it," Denko said. "Seven tonight and Thor comes alone with the dog. He parks at the Wally Park and walks. And I'll know if he's not alone."

"Wait, what?" Zeus growled, examining the map. "Thor alone? In a place like that? Not happening," Zeus said.

"Are you fucking kidding me?" Odin spat.

"Well, there will be only one of me," Denko said. "I haven't forgotten the last time there was only one of me and four of you. Excuse me if I don't feel like a repeat performance."

"Oh, it was no performance," I said, all sassy.

"It's fine," Thor said. "I've got this."

"It's not fine with me," Zeus said, and clearly it was not fine with Odin, either.

"These are the terms," Denko said. "Do you want the bag?"

"Do you want your dog?" Zeus asked.

"Those are my terms."

"We don't accept those terms," Zeus said. "We'll keep the dog. We like her."

I widened my eyes. We couldn't keep a dog. And more to the point, we needed the proof!

"Don't be assholes," Denko said. "I'm not asking a lot."

"Let Thor walk into a place like that alone?" Odin said. "Shit like this? The gang does this together. That is how we roll."

Denko said, "I'm offering you a tackle bag that contains original footage, copies of emails, and passwords to files full of verification. Are you no longer interested in it?"

"We're definitely interested in it, but we're not complete fools; that's the problem that we have here," Zeus said. "Us not being complete and utter fools."

"I'm interested," Thor said. "I think it's worth it."

"It's not," Odin said.

Thor shot him a hard look.

"Show up with Doris and we'll do this, Thor," Denko said.

"If we can't name the place, this doesn't happen," Odin announced.

"Look, I did some risky fucking things to get this evidence out of where it was, and if it ends up that I don't have a use for it, I need to get it back by tomorrow morning before people miss it," Denko said. "The only way this deal gets done is on my terms in ninety minutes. Take it or leave it."

"We're taking it," Thor said.

I gasped. "No, Thor!"

"Not happening!" Zeus said.

Denko hung up.

Odin aimed a furious frown at Thor.

"Thor!" I gasped. "How could you even think of taking that chance?"

"We can't cover you in that place," Zeus said. "You could be walking into a trap."

"But on the other hand, we could have that evidence in a few hours," Thor said. "This could be over."

"Other hand?" Odin barked. "What the hell is that? Think,

Thor. Before that tackle bag was in play, would you ever have agreed to meet Denko alone? For any reason whatsoever?"

"I can answer that one," I said. "Not in a million years. We would have laughed about a suggestion like that."

Thor glared out the window. "The tackle bag *is* in play, though."

"You can't do it," I said.

"What if the evidence is bullshit?" Zeus asked. "What if this was a trap from the start with the goal of nabbing you to use you as bait for us? He knows once he has one of us, he has all of us. It could be a full ZOX plan, with Alfred in on it. Didn't that mystery seem a bit easy to solve?"

"Though to be fair, we are *fucking-g* brilliant," Odin said.

"You said that he recognized the smell of Denko's sock," Thor said. "Doris is obviously Denko's dog. Alfred obviously wasn't playing around. This thing is real."

"Okay, maybe Doris is Denko's dog," Odin said. "But what if Denko is willing to gamble her in order to capture us? Would you put it past him?"

"That would be pretty extreme," Thor said.

"Everything about this situation is pretty extreme," I said, feeling upset.

"If he's trying to pull something, why ask for me? Why not ask for you?" Thor said to me. "You'd be better leverage. We'd crumble right away."

Zeus barked out a laugh. "We'd never allow Ice to go into a situation like that, and Denko knows it. And Odin and I are trained to fight our way out of situations like that or take a lot of people down trying. You're a good fighter, Thor, but your training isn't what ours is. And you walk in, and the fighters come out of the woodwork, and they have us by the balls. And you have one hostage—a dog who you'd never harm in the first place."

"I just got an awful thought," I said. "Could he even have adopted Doris just to build this scenario?"

"Listen to yourselves," Thor said. "You're paranoid! Did you hear what he said? He doesn't want to be at our mercy again, that's all."

"We'd have to break you out of wherever they'd be holding you," Odin said.

"No, you wouldn't. I forbid it," Thor said. "It would be a suicide mission for you."

"What about you?" I said.

"Unlike you all, I choose to take Denko at his word, and that's my right," Thor said. "We like to say we're all about freedom—shouldn't I be free to take this chance for us? Shouldn't I have that option?"

"You're not going," Zeus said in the finalistic way he sometimes did when he decided things as our leader. "Doris is staying right here. You are, too."

"Didn't you hear him? He has to put the evidence back if he doesn't use it. There's a window, and it's closing."

"So he says," Odin said.

"Either way, since when did a closed window ever keep us from getting in somewhere?" I asked.

"Once this evidence leaves Denko's hands, it may as well not even exist," Thor warned. "We need it. This has to end."

"Does it?" I asked.

"Yes," Thor said.

My pulse raced. Did he hate our lives so much? I went over and wrapped my arms around Thor. "These have been the best years of my life," I said. "Can you really not say the same?"

"I can't," Zeus said. "Wait—I can't *not* say the same."

"I can't not say they have been my best years..." Odin said. "Wait..." He frowned. "Why the fuck did you say it like that, Ice?"

"Just to clarify," I said breezily, letting Thor go. "We three *can* say they *have* been the best years of our lives, aka, we can't not say it, and they wouldn't have happened without you."

"You have to say that," Thor said. "This is what we do, this is what we are amazing at—taking a shit situation and turning it to our advantage. Most people on the run have bad lives, so yes, I'll grant you we turned it to our advantage."

"You can't do any better than that? That's the best you have to say? That we turned a shitty situation to our advantage?" Zeus asked, sort of kidding, but sort of not.

His feelings really were hurt.

Thor just grunted. Usually I could read Thor, but for once I didn't know what he meant. What was the grunt all about? Was it an agreeing grunt or a disagreeing grunt?

I exchanged glances with Odin who could also usually read Thor. All I saw were his soft golden eyes full of sadness.

Everything began to feel ominous. Panic welled up inside me.

Here we were, hopes dashed. And now we were at odds again.

Doris snoozed in the corner. Waves crashed faintly in the distance. A small plane droned overhead.

I looked at my guys, one and then another. Zeus's hard, concerned frown. Odin's somber brooding. Thor so lost and alone.

I felt like my heart might be breaking.

Also, since when did we run out of things to say to one another? How was everything suddenly so pained and awkward?

I said, "Enough to make a person want to taste-test butthole spurge."

Zeus groaned.

Thor snorted. I felt such relief at that, I can't even say.

"Still not explaining it to you, goddess," Odin said.

I pouted. "Pleeeeeeeeeease?"

"Nope."

Joking was how we always repaired things. Together, we could get through anything. We were the God Pack, dammit!

Zeus sighed. "Here is what we're going to do. Odin is going to season those steaks for grilling and make his amazing salmon cakes. I'm guessing Ice is going to probably read her book in the hammock, and, Thor, you and I are going to drink some beer and throw the ball for Doris. And Denko can go to hell."

"And we are brilliant fucking-g outlaws, and we'll get that evidence another way," Odin said.

"We're keeping Doris?" I asked.

"Doris can hang with us until we decide different," Zeus said.

I grinned at Thor, wishing he could feel the love we had for him. He smiled back, but it looked a little fake. I got up and kissed the top of his head, wanting to infuse him with my love.

"It's all good," he said.

Odin got busy in the kitchen. Thor grabbed beers for him and Zeus. I staked out the hammock with my book and watched Thor and Zeus and Doris. From the outside, we looked like the happiest family ever. Maybe this was how we got it back—by acting as if.

Eventually, Odin emerged from the kitchen with a platter of food.

"Finally." Thor grabbed the food and grilling implements and went over to work at the grill, arranging the grates or whatever guys do at the grill.

I told myself that food would help. That things would be fine, though I'm sure we were all thinking about that tackle bag. Right about now, Denko was probably packing it up to bring to that sketchy meeting place. Or maybe he was overseeing the trap, and ZOX guys were climbing up onto building rooftops to wait.

We'd never know, I suppose.

Thor threw a Frisbee with Doris, who sadly couldn't catch Frisbees that well. Odin made me a Pink Barbie cocktail, and I went back to my book.

Minutes later, a deafening *bang* crashed the silence.

On instinct, I spun out of the hammock and dove behind a bush, ears ringing. Odin came over and dragged me behind a boulder. There were more loud pops—*pop-pop-pop* like gunfire.

I peeked around to see the grill blazing like an inferno. "Did somebody shoot the grill?" I asked.

Odin was surveying the area. We waited while the grill blazed. "That wasn't gunfire," Odin said, rising.

"Odin, get the fire extinguisher!" Zeus barked. "Ice, go get a pitcher of water. Thor, see if you can find a shovel or another fire extinguisher that's in the front hall."

Ears still ringing, I rushed to get the pitcher and brought it out just in time to see Zeus shove the top of the barbecue off with the fireplace poker. Odin sprayed the thing down with the fire extinguisher. Eventually, the flames subsided.

"What the hell?" Zeus grumbled, drawing nearer to the thing. He lifted a charred, limp, black mass up with the poker. It was some kind of fabric thing from the looks of it, burnt to a crisp.

"Kerosene," Odin said. "Kerosene and firecrackers."

"Was somebody trying to hurt us?" I asked. "Was this an attack?"

"The only reason you do something like this is for a diversion, but what purpose—" Odin and Zeus exchanged glances. As if on cue, a car engine rumbled from the other side of the place.

Zeus swore. He and Odin took off around the side at top speed. I followed them and caught up just in time to see Thor peeling out in our car—with Doris in the front seat next to him.

He was heading to the meeting site! It was just after six o'clock —still plenty of time to make it there.

Zeus and Odin were chasing him on foot, but Thor had an obvious advantage, what with driving a car.

I got a sudden brainstorm and took off in the other direction, remembering a path I'd spotted down the hill in back, leading down to intersect with the main road where it twisted around the hill.

I scrambled and slid down the hill, skinning my palms and nearly taking a horrible tumble. I made it down just in time to get to the middle of the road.

I saw Thor take the hairpin turn, zooming toward me.

Sucking in a breath, I put out my arms, making myself big. With a screech, he slammed on the brakes.

"Get out of the way, Ice!" he yelled through a cracked window. "Don't make me run you down!"

"Run me down," I heard myself say. It was here I knew—I would lay down my life to protect these guys. "You go ahead and run me down!"

"I mean it!" he yelled, laying on the horn.

I shook my head.

"You have to let me go, Ice," he begged.

"Forget it! Not worth it."

Zeus and Odin were running up the road behind him.

"What the fuck!" Zeus was the first to reach the car. He yanked open the driver's side door and pulled Thor right out of there. The car started rolling.

"Omigod!" I dived out of the way.

Odin jumped onto the car and swung into the driver's side and stopped it from careening off the side of the hill. He grabbed Doris and came out, handing her leash to me.

"You can't keep me a prisoner," Thor said, getting right in Zeus's face.

"We can do whatever we want," Odin said, stalking over to him and getting right in his face. "We're outlaws, motherfuckers!"

"We will keep you prisoner forever if it keeps you safe," Zeus said.

"Fuck you!" Thor said.

"You'd prefer capture or death to this?" Odin asked.

"Yeah, I would," Thor said.

"Stop it!" I said. "Don't say that."

"This is for me to do," Thor said. "It's mine alone to do, and it's not right for you to stop me."

"What?" I asked, shocked.

"You heard me. I take this way out or die. This is what's mine alone to do."

"You're not making any sense!" I said, eyes misty with tears.

"Don't you dare make her cry," Zeus warned.

"Nothing is yours alone to do," Odin said. "We're married, motherfucker."

"You all need to let me go," Thor said.

"Is this connected to the man you shot?" I asked. "Because no —just no!"

"It's the whole thing, don't you see?" Thor said.

"No, I don't see!" I said. "How about you explain it? None of us get it."

"Everything that has happened is my fault. I went somewhere I shouldn't have," Thor said. "I knew I was heading for trouble—I knew it! I'd heard the rumors swirling around the refugee camp, but I had to stick my nose in anyway, didn't I? I knew I'd see something I shouldn't see and I did. And then I was oblivious enough to report what I saw—"

"You witnessed an atrocity, and you spoke up about it," I said.

Zeus grabbed hold of him. "You're coming back with us. This is ridiculous."

Thor pushed Zeus off of him. "I started a chain of events that destroyed how many lives? What good did it do? Answer me that! Can any one of you answer it? I killed a man. I have two brothers who tossed their futures into the trash to save mine, Venus is dead, and the woman we love tossed her future in the trash soon after."

Zeus's expression darkened. "Are you telling me that the choice we made back there was tossing our lives into the trash? That had better not be what you're saying, because if that's what you're saying right now, we have a big motherfucking problem."

"That's exactly what I'm saying," Thor said. "Why are you all so dense? Our lives are trash. This is all trash."

In a blur of motion, Zeus was on Thor, knocking him to the dirt on the side of the road. "You'll take it back!"

"Fuck off," Thor said.

Doris barked. I held on to the leash with both hands as they struggled, fighting, rolling in the dirt. Eventually Zeus had Thor pinned.

"Our lives are not trash," Odin bit out.

"You gave up your lives and everything you ever could've had to save my ass," Thor gasped. "You gave up your dreams."

"Leading to the best fucking-g time in our lives," Odin said. "I was lost before this. I was the walking dead before you three."

"And, Ice, you got dragged into it…" Thor said.

"I wouldn't have wanted anything different," I said. "I was dying before I met you all."

"You all just *have* to say that. You know what's happening as well as I do. All the in-fighting. Trapped in this tinderbox together." Thor began to struggle like mad to get away.

"I'm gonna pin you here until it's too late," Zeus said.

With a shocking burst of energy, Thor heaved Zeus off him and hit him square in the jaw.

Zeus hit back. They pounded on each other, every hit sounding out with an excruciating *whack*.

"Stop it!" I screamed. I felt like I might throw up, the way they were all-out fighting.

Suddenly they were wrestling on the ground, both of them panting, all dirty and bloody. "Fuck you, Thor, we love you!"

"Fuck off," Thor said, fighting back.

Then Zeus was bearhugging Thor. Was he trying to suffocate poor Thor like a python? Then he growled, "We will never fuck off."

Right then the energy changed.

Thor stopped struggling. His face seemed to soften, and it was like the whole universe shifted.

"I'm sorry, I'm so sorry," Thor said, half sobbing.

"No, I'm sorry," Zeus said. "You were carrying this all alone, all this time? I didn't realize you were carrying this, man."

"I put you into this, I just wanted to get you out."

"What you were carrying, it is ours to carry together," Zeus said. "You understand?"

He pulled back and looked Thor in the eye. There was something about his tone right then, noble and resolute, that got me in the gut, that made me feel so much love for Zeus.

For Thor.

"I wouldn't be half the man I am if you hadn't happened along," Zeus said.

"You'd have your little house. Your peaceful life..."

"You really think that's what I want my life to be about? Peace and creature comforts and all of that shit? You think that's what life is for?" Zeus demanded.

"It helps," Thor said.

"Fuck that," Zeus said. "Life is not about comfort; it's a journey of discovery, of finding out who you are inside, of knowing your own heart and fighting for what matters. If that means walking through fire in excruciating pain, I'd choose that every time over comforts and ease and sleepwalking through this life. Wherever you all are, that's my heart. There is no more perfect life than what we have now, and wherever you all are, that is my home."

"Hell yes," I said, a little to my guys and a little to myself.

"I would rather have my face clawed off by hyenas a thousand times a day than to live as a bitch to comfort and ease," Odin said.

"That, too," I said.

Zeus stood. He stretched out his hand. Thor slapped his palm into Zeus's palm and was hauled up to his feet.

"You make us know our own heart," Odin said. "You gave us that, Thor."

"A hundred percent," I said.

Chapter Twenty-Four

BACK AT THE AIRBNB, I SAT SIDEWAYS ON THE COUCH, my legs in Odin's lap. I was sipping yet another drink, and the sun was setting in its usual fiery show. We watched Zeus and Thor reassemble the parts of the grill after having cleaned them.

"They are being very thorough," I observed after a bit. "I'm going to go out on a limb here and predict that there won't be the tiniest speck of soot on the tiniest screw. Not to mention fire extinguisher foam. There definitely won't be any of that."

"Good," Odin said. "We still have to cook the salmon cakes that I made, and they have a delicate *fucking-g* touch of saffron that I don't want ruined by the taste of foam or soot." He said this all growly, of course, but I think he was as touched by the scene happening in front of us as I was.

Not just because it was so massively satisfying to watch these two men toil in a manly man way, skin glistening with sweat and all that.

No, there was something about Zeus and Thor carefully breaking down that hot grill, cooling it down and shining it back up and putting it back together that was like they were repairing something about us.

Like the grill was a metaphor for the four of us. It had caught fire for a bit, but we put it back together, better than ever. We would go forward.

It was important. Especially to Thor.

Thor needed to heal us, to help us—not just other people, but *us*. I saw that now.

When we hurt, Thor hurt on another level. More than anything, Thor wanted to help Odin with his sleep problems. But that just wasn't possible at the moment, and maybe he'd never have that, but we'd get through that together, too.

He'd come to see that what he did for us was enough, that the love he offered us was enough.

Discreetly, I glanced at my phone. Three minutes after seven.

If Denko had been telling the truth, he'd be waiting alone in that warehouse with a tackle bag full of evidence that would have gotten us free.

"This is how we survive," Odin said, understanding perfectly the direction of my thoughts.

"Yeah," I said. "It's hard not to picture him alone there, waiting, that's all."

"I know," he said. "No taking stupid chances. Some rules were not made to be broken."

I grinned at him and shoved at his thigh with my heel. "Listen to you, Mr. Rule-hater!"

He squeezed my big toe. I laughed and kicked off his hand.

Thor looked up. "Can't you two behave for one second?"

"That's what I keep asking myself!" I said.

Zeus growled.

"The grill is going to look newer than when Sue bought it," I said. "She is going to keel over."

"What can I say? We are amazing Airbnb renters," Odin said. "The most amazing. We make all other Airbnb renters look like scoundrels from the pits of hell."

I shoved him again with my foot. "Scoundrels from the pits of hell! I like the sound of that! Where can I meet these scoundrels?"

Odin smiled. His smile was increasingly rare these days, so I let myself enjoy it. I didn't know how well a man could function on so little sleep. I didn't know how Thor would get past the pain of seeing Odin suffer and being unable to help him. I didn't know how I could look at a life of never seeing my sisters. But we were in this together.

If nothing else, we were the most amazing Airbnb renters in the world. Not only did we leave the grill shiny and sparkling, in a barely used condition, but we left behind a priceless piece of dog art for Sue, gift-wrapped and everything.

Epilogue

A MONTH LATER
Somewhere on the Oregon coast

Thor and Zeus and I were power lounging out on the rustic stone patio of our lavish backwoods rental, sprawled side by side on comfy loungers we'd pushed together.

Zeus had settled his head in my lap and had just begun to snore lightly.

I was reading a book on my phone, balanced on Zeus's head.

Thor was watching Odin play fetch with Doris out on the huge field behind us, yelling encouragements to Doris now and then. Odin had bought a Big Bill tackle bag as a toy. It seemed a bit perverse, being so fraught with significance, but Odin had strange ways. Maybe he wanted to see it all chewed up.

And of all the toys that we'd bought for Doris, the tackle bag was the one Doris seemed to prefer for whatever weird reason; maybe she liked it because there were so many ways for her to grasp it in her teeth. Or maybe she felt that it was weighted with significance for us. More likely, she sensed that it was Odin's favorite.

In any case, the games they played with it were extensive and elaborate. Odin would take the tackle bag and hide it in different places in the house and out on the property, and when Doris would find it, she'd race around looking for Odin. Sometimes Odin would take off on a run after hiding the tackle bag in the house, and if Doris found the bag while he was gone, she would try desperately to escape the house in order to find Odin. Sometimes he would lock Doris in the car with the tackle bag and she'd have to get out.

Sometimes a dog whistle seemed to be involved.

"He's going to miss that dog something awful," Thor said.

Zeus mumbled his sleepy agreement from my lap.

Thor kept watching. He was still worried about Odin.

We'd reached a new level of commitment and acceptance back there in Malibu. It had been amazing, feeling like we'd embraced each other harder.

And Thor had gotten past his strange guilt.

But it didn't keep Odin's sleep issues from getting worse. It didn't keep Thor from worrying about that.

Whatever came, we'd deal with it together.

Still.

We'd kept Doris around, hoping that Denko would feel worried about her and change his mind and do another trade, one that wouldn't be foolishly dangerous. Zeus even threatened to drop Doris on a roadside somewhere where Denko would never get to her, not that we ever would.

Over and over Denko refused, claiming that the evidence was now off-limits to him.

What did that even mean? Was his access to it intermittent? Or did Denko have it, but he never planned to turn it over?

One thing was for sure—Denko wanted his dog back. That had become evident over the ensuing days and weeks.

So we were at an impasse.

Denko sent along a message one day asking again for Doris and offering to trade something else—anything. "Pick something I can actually deliver," he'd demanded. "Let's end this."

"What the hell else would we want from you?" Zeus had asked. "Start shopping for another dog, because this one's coming to Timbuktu with us."

In truth, we couldn't take Doris on the run with us—it would be dangerous for all involved. Denko knew it.

A week later, Denko messaged to suggest he could drop some charges that had been filed against the Gigis. Apparently, Macy and Jenny had gotten into some trouble connected with a heist they'd done. They weren't indicted for the heist itself, but they might have to do time off of lesser charges.

That was interesting to us, needless to say. Not as interesting as the exculpatory bag of evidence, but if Denko really couldn't get at it anymore, helping our dear friends was something.

It was on a rainy Wednesday afternoon, sitting inside around the fire, that we all four voted to take Denko up on the offer.

It was a big decision. Earth-shaking, in a way, because it was letting go of a possibility we'd embraced. Zeus got quiet after we made it. Odin looked upset, even though he agreed it was the only option. Thor seemed distant. I felt a little bit lost.

True to his word, Denko arranged for the charges to be dropped.

The Gigis agreed to come by the following Saturday and pick up Doris. They were to deposit her at a to-be-named doggy hotel. The Gigis would be able to handle the logistics with Denko once they had Doris.

We'd all miss Doris, but Odin would miss her the most. He'd stopped talking about his sleeping thing, which was a bad sign. Now he'd lose his new friend.

Thor didn't say anything, but I could tell he wished he could alleviate our suffering. He wanted so badly to make things better for us, and there was no way he could.

The Gigis showed up like clockwork that weekend, along with

a feast of gourmet takeout food and lots of booze and sparkles. They lifted the mood, as usual, and the seven of us had a fun night around the bonfire. Odin showed off the tricks he'd taught Doris, and the Gigis were stunned and impressed. They stayed over; we definitely had the extra bedrooms to spare.

The next morning, Zeus and Thor made the whole gang breakfast.

I went off for a long walk with Angel, and we downloaded about everything that had been happening, dishing fondly about our respective gangs the way we always did when we were together.

Eventually it was time. We said our goodbyes to the Gigis and Doris, and the four of us sat together on the stoop watching them drive off, keeping sight of Doris's sweet face in the back window until they took a corner and turned out of sight.

It was indescribably sad.

Our leverage for the tackle bag was gone for good, and now Doris was gone, too.

I put my arm around Odin. "At least we can go to five-star hotels again," I said.

He mumbled sleepily. Maybe all his energy had left with Doris.

"Hot tubs," Zeus said.

"Plush bathrobes," I said.

Thor just picked up a stone and chucked it into the woods.

"Room service," Zeus said.

"Badass takeover robberies with awesome fucking afterwards," I said.

I waited for Thor or Odin to add something positive, but they remained quiet.

The four of us had a subdued dinner together—grilled shrimp and squash risotto, a recent favorite, but even that didn't lift the mood.

I kissed Odin goodnight, saying a silent prayer that he'd have a peaceful sleep for once, and headed off to the room that Zeus and

Thor and I shared, snuggling deeply under the covers of one of the big beds that we'd pushed together.

Thor came in with his book soon after and started reading by the light of the little table lamp. I could hear Zeus locking up for the night with Odin. They would've checked the perimeter traps and alerts and deemed us safe.

I sighed and grabbed my ereader, flipping through to find something that would match my melancholy mood.

Zeus came in and got on the other side of me. I tried not to let myself dream of the four of us in that bed.

Our time was up soon in this place, so Zeus was looking through travel websites, thinking about where to make our next move. The whole world was our oyster in a lot of ways, but that could sometimes feel overwhelming. Too many choices could sometimes be as bad as too few.

"How do you guys feel about cross-country skiing? Or maybe snowshoeing?" Zeus asked.

Thor groaned.

"Don't knock it until you try it!" Zeus said.

I said, "If there's an outdoor hot tub and plenty of hot chocolate, plus a nice sauna, I might be into that."

"Picky," Thor said.

"Here's a place that's an igloo," Zeus said. "But it looks really posh. An igloo Airbnb—"

"Dude!" Thor said. "I'm drawing the line at an igloo."

"I'm drawing the line at an igloo, too!" I said. "Gimme that!" I tried to wrest the phone from Zeus's hand. He held it in the air, and I kept trying to get at it. Eventually the two of us were standing on the bed, laughing, with Thor complaining about the bouncing.

"What's this about staying in a *fucking-g* igloo?"

We all stilled.

Odin stood at the door in his pajamas, wrapped up in some

kind of giant puffy thing that I quickly recognized as one of the Paris Hilton comforters.

Come over, come to bed with us!—the plea was on the tip of my tongue.

I kept my lips zipped. I'd asked too many times. Begged too many times.

"Hey," Zeus said.

Odin stood there, looking unsure. Then, "Got room for one more?"

My pulse raced. "Of course we do!" I got back down and patted the spot on the other side of me from Zeus and Thor, Odin's traditional place to sleep from the beforetimes.

"If we could use this…" he said, bringing the quilt. "It's the one Thor had made."

"Of course!" I said.

Thor sprung up from the bed and tossed aside the plain quilt. "Get in," he said. "I'll put it over you."

Odin got in and Thor settled the quilt over us, pressing the heavy end around Odin. Thor was acting all casual, but I knew how huge this was for him. He'd wanted more than anything for Odin to try his quilt.

What had changed?

Thor flipped off the bedside light and got in. I didn't dare open up my ereader. Was this for real? Was Odin giving it another shot? Was he going to let himself fall asleep with all of us there? Did he think the quilt would work?

"I know you guys are probably worried, like what happens if I fall asleep," Odin said, breaking the silence.

"Not at all!" I said quickly.

Odin said, "No, you'd be right to worry, but I need you to know something. Thor, remember all the stuff you tried with me?" He turned onto his side, addressing Thor from the other end of the bed. "The meditations, the progressive relaxation, the lavender, all of it?"

"Of course," Thor said.

"I've been doing tests and trial runs. Combining the techniques," Odin said. "In isolation, no one thing worked, but it came to me then to try them together. Different things at different times of day, plus the quilt. They seemed like they were having an effect, like a real, genuine effect when I used them together."

I sucked in a quiet breath. On the other side of me, I could feel Zeus still.

"I started filming myself sleeping at night," Odin continued. "I told myself I could only trust it after one full month of peaceful sleep. One month of no thrashing."

"And?" I asked.

"I'm twenty-nine days in, one day shy of a month, but I thought under the circumstances..."

"It's decided, then," Zeus said. "We're doing this."

"February only has twenty-some days," I reminded him.

"My stuff is really helping?" Thor asked, voice cracking with emotion. "Twenty-nine days without sleep disturbances?"

"It's been fucking amazing, Thor," Odin said. "To be able to close my eyes. To sleep. To experience this peace. And now that I can sleep with you all, it's even better."

"Twenty-nine days," Thor said, voice full of amazement.

I threw my arms around Odin's neck and buried my face in his shoulder, holding him tightly. There were no words. We could sleep together as a family.

"And sleeping next to you, that's another layer of peace, goddess," Odin said. "We'll sleep as an actual family, in whatever configuration..."

I snorted and sat back up, quickly scrubbing my face, not wanting to be sappy. "If there's one thing we have no shortage of, it's configurations," I said.

Zeus was laughing now, supposedly at my joke, but I think he was feeling the joy and relief that I was feeling. He reached over and clapped a strong hand on Odin's shoulder.

Odin leaned over. "Thor," he said. "I don't know how I can ever thank you for the gift that you gave me. Introducing me to the research and methods you dug up. I didn't tell you because I didn't want to get your hopes up. I'm obsessed enough with my sleep as it is."

Thor said, "I want to hear about the specifics. Maybe tomorrow."

"We'll fine-tune," Odin said. "You gave me my sleep back."

"It's nothing," Thor said.

"No, seriously," Odin said. "It's like you gave me my life."

Thor nodded, eyes shining.

I slid back under the covers with a sigh, snuggling in, practically wiggling with happiness. My guys followed suit.

"This is nice," I said.

We talked about the day. About the Gigis. Igloos.

Suddenly a snore ripped out from my left.

Zeus.

Thor snorted, and Odin and I snickered softly.

Another snore, and then there was calm from the Zeus side. We said nothing more.

Odin dropped off. Then Thor.

Soon there was just the sound of breathing. Peaceful sleep breathing.

Except for me. I stayed up, watching my guys.

We'd missed our chance at freedom. If it had even been real. Even so, somehow I knew that, sure as the matching tattoos that adorned our arms and ankles, we'd have our day in the sun. And on that day, we'd celebrate and live large out in the open, wild and free. We'd blast back into our Hollywood home—after kicking out the James gang, who were using it at the moment. We'd dance and celebrate. Be in the world.

But it wouldn't be that day I'd look back on with the greatest fondness; it would be times like this. Us as a family, making our way. Helping each other journey through life.

Yet another epilogue

One month later

Odin and I were strolling along the beach one morning...yes, the Southern California beach. With all of the places that we could have gone, that's where we ended up.

Weird, I know. It was Odin's idea to come back to L.A. not too long after we'd sent Doris back with the Gigis. I think we were all just excited that he was back in the land of the sleeping together that we would have done anything for him.

We'd rented an out-of-the way bungalow near Huntington Beach. It was nice, with some amazing fruit trees out back. The Wisconsin farm girl in me still got very excited about being able to pick fresh lemons and dates right from the yard. It seemed so unbelievably exotic.

And there was the beach. The beautiful Pacific.

I stopped to pick up a pretty shell and went into the water to wash it off while Odin fussed with his phone. He was spending a lot of time on the phone these days, monitoring various kinds of official communications channels. It's like he was obsessed with hearing all of the chatter from every government agency. When Zeus asked him about it, he just said it's his new hobby.

"You're like those guys who obsess about the police scanners," Zeus had said. "Nothing important gets said on a scanner. It's ridiculous. You need a different hobby."

"Dude, you can't choose another person's hobby unless that person is under five years of age," Thor reminded him.

"Anyway, hobbies are supposed to be ridiculous," Odin said. "Do you think I should go back to video games? Do you think that would be a less ridiculous hobby?"

"Yeah, I think it would be less ridiculous," Zeus said.

"I don't think it's ridiculous to be interested in the world," I said. "Odin is interested in the world around us."

Zeus just grumbled.

We strolled along in the sand right where the water rushed up, washing our footsteps away as we went. Odin pocketed his phone and I showed him my shell. It was a perfect pink and white one, small and bright.

"Your favorite kind," he said.

I closed my fingers around it. I'd keep it until we had to move again. Even little things like that shell had to be left behind when you lived on the run.

Just then Odin's phone beeped. He stopped dead in his tracks and pulled it out.

"That's a weird alert," I said. "What does it mean?"

He just stared at the phone, wide-eyed.

"What?" I asked.

"Just an alert I set up." He grabbed my hand. "Come on!"

"Where are we going?" I asked.

"A little mission."

We ran back to the car. Odin got behind the wheel and poured on the speed, racing up the surface streets, breaking laws, passing illegally over my very extreme protests. Twenty minutes later we were getting out at Venice Beach.

"You're gonna get the car towed," I said pointing out that we were parked illegally.

Odin grabbed my hand. "Come on!"

"I don't understand," I said. "Did you just really hate the other beach?" I asked. "It's not that different from this one."

We were out near the boardwalk now. Odin pulled something silver from his pocket and blew into it.

"Is that the dog whistle?" I asked.

He nodded and ran up the beach blowing the whistle every few yards with me running after him. Dogs all around us began barking like crazy.

What was he doing?

He kept running on and on toward Santa Monica, running and blowing the whistle. I could hardly keep up, but I felt like I needed to. I was a little worried about this new behavior, frankly. We weren't in our proper disguises—hats and sunglasses only. It was not a good time to be drawing attention to ourselves.

"Odin, slow down!" I pleaded, running after him.

He wouldn't slow. He was a man on a mission.

Suddenly I saw a grey blur, barreling toward Odin from the north.

Doris.

She had something yellow and black in her mouth—it looked like their tackle bag toy that they were incessantly playing with. But where had it come from? Where had Doris come from?

Odin reached Doris first. He collapsed to his knees, hugging her, petting her.

The tackle bag was in the sand next to them. For a second my mind didn't make sense of it. It looked like the tackle bag they played with all the time, but this one was a lot newer.

No scuffs. No tears. No drool spots.

When Odin looked back up at me, there were tears in his eyes. "Get that in your purse. We have to get out of here!" he said.

With shaking hands, I picked it up. It was heavy. Full of stuff. This wasn't the toy at all. Not at all.

"This is the real thing." I said.

"Sure fucking-g is, goddess."

We raced back to the car, which miraculously was still there.

I got into the back with Doris, petting her and keeping her distracted as we headed back to the bungalow, not an easy feat, because all Doris wanted to do was lick Odin's face, which, to be fair, I could definitely relate to.

"Can I look inside?" I asked.

"We'll all look at it together," Odin said. "We need to get off of the road fast. Let's concentrate on that."

"This is so exciting!" I said to Doris in my most exciting voice.

Doris panted.

"We'll see," Odin said.

"We'll see?" I complained. "Pull-ease!"

We found Zeus and Thor playing lawn darts in the backyard.

Zeus's eyes were wide as saucers as Doris bounded up. "Where did she come from?"

"Doris!" Thor said, petting her scruff.

I pulled the tackle bag from my purse and handed it to Odin, who held it up like a prize. "She missed her games," he said. "Poor baby."

Zeus's green eyes went wide as saucers. "Is that..."

"The tackle bag? Why, yes, my friend," Odin said.

Thor stood. "The bag."

"If you have to pee, you'd better pee now," I said, because I felt half crazy—from relief or happiness or shock or I don't know what.

"It's the evidence," Thor added.

"You didn't," Zeus said to Odin.

"What?" Odin grinned. "I didn't train Doris to be our inside asset? Why, actually, yes, I did."

"How did you think this up?" Thor asked.

"A guess that I made about Denko." Odin knelt down to pet Doris. "The more we dealt with Denko around this, the more it came to me that we weren't the only ones who valued the tackle bag of evidence."

"It was Denko's insurance policy," Thor guessed.

"Exactly," Odin said. "He was holding onto it this whole time, but he didn't want us to know that, and who can blame him? I wouldn't want us to know it, either."

"We'd wouldn't stop until we had it," Zeus said.

Odin said, "I think he panicked when Doris was stolen, and then when we found her, he changed his mind about giving this thing up. Maybe he never intended to hand it over."

"He knew we'd never hurt Doris," I said.

"Right," Odin said. "I think that the night he wanted to meet us, I think it really was a trap. I think he told his colleagues that he'd invented some bullshit evidence that we were after. But I always felt like it existed—the idea of this tackle bag had the ring of truth. I also felt pretty sure that he wouldn't keep it around his home, but rather somewhere offsite, somewhere he could get at easily. There are probably instructions of some sort that it gets released to somebody upon his death—that's the kind of insurance policy he would need in an organization like ZOX."

"Of course," Zeus said. "Swimming with the sharks."

Odin nodded. "Denko's careful. The kind of guy who might move it from time to time. And what else do we know about him? He's the kind of guy to take Doris wherever he goes."

"So that's why you taught her to escape from a locked car," Thor said.

"With her nose," Odin said, grinning. "Open the door, grab the bag, find me."

"You are diabolical!" I said. "In the best way!"

The group of us headed inside. After feeding Doris something delicious, we emptied the tackle bag onto the table. There were thumb drives in little baggies, a couple of SIM cards, a small digital recorder, and a short cardboard tube that had a lot of papers folded and rolled up inside that turned out to be copies of emails.

Thor flattened them out on the table and we all crowded around, reading. The language was cagey. There were lots of vague terms and code names, but it was dated back from the time where the whole thing had begun. It didn't mean a lot, but Odin thought it would after we went through the rest of the evidence.

Zeus held up a small recording device. He hit play and we heard two male voices discussing the need to get rid of loose ends. They were hatching some sort of a plan. Something was going down in upstate New York.

"This would have been five years back when we were in Ithaca, before your time, Ice," Thor said. "Remember that attack?"

Odin nodded grimly.

Zeus rewound the recording device to the beginning. That's when we hit the jackpot. An angry meeting, male voices arguing. People blaming each other for not keeping somebody they referred to as "Snapdragon" under control. They blamed each other as the conversation wore on. It became clear that Snapdragon was some kind of a double agent, and he was also the person who was responsible for "Incident A" aka the hundreds of deaths that got blamed on my guys.

They were talking about what to do about the doctor.

"Thor," I whispered.

Everybody agreed that the doctor needed to be handled after Snapdragon was sent away. The doctor was in the wrong place at the wrong time.

"Collateral," one person said.

"War is hell," another voice said.

"Let's send Rashad," another said.

Zeus clicked it off. "This is everything. Just this alone will get the case against us eviscerated. They can voiceprint this. It's a smoking gun."

"Oh my god, it is," I whispered.

We sat there, silently absorbing the hugeness of what we had. The moments ticked on. My guys sat there, stunned, I suppose.

Screw that!

I sprung up from the table and went around and pulled them into a hug, all my three guys at once.

Zeus snapped out of the stoic thing suddenly, rising up with a roar. He hoisted me up into his arms and spun me around the living room. "Fuck. Yes!"

"Yesssssss!" I said.

"It's everything!" he said.

"In the right hands it's everything," Odin said.

Thor stood up and hugged me and Zeus, and then Odin stood up.

"Group hug!" I screamed.

Odin complied. "We have to be smart about this," he said, pulling away. "Denko's gotta know we have the bag, and he's not going to want to lose his little policy. The manhunt that's on for us right now is going to make past manhunts look like a toddler's Easter egg hunt."

My guys went to work, copying the contents, making multiple sets of evidence. The plan was that Odin would take one set personally to his contact at the CIA. Zeus would accompany him out to Washington, D.C., but he'd bring a set of evidence to one of the congresspeople who had been on the committee looking into the incident. Thor and I would offer a set to an *L.A. Times* team of journalists who had been following the story since the beginning, a team who was familiar with a lot of the players. Of course they believed my guys were the culprits.

"They're going to be shocked when the murderers themselves walk into the newsroom," Zeus said. "But they'll be very pleased when they verify this stash."

Other copies were earmarked for other people. And we made one set to give to the Gigis. Just in case.

An hour later, Odin and Zeus were in a car headed for Phoenix. They'd hop on a plane to D.C. from there.

Thor and I stayed back with Doris. After dropping a set of evidence off at the newspaper offices in El Segundo, we hung back and kept a low profile, making simple food together, taking lots of walks in a nearby park. We lived for the check-ins from Zeus and Odin.

They'd had good meetings with a few people.

Rumors were starting to fly.

Heads were going to roll.

Epilogue number 3

They say people who have their backs against the wall are more dangerous because they fight harder.

I couldn't help but think about that when the next text came in from Zeus and Odin:

Stay out of sight. Shit hitting fan.

A day later we managed a call over a burner phone.

"Things are getting hotter," Odin said. They had decided to drive back—that's how hot air travel was for them now. He suggested we stay indoors except for letting Doris out to poop.

We spent the next few days ordering pizzas and watching movies. I worked on a new module for my Swiss cheese masterclass —everything you ever wanted to know about making Swiss cheese —with my real face being shown. It was a gesture of hope.

"I can re-record the parts with my disguise face later," I said when I showed Thor the new module. "If things don't work out."

He put his arm around me. "I have a feeling you'll never have to put those chipmunk cheeks in again," he said.

I liked hearing him sound hopeful. It was such a change from when he didn't want us to talk about the future.

"Do you think they'll reinstate your license?" I asked.

He didn't know. We'd done a lot of bad things.

The next day we got a frantic text from Zeus and Odin. They were coming in hot.

"Uh oh!" I said.

We slammed into the car with Doris.

They needed us to wait for them in a running car in a place we'd identified earlier as a great place to switch vehicles during a car chase. We always found at least one of those near every place we stayed; sometimes we even rehearsed.

We got into the spot and waited. It was an illegal spot, but the best thing about illegal spots is that they're always open.

"We have to find a place for Doris," I said. "She is not a fan of these crazy car rides."

I wasn't either.

"I'll keep you safe," Thor said. "Both of you."

The parking spot was well-obscured with sightlines blocked from every angle. I winced as I heard a chopper overhead.

"We got this," Thor said. "They'll lose them on the covered walkways."

The plan with spots like this was that Odin and Zeus abandon the first car and go off on foot, running up walks between shops and hopping into the new car, we'd whisk them off while their pursuers held a foot chase.

The chopper got louder. Sirens wailed. I made sure the doors were unlocked for the umpteenth time, and then crouched with Doris in the middle seat, holding fast to her leash. She whined and pawed at the floor of the car.

"It's okay, honey," I said to her.

Five minutes later, the doors opened. Zeus and Odin dove in on either side of us.

"Drive!" Zeus panted.

"Down!" Odin said.

The three of us crouched on the floor of the back seat with Doris while Thor pulled out and joined the calm stream of

Saturday traffic. He had on a Lakers cap, making him look like every Southern California dude out there.

"Anything?" Zeus asked. "One of the pursuit vehicles was an unmarked red Subaru."

"So far so good," Thor said.

It was nerve-wracking to drive slowly, but we'd done this a hundred times. The sirens seemed to get louder at one point.

Suddenly a police car came up behind us. The guys argued about whether to make a run for it. "He's running the plates," Thor said. "It'll check out."

"You sure?" I squeaked.

"The plates will check out," Thor said evenly.

I breathed a sigh of relief when the patrol car zoomed past us.

After a nerve-wracking drive with choppers and sirens going everywhere, it seemed, we got out of L.A., driving through the night until we reached Las Vegas. After finding a doggie boarding kennel, we checked into a posh room at Caesar's Palace.

It was like old times, except really, really not.

Odin had a million alerts on his phone, but it was all just more trouble. We ordered room service. Paid in cash. Roamed around in disguises.

The weather was bright and sunny on the fifth day. Zeus and I came back from our walk to find Odin and Thor glued to the TV.

"Arrests!" Thor said.

We crowded in, all four of us on the small hotel couch. In the corner of the screen was footage of what looked like a mass grave. The main picture was lawyers and security leading a group of men through a crowd of reporters. You couldn't see the men's faces— they had coats pulled over their heads—but it didn't matter. We knew who they were.

ZOX.

One of the figures looked familiar, walking hunched. "You think that's Denko?" I asked.

"If there's karma," Zeus said.

There was karma, as it turned out. Lots and lots of it.

The papers the next day were full of accounts of arrests "stemming from a decades-old cover-up." A giant swath of the top brass of ZOX was being held without bail. Congressional hearings were scheduled. There was talk of war crimes.

"Can we celebrate yet?" I asked.

My guys thought it was premature. Odin wanted proof our names were clear—of everything.

"Blanket immunity," Zeus said. "That's what I want to hear."

Odin was in constant contact with his guy in the CIA. Why was it still going on? Why did we still have to hide?

Finally one afternoon there was a call. A team of federal attorneys wanted us to come down to the Las Vegas courthouse.

Zeus got on the phone and argued. He informed them that they would be meeting at a restaurant, and it would be him alone with a lawyer, and that the three of us would stay back. There were lots of arguments.

"Excuse me if I am not in the mood to trust the goodwill of the United States government," he said at one point. He informed them that he'd be heavily armed. "And if you screw me, I will go full Rambo."

"I don't like it," Odin said once he hung up. "It doesn't seem safe."

"Life isn't safe," Zeus said. "But we have to trust somebody at some point. We saw the arrests."

The restaurant they chose was a small fine-dining restaurant a block off the strip. There were white tablecloths, candles, and heaps of pasta, rich with oregano and garlic.

Odin and I were dining in a dark booth, both in wigs. Thor sat up at the bar in his hat wig. Three feds—two men and a woman—had settled into a corner table some time ago. Those were the people Zeus was meeting.

Zeus strolled up wearing a suit and tie. He was with a woman with black and gray hair and a no-nonsense expression. Our lawyer.

The five of them shook hands and sat. Appetizers and drinks were set down. The meeting looked lively. Intense.

"I like the body language," Odin said. "The feds look apologetic."

"As they should be," I said. A waiter brought us bruschetta and fried shrimp. I dug in. Thor watched from the bar.

Finally the meeting looked to be over. The check was brought. iPads were put away.

When Zeus stood up, he was smiling. People shook hands. The feds left as a group. A few minutes later, Zeus strolled out with the lawyer, presumably to say goodbye and discuss next steps.

Moments later, he strolled back in and joined us at the table, with the biggest, most beautiful grin.

"Well?" I asked.

Zeus picked up a fried shrimp from the plate. "Shrimp? Please. This occasion calls for frog legs!"

"What does that mean? What happened?" I asked.

Thor came over to join us. "That took forever. I was sweating bullets."

"Full immunity?" Odin asked. "Did we get it? All crimes?"

"Full immunity?" Zeus said, grinning from ear to ear. "They're giving us full immunity...for *starters*."

"What does that mean?" I asked. I sort of knew, but I wanted it spelled out.

"We are getting full immunity for all crimes up until today. Plus, we're gonna get a few awards, my friends. And there will be a settlement. Money. Lots of it." He turned to Thor. "You get your license back. I told them there was no deal without that."

"Just like that?" Thor asked, aghast.

"Just like that," Zeus said. "I watched the paperwork get filed. I e-signed. How about you check your email."

We all checked our email. There were things for us to sign, too.

"Click the little pen and type your name," Zeus said, pointing at my phone.

"It seems too easy."

"Just do it!" he said.

We all e-signed and sent the docs.

"Sooooo...we're free?" I whispered.

"We're free," Zeus said.

I grabbed a glass off the table. It was a water glass but who cares? I raised a toast there in the middle of the restaurant. "Woo-oo!"

A few people in the restaurant clapped uncertainly.

Zeus was just laughing. "That's your toast?"

"I don't know, they don't write toasts for people like us!" I raised my glass again. "No more running from the law! Woo-hoo!"

"Fuck that!" Odin grabbed a glass and raised it high. "I toast our enemies now rotting in jail, who falsely accused us, and relentlessly pursued us! You wish we were dead, motherfuckers, but we survived!"

People were clapping now; our exuberance was contagious. Zeus bought drinks for the whole restaurant. Odin said more outrageous things. Some tabletop dancing was done.

We took the party back to the hotel room. We talked all night. Made plans. Enjoyed the hot tub, and by enjoyed, I mean *enjoyed* in the dirtiest and funnest of ways.

Most of all, we couldn't stop planning for the future. How would it feel to never look over our shoulders again? To have a home?

It was too late to call my sisters, but it's the first thing I planned to do.

Tomorrow we would rejoin the world.

One Year Later

Flower garlands decorated the entryway to the Severride Fine Arts Gallery in downtown Los Angeles. It was a sprawling place on the top floor of a historic building. There were several verandas and a rooftop entertainment area.

Vanessa ran up and pulled me over to one of the cheese and wine stations. Because of course, what could go better with an art exhibition than the best cheese in the land?

"What? It looks perfect," I said.

"I feel like we're going to run out of the gouda," she said.

"You worry too much!" said Kaitlin, coming up to join us, pulling Candace by her purse strap. "Plus, if we run out, it will just make people want to buy more for themselves."

I looked at my three beautiful sisters, wanting everything perfect for our big night. I couldn't believe how lucky I was. "I missed you guys so much," I said.

"Not this again," Candace moaned.

"Yes, this again," I said. "And again and again and again."

Waiters were beginning to circulate with trays full of drinks.

"I'm so sorry for all that I missed," I said.

"You protected us," Vanessa said, taking a champagne. "If you hadn't done what you did, we would have lost the farm."

"Yeah, you didn't just protect us, you showed us how to follow our hearts. You showed us how to fight for love," Candace said with all the idealism and confidence of a college sophomore. But I suppose she was right.

Fighting for love.

You can't do better than that. I waved away the champagne and grabbed a flute of orange juice.

Needless to say, I'd hopped a plane to Wisconsin as soon as our paperwork for immunity had been officially filed. Walking in that farmhouse front door as a free woman, it was an experience I'll never forget. I think we might have spent an hour just screaming and crying and laughing together.

I couldn't get enough of hanging out there in the days the followed. My guys came by a week later and we worked on the farm. I wanted to do everything—fix the fences, knit with Vanessa, hear about Candace's classes over big juicy mushroom burgers. I even drove Kaitlin to the University of Madison and helped her set up her new dorm room.

The settlement we'd gotten from the government really was huge. I think they were just relieved that we didn't sue them.

Thor had taken a big chunk of his part of the settlement and created a state-of-the-art free community clinic in downtown L.A. I've never seen him happier than when he was interacting with people and improving lives. His amazing clinic was able to attract some of the top doctors and specialists across the nation, plus lots of big donors. He was in heaven.

I'd asked him one day out on the beach if he thought about going back overseas to work as a volunteer doctor again.

"Maybe," he'd told me, "for a short amount of time, not months on end like before. It was okay the first time around because I didn't have a family. Now I do."

Thor and I strolled around the gallery greeting old friends and looking at the massive canvases that Odin had painted. We'd built an addition onto the hills hideaway where the four of us lived, creating a huge bright studio for him to work in. His studio had so many windows, it was almost like a greenhouse, and he took to painting in there like a madman, creating this amazing, colorful body of work. He also continued to tinker with his tech inventions, of course, being the ultimate Renaissance man.

The four of us had taken a trip out to Rabat, Morocco, where Odin had grown up. We met his extended family and visited his childhood home. We had hosted one of his Moroccan nephews recently, a handsome, curly-haired boy who was clearly going to grow up as devastatingly handsome as his uncle.

The gallery doors weren't officially open yet, but lots of familiar faces were starting to appear. Sue from the Airbnb already had dibs on one of Odin's paintings—we'd let her in early. We'd felt bad when we found out how many dogs-playing-pool pictures she'd purchased because of us.

The Gigis were out on the veranda, dripping with jewels. They were frequent fixtures at the house, and the four of us women had a standing date for yoga class. Some of the Guvveys gang had already shown, including Bentley, Stamos Strong, and even Matteo. The Gigis promised to make Matteo do a robot dance later.

I caught sight of Zeus across the room in his tuxedo. I waved and he strolled over and kissed me. "You're not overexerting yourself, I hope," he said.

"Yeah, this diamond tiara is so heavy on my head. How do I carry this weight one step further?" I joked.

Thor grinned.

"You know what I mean," Zeus said.

"How's the case?" I asked him.

He shook his head all stormy and proceeded to tell us how baffling it all was. He was trying to solve a cold murder that the police had given up on, and it was driving him crazy. In other words, he was loving it.

In addition to starting his own detective agency, Zeus had bought the little house he'd grown up in. He'd fixed it up and then sold it at a deep discount to a struggling family. It was just like him.

I reached up and wiped and nonexistent crumb off his lapel, just wanting to touch him. "You should have worn it!" I teased.

He rolled his eyes. "Stop it!"

"It would look amazing with this whole outfit," I said.

He snorted like I was being so silly. I was talking about the Medal of Honor, of course. The three guys had all received one in a big ceremony a few weeks after the arrests had happened. It was a powerful event. I feel like I didn't fully grasp everything we'd gone through until we were standing there, the four of us side by side, with all those people clapping.

It's not that the medals weren't important to Odin and Thor, but Zeus's medal meant everything to him. He'd grown up wanting to dedicate his life to enforcing the law, after all, and having that Medal of Honor was an acknowledgement that he'd done the right thing in defying those corrupt orders all those years ago. Him and Odin. And Thor had told truth to power.

And I believed in them. I knew their hearts from the start.

The whole world had said they were wrong, over and over. It had felt like everyone had been hunting us.

Now everything had changed. There would be no more hunting—not ever!

Unless you counted the kind of hunting that took place with my guys wearing leotards and Robin Hood types of outfits. And me in a sexy elf girl costume. That type of hunting was alive and well, hopefully never to end.

The week we were in D.C., we thought about visiting Agent Denko, who now lived in a maximum-security prison. There had been times where we would have relished the opportunity to go face-to-face with him and taunt him. The man had that exculpatory bag the whole time. He could have turned in the evidence and saved our asses at any point, yet he chose not to.

But when we talked about visiting him, it just wasn't that important anymore.

We were happy.

Everything was new now.

I waved at a woman from across the gleaming hardwood floor —I recognized her as one of the regulars at the climbing wall. A few months ago, I had done this big rock-climbing and bungee-jumping excursion in the Rockies with a group of badass women. It was unbelievably exciting, and I definitely planned on doing it again at some point, although probably not in the next year or two. I would be sticking to my cheese-making classes and preparing our home in the hills. A bit of redecorating.

I spotted Odin across the gleaming expanse of hardwood floor. I grabbed Zeus's and Thor's hands and pulled them over to Odin.

"This is amazing, baby!" I said to him. "I can't stop looking at this collection altogether. Everybody is loving it!"

Odin turned to me giving me a simmering look.

"What?" I asked.

Slowly he pulled off his glasses.

"Oh my god," I breathed. "Be careful or I might drag you out of your own art opening."

"Stop causing trouble, Odin," Thor warned.

Odin snorted. We still called each other our on-the-run names. Everybody else did, too. It seemed right, with all we'd been through. Like the names you get at the end of a trial by fire.

The four of us stood staring at the biggest canvas of all, as big as a car. It was a self-portrait that Odin had done of us with Doris, who we had adopted. We were a family. I couldn't believe how good it felt.

"How many people have offered to buy this one?" Zeus asked, grabbing a flute of ginger ale from a passing tray.

"It doesn't matter, this one's not for sale," Odin said. "It stays in the family."

"Your bungee-jumping friends are here," Thor said, pointing

across the room.

"No way," Zeus said. "You can't let them talk you into anything."

Odin turned to me. "You gave your word you'd stay away from bungee jumping."

"I know!" I said.

"And rock climbing and ski jumping," Thor said.

"No extreme sports," Zeus said.

"Yes, yes," I said, beaming at my guys. They'd been so doting and caring.

"All risky activities," Odin said.

I winced. "Bad news—I can't promise you that," I said.

"What?!" Thor frowned. "What do you mean?"

"I'll never stay away from all risky activities," I said. "Because love is the ultimate risk, and I plan to keep plunging myself into that risk every day with you. Bravely, honestly, truly."

"Goddess," Odin said, tucking a strand of hair behind my ear. "I will always be by your side in that risk."

I grinned.

"Me too." Zeus put out his hand. "*I promise to always love this family. And to fight for this family, and fight for our dreams. And if anybody ever hurts our baby, I will destroy them.*"

Odin put out his hand. "And I will never stop protecting our right to be as messed up as we want to be."

Thor put out his hand. "Me, too. And our baby will know what it's like to be wild and free and loved completely."

"You guys are gonna be the best fathers," I said. "I can't wait."

The truth.

In two months, I was going to have the luckiest baby in the world.

"God Pack forever," I said, clasping hands with my guys, four hands joined together for all time.

~ The End ~

I hope that you enjoyed reading The Best
Trick!!

Thank you so much for being on this journey of
love and bravery and fluffy hotel bathrobes.

Thor, Isis, Odin, Zeus and I send you heart
eyes!

xox

Annika

DANGEROUS ROYALS

Dark and edgy mafia romance; read in order

Dark Mafia Prince

Wicked Mafia Prince

Savage Mafia Prince

Annika Martin writes in many genres; find a complete list of her books, audiobooks, and translated works at www.annikamartinbooks.com

All the Annika deets!

Annika Martin is a New York Times bestselling author who lives in Minneapolis with her non-bank-robber husband. In her spare time she enjoys taking pictures of her cats, consuming boatloads of chocolate suckers, and tending her wild, bee-friendly garden.

newsletter:
http://annikamartinbooks.com/newletter

TikTok:
@annikamartinauthor

Facebook:
www.facebook.com/AnnikaMartinBooks

Instagram:
instagram.com/annikamartinauthor

website:
www.annikamartinbooks.com

Reader group of awesomeness
www.facebook.com/groups/AnnikaMartinFabulousGang/

God Pack forever!!

www.ingramcontent.com/pod-product-compliance
Lightning Source LLC
Chambersburg PA
CBHW070454200726
48293CB00007B/2195